IT'S NEVER TOO LATE

It's Never Too Late

Donna MacQuigg

FIVE STAR
A part of Gale, Cengage Learning

GALE
CENGAGE Learning™

Detroit • New York • San Francisco • New Haven, Conn • Waterville, Maine • London

GALE
CENGAGE Learning·

Set in 11 pt. Plantin.

Printed on permanent paper.

LIBRARY OF CONGRESS CATALOGING-IN-PUBLICATION DATA

MacQuigg, Donna.
   It's never too late / by Donna MacQuigg. — 1st ed.
    p. cm.
   ISBN-13: 978-1-59414-778-4 (alk. paper)
   ISBN-10: 1-59414-778-7 (alk. paper)
    1. Middle-aged women—Fiction. 2. Fathers and daughters—Fiction. 3. New Mexico—Fiction. I. Title.
   PS3613.A283I87 2009
   813'.6—dc22   2009001226

First Edition. First Printing: May 2009.
Published in 2009 in conjunction with Tekno Books.

Printed in the United States of America
1 2 3 4 5 6 7 13 12 11 10 09

This book is dedicated to John Helfers and Tiffany Schofield. Thank you both very much for your loyalty and support.

ACKNOWLEDGEMENTS

I've been very fortunate to have two very wonderful women lending their expertise to make me a better writer. They are Kathryne Kennedy and Alice Duncan.

I met Kathryne Kennedy at a conference in Arizona where I saw from a distance this woman with a mass of long, curly hair. I didn't see her face, only her waist-length blond, curly hair as she walked among the other women toward the conference rooms. Fate stepped with me into an elevator where I met the woman and helped her get some books to a signing while she met with an editor. A small favor, but one that's been returned ten times over. We became critique partners, and now are best friends even though she lives in Arizona.

There's another person who has played an important role in my writing career, and I've never been fortunate enough to meet her face to face. We've met only through emails. She's my editor, Alice Duncan. Since that first email, Alice has edited each one of my books, and through her patient tutelage, I am learning the proper usage of commas and scene breaks. Only Alice knows my dark grammar-challenged secrets because by the time my books get to print, she's taken care of my mistakes.

So, to Kathryne and Alice, thank you both very much. I'm a very lucky person.

CHAPTER ONE

Present Day Baltimore, MD

Kathryne Sheldon-Wilcox glanced at her Rolex. Her husband, Doug, was late. A little nervous, she motioned to the waiter and when he arrived, ordered a glass of red wine. Her drink had just been delivered when Doug came in, saw her, and headed toward the very private corner table in their favorite Italian restaurant.

"Wow, this is nice. I almost forgot it was Valentine's Day," her husband said as he placed a quick kiss on her cheek. He took off his coat and draped it over the burgundy velvet chair across from hers. After he smoothed back his sandy brown hair, he loosened his tie. "Had I known you'd choose this place, I would have sent roses," he teased with one of his *knock 'em dead* smiles.

"You never have before," Kathryne replied, nervously tucking a strand of honey-blond hair behind her ear. "Why break tradition?" She forced a stiff smile when he laughed.

The waiter returned, and Doug ordered his usual drink, a scotch and soda. After the young man left, her husband reached over and put his hand over hers. "You look upset. Hey, I'm sorry I'm late. I had something come up at the last minute."

Kathryne slipped her hand free, took a calming breath, and pushed a large manila envelope toward him, ignoring his questioning look. "Open it," she said softly.

Doug's smile slowly faded. "It's kind of big for a card. What is it, another brief?" He started to push it aside, but she stopped him.

"Doug, open it."

"Come on, baby. What do you say—let's just relax and enjoy dinner. Let's leave work behind for a change."

The waiter returned with Doug's drink, placing it before him. "Are you ready to order?"

Doug reached for the menu. "I think—"

"No." Kathryne shook her head, smiling at the waiter. "Not yet. Give us a few more minutes." She felt her husband's gaze but refused to acknowledge it until they were alone again. "Please. Open the envelope."

He frowned. "All right. If it's that important to you, I'll open it."

Kathryne took a sip of wine while he undid the string around the button. His expression turned from slight annoyance to one of complete shock, then, almost as quickly, to one of anger. He cast a quick glance over his shoulder to make sure no one watched, flipped through several more of the photos, and then shoved them back inside the envelope. He grabbed his drink and took a long swallow. "Is this your idea of a joke? Having me followed like some . . . some kind of criminal? I messed up. So what?"

"Messed up?" she repeated, thankful her voice didn't betray the rage welling inside. She took another sip of courage, and then slowly put down her glass. "Those pictures, in case you didn't notice, are of several different women. I'm sure I don't need to tell you that they can and will be used against you in court."

"Ah shit, Kate, stop with the legal crap. I'll admit we've got some problems, but it's nothing we can't work through."

"Can't and won't, Doug. I'm tired of pretending that you're a good man." She leaned closer and lowered her voice, fighting against tears. "You're not. You're a bastard, and I'm going to enjoy exposing your true character."

10

"We've both got a lot to lose, Kate. I'd think this over if I were you."

She'd expected his reaction. She reached over, took the envelope and with trembling fingers, withdrew a smaller, white envelope, then placed it on the clean plate before him. "Remember this—the prenuptial my father insisted you sign the day we were married? From your expression, I would say you do." She grabbed her purse and stood, grateful that her shaky limbs functioned perfectly.

Doug grabbed her wrist, looking up at her. "Twenty-five years in the toilet? Just like that? Can't we just have dinner and talk things over, for God's sake? I'll even go to counseling if that's what you want. Don't do something you'll regret, Kate."

Kathryne steeled herself and raised her chin ever so slightly. "I've already had the locks changed on our apartment, so don't bother coming home. I've also taken care of the check, so eat up." She leaned down, placing a cool kiss on his cheek at the same time whispering in his ear, "And I hope you choke on it."

The sound of her own pitiful sobs jarred Kathryne awake. For a moment she was confused, groggy, wondering why she felt so terribly alone. She took a long, deep breath, then after she clicked on the bedside lamp, reality set in—a reality as painful as reliving the stillbirth of her child in the nightmare that woke her. Sitting up, she angrily swiped at her eyes before she wrapped her arms around her ribs in an attempt to regain control.

If Douglas were here, she thought miserably, he'd put his arm around her and tell her to be strong. But he wasn't. He was across town in some fancy hotel, and probably not sleeping alone.

A quick glance at the clock on the bureau made her feel a little better. She had several hours before she'd have to get up and get ready for work. Still shaken, she slipped out of bed and went into the bathroom to splash some cold water over her tear-streaked face. After a few moments, she patted her skin dry, looking at her disheveled reflection in the mirror, seeing her red-rimmed green eyes, feeling more alone than any other time in her life.

Twenty years ago she'd lost her baby. Ten hours ago she'd lost her husband, and now, somewhere along the way, she'd lost her youth.

Slowly, she stepped out of the bathroom still too depressed to sleep and thinking a snack might help. She went to the walk-in closet to retrieve a warm robe. The moment she stepped inside, her gaze fell on the neat row of clean, pressed, personally tailored linen shirts.

Douglas's favorite monogrammed shirts.

Grabbing an armful, she flicked off the light and went into the living room and dropped them on the couch before going into the kitchen. Several minutes later, she returned with a glass of milk, four chocolate-chip cookies and a pair of scissors.

Two months later, Kathryne stared at her computer screen, but she didn't see the contract she'd been working on for the last two weeks. The long, boring contract. God, could her life get any worse? She should have studied criminal law in school. She took a deep breath in an effort to ease an abrupt tightness in her chest that had claimed her full attention.

Indigestion, she calmly told herself, taking another deep breath and letting it out slowly. Yet she'd skipped breakfast, choosing in its stead a tall cup of half-decaf and half-regular coffee with two sugars and a generous splash of cream. As it was, she'd thought she was doing well to mix the decaf in her favorite brew.

That was two hours ago, on her way to the office. But now

what? What was this? Had it been brought on because of another restless night filled with bad dreams? Was it heartburn or heart attack? Good grief, wasn't she too young to be having a heart attack? So if not indigestion, it must be something else— something that could cause her to feel bad.

"Damn it, Douglas," she muttered, rubbing her breastbone with her knuckles. "This is your fault. I should have insisted you leave the building. What was I thinking, renting you an office?"

She frowned. She'd always been as healthy as a horse. It was so unlike her to let his antics get her down. Now that the divorce was finalized, she should be feeling great, not having chest pains. Maybe she should have left the building instead.

Indigestion, she reaffirmed, even though she had enough doubt in the back of her mind to make her momentarily ignore the beeping intercom. Instead, she flexed the fingers of her left arm, remembering that she'd read somewhere that left-arm pain was a common symptom of heart attack. She was much relieved to find her arm felt fine. So did her back. No problem there either.

Except for her annuals, she wasn't the type to run to the doctor at the slightest whim. Yet she couldn't deny that only a few moments ago, she'd experienced a pretty severe bout of pain. She took another indecisive breath. The intercom on her desk beeped again, and this time she answered. "Yes, Helen."

"Doug's holding on line one. Do you want to talk to him, or do you want me to get rid of him?"

Kathryne hesitated for a moment. A few short months ago, she would've dropped everything to take his call. Now she wondered if she should take Helen up on her offer or just take the call and be done with it. "I'll take it."

Never one to run from a challenge, she stared at the blinking green button for several moments to collect her thoughts, *and* her courage. She lifted the receiver. "What is it this time, Douglas?" she asked with false bravado. "Visitation rights for the cat?"

She was quiet for several moments. "It was a joke, all right? I know we never had a cat. You never wanted a pet. It might have soiled the rug."

She heaved a tired sigh, reminded that she didn't get much sleep after another baby dream. While she listened, she picked up her pen and began drawing circles on a blank pad of paper. "I think you made that decision a long time ago. We've made our beds . . . all right, I'll listen, but don't expect me to give you advice when I haven't even seen the contract."

She patiently listened to him rant on about a real estate prospect he was interested in while she doodled, curling a black line steadily inward toward the center.

"It sounds risky," she continued, staring at her drawing. "I don't want to take on anything risky right now . . . no, not even if there's a profit to be made. Why? Because I don't feel it's in the best interest of the corporation. *Or myself.* We're through, over and done with, remember? Those were the words you used—"

His voice grew louder, causing her to move the receiver slightly away from her ear. At the same time she studied her doodling—a doodling that very closely resembled a target.

A target? She smiled at the plans bubbling up from her subconscious. Did she really feel angry enough to shoot her ex-husband? If she killed him, she couldn't torment him, couldn't exact her revenge with little insignificant things that thoroughly annoyed him. Things only she could know after so many years together.

What was that joke she heard? *Married for twenty-five—happily for seven.*

She pondered her drawing a moment, thankful she still had her sense of humor, coloring in the bull's eye while her ex-husband rambled on that she never took chances, and if she wasn't so stubborn, perhaps things would have worked out differently. She almost reminded him that taking no chances had paid off, especially concerning their divorce.

Had she not kept the prenuptial agreement, Douglas Wilcox would have kept his controlling interest in her family's law firm. Now she was the sole senior partner, and he blabbed on the phone, asking for financial backing.

"Listen, I'm really pressed for time," she broke in, aware that even the slightest interruption while he spoke infuriated him. A slow, satisfied smile teased the corners of her mouth. "Yes, Douglas. I know you were speaking."

She leaned back in her dark green leather executive-style desk chair—the one she'd ordered to match his when their offices had been next door to each other. "Nothing will be accomplished if you act like a child."

More like a jackass, she silently amended. Funny, most of her married life Douglas had been the one who made her feel childish, but since the divorce, their roles had reversed. Now, the more he ranted and raved, the more calm she became—which only served to enrage him more. She smiled again, pleased that the anger management sessions with her therapist were finally paying off.

If only it could be this easy at night when she longed to have him hold her and kiss away the pain of betrayal. Nighttime made her doubt her decision. Lying awake in the dark made it difficult not to wish for her old, comfortable life—being married. Even if she hadn't been completely happy, she had always felt safe. Her therapist said the bouts of loneliness would happen and even gave her tips on how to deal with them, but it was much more difficult than Kathryne had expected.

When you feel sad or angry, picture something funny or enjoyable and focus on it until you feel better.

She drew a head on the target, picturing Douglas in his office on the west side of the building they'd designed together. The face she scribbled matched the flustered sound of his voice as he sputtered how blind she was to reason. Resisting the urge to laugh when his voice cracked in mid-sentence, Kathryne cleared her throat, somewhat surprised when he took it as an assault on the fact that he was having a bout of laryngitis.

Pushing him to the brink usually gave her a liberal measure of satisfaction. But not so much this time. Not when she had just been wondering if she should've called 911 or taken an antacid. She picked up the pad and began to wave it slowly back and forth near her face—feeling uncomfortably warm, wondering if Helen had turned up the heat.

"Douglas, listen. I'm in complete agreement with you. We're through both personally and professionally. You don't need my opinion . . . at least you never asked for it before, and if you did, you never listened. No. I have absolutely no desire to invest in a repossession, especially out of state. I see hundreds of repos a week, and they're usually in such bad shape it would take a small fortune to renovate."

Not surprisingly, he changed the subject to the one that he knew cut her the most.

"No, I didn't know," she replied. She closed her eyes for a moment, fighting the unexplainable urge to cry as the man she'd loved for over twenty-five years told her about the plans he'd made with another woman. "I hope you have a wonderful time," she said, thankful her emotions weren't revealed by her voice. *Yeah, right,* her inner voice countered, *just like you hope you owe more on your tax return.*

"I can't discuss this any further. I've got an appointment." She didn't wait for his response; she just hung up, and then turned her chair around to gaze out the large glass window, all the while fanning her face and attempting to think nice thoughts while trying to get past the hurt and humiliation of his latest conquest.

Using a fair amount of determination, she directed her thoughts away from Douglas to what was happening outside the window. Since the divorce, she'd spent a lot of time looking out the window instead of at the contracts on her desk.

What a beautiful day. Even from the twenty-first floor she could see the city park and an occasional glimpse of joggers, bike-riders, and other people out for a brisk walk, reminding her that she should put *getting more exercise* at the top of her to-do list. Her reflection told her again her that she shouldn't ignore the pain she'd experienced a few moments ago. It was better to face it, find out what it was, and deal with it. She turned around and poked the intercom button. "Helen, has Mr. Madison arrived for our meeting?"

"Not yet. He's got another fifteen minutes."

Kathryne glanced at the brass clock on the wall. "Oh, you're right. I'm ahead of myself. Let me know when he gets here, and . . . check the heat. It's kind of warm in here."

She stood, and then strode to the black marble-and-brass bar built into the ceiling-high bookcases on the north wall of her office. She prided herself for choosing the east-side office for the delicious amounts of early morning sunshine that came in through the windows.

She retrieved a bottle of ice-cold water from the black porcelain mini-fridge concealed under the bar, taking several sips as she made a mental note to get some antacids the next time she went shopping for the office. Meanwhile, she tried to decide if her chest felt heavy or if it was just her imagination.

"I'm not old enough for this . . . am I?" she muttered as she stepped into the adjacent private restroom to run cold water on her wrists and hands in an attempt to cool down.

After she dried her hands, she took the damp paper towel

and pressed it against her neck, glancing in the mirrored medicine cabinet. She looked a lot better than she had last night. Out of habit, she checked her make-up, then tucked a strand of hair back into the neat chignon at her nape, pleased that the soft highlights looked natural and drew out the gold flecks in her green eyes.

She smiled, finding some comfort in the fact that with a little make-up she didn't look her age. Even some of her staff had commented that she looked great the week before, when she'd returned from the salon with her hair down in soft curls around her shoulders.

"I suppose so," she murmured, continuing with her self-scrutiny. "Considering that most of them are in their twenties, *and* I sign their paychecks." For a moment, she thought to pull out the pins and shake her hair loose, but she knew that her clients expected the firm, no-nonsense, strictly professional look.

"What's this?" Kathryne muttered, leaning closer to the mirror. She quickly opened the cabinet and retrieved a small pair of tweezers, plucking a small, coarse, white hair from her brow. Frowning, she studied it a little longer, and then washed it down the drain. After she adjusted the collar of her rose-colored silk blouse and smoothed her cream-colored skirt, she took one last deep breath, just to check how her lungs felt.

Satisfied that her incident, whatever it was, had passed, she stepped out of the restroom and began to straighten up some papers on her desk, trying to forget what had just happened.

A soft knock sounded on the door. "Kate," Helen said as she poked her head through the opening. "Mr. Madison is here."

Kathryne glanced up. "Thanks Helen. Put him in the east conference room and bring—"

"Coffee," Helen finished with a knowing nod. "Already done. On both accounts. Danish too. If memory serves, he liked cherry-cheese filled. And I got a couple of bear claws from Clancy's." Helen's smile faded. "Are you all right? You look a little pale."

It was like Helen to notice, Kathryne reflected. Too bad Douglas hadn't been as thoughtful, but she'd known he wasn't the type to pay any special attention to her even before they married. She'd consoled herself with his occasional *I love you too,* spoken *after* she'd said it to him.

He'd proven himself a bastard, so why did she miss him so much?

"Kate?" Helen said with a concerned frown.

"I'm fine."

"Sure you are." Another knowing perusal from Helen. "That's what I admire most about you. You always land on your feet." Helen stepped aside, holding the door open. "Don't forget you've got a dental cleaning appointment at one and dinner with Liz at Murphy's at six."

"I won't." Kathryne shrugged on her matching, cream-colored jacket. "I need—"

Helen held out a thick file. "This is the last of the old pre-divorce contracts. Akins and Roberts have already approved the proposed merger, but so far, I haven't heard a word from Douglas's team. They don't seem to want to make a decision without consulting Doug, even though he's no longer associated with the firm."

Kathryne took the file. "I doubt you will. Doug's leaving tomorrow on a cruise to somewhere . . . I can't even remember, with someone I'd like to forget."

"Vicky from records," Helen confirmed with a nod. "Sorry, but it's all over the complex."

"Great," Kathryne replied, relieved that her voice didn't betray the gut-wrenching hurt of yet another betrayal. "Let me guess. She's probably platinum blond, good looking, her bra size is thirty-eight D and, she's under thirty?"

"Yes to all of the above."

"What does this make it . . . number three?" Kathryne asked bitterly. "I've lost count." She opened the door leading out to the hall. "Oh, and call Hill Crest Clinic and see if you can make an appointment for me with David Anderson for tomorrow. Tell him I've been having some indigestion lately and I'd like to talk to him about it."

"Ah-ha. I knew you weren't feeling well." Helen hurried to her desk and plugged in her headset. "I'll get right on it."

As soon as Kathryne's dental appointment ended, she noticed a message on her cell phone to call the office. Helen had worked her magic—must have told poor Dr. Anderson's receptionist that she was dying in order to get an appointment for the same day. Nevertheless, she had just enough time to make it across town for her appointment.

Kathryne checked in and took a seat. She picked up a magazine and began to thumb through the latest copy of *Country Horseman*. It was like David to have equine magazines in his lobby. A kindly older man, he'd often told her that he enjoyed horseback riding whenever he could steal away to his estate up north in Connecticut.

Looking at the pictures of horses reminded Kathryne of her grandfather's ranch and the summer's she'd spent there with her father, learning how to ride and helping with the care of her grandparents' menagerie of farm animals. She continued to stare at the page, but her mind had carried her back to a time of innocent happiness.

"Kathryne Wilcox?"

"That's me," Kathryne replied, placing the magazine aside. "You can call me Kate if you'd like."

Kathryne smiled, but the stocky nurse never looked up from

her chart. "Is Corinne off today?"

"Retired last summer. You're way overdue for an exam, but since we're working you in, you'll have to schedule later. Follow me," the woman said, marching toward a scale at the end of the hall.

Can this get any worse? Kathryne thought as she quickly shrugged out of her suit jacket, and then put it with her purse on the floor before stepping on the scale. Why did they have to weigh her anyway? She watched the nurse adjust the counter weights, inwardly wishing that she'd worn different shoes and hadn't splurged the last few days, cringing at the memory of the decadent bear claw she'd consumed earlier.

"How tall are you?" the nurse asked as she wrote something down.

Lost in her thoughts of lighter shoes, Kathryne glanced over at the nurse. No personality, and no smile. "I'm sorry, what did you say?"

"How tall are you?" the woman repeated impatiently.

"Five-eight," Kathryne said cheerfully, sure that her height would counter her slight weight gain. "My ex-husband always said I was too tall," she added. "But since the divorce, I think he's too short." Kathryne gave a weak laugh, embarrassed that she'd only just noticed that the nurse was short as well as stocky. "I'm sorry. I don't usually make short comments . . . to ah . . . other people. I'm recently divorced and I guess I'm—"

"In here," the nurse motioned, opening the door. "Take a seat on the examination table."

"Sure," Kathryne murmured, wondering if the woman had worked for the marines in her younger days, or perhaps the Spanish Inquisition in a previous life. A blood pressure cuff was wrapped around Kathryne's arm, and pumped up to the point of pain. *Payback?*

"Why are you here today?" the nurse asked.

21

"I had some chest pains this morning, and I thought I'd better get checked out." Kathryne blanched at the shocked look on the nurse's face.

"You had chest pains this morning, and you waited until this afternoon to come in?"

"Y-yes . . . I had a meeting that couldn't be postponed, and this was as soon as I could get an appointment. Where's Marcy, Dr. Anderson's other nurse?"

"She's sick. I work for a temp agency."

"I see," Kathryne said. "Well, I'm not an alarmist. I think it's just a bout of indigestion, but I want to—"

"A woman your age . . ."

The nurse kept talking, but Kathryne didn't hear. *A woman my age? What is that supposed to mean?* "I just turned forty-four," Kathryne replied defensively, expecting the nurse to comment on how she *didn't look her age.*

But the nurse just scolded her about ignoring signs and went on about how symptoms of heart attack differ in women from men, and if she'd had pain, she should've gone straight to the emergency room.

The nurse asked a few more questions, mentioned that it could be the onset of menopause, and then jotted a few things down. On her way out of the room, she muttered, "The doctor will be here in a few minutes."

Emergency room? *Menopause?* Kathryne blinked, swallowed, and then glanced around the small room at the pictures and charts of hearts and veins, feeling a bit apprehensive.

Dear God, where had the time gone? *I'm too young for menopause.* Sure, menopause was better than a heart attack . . . but not by much. There were pills for menopause. And, if she didn't want to take pills, she could tough it out, just like she had when she'd lost the baby. In and out of the hospital—no long labor, no complaining—no tears. Especially no tears. Just an, *it's better this way . . . you'll see,* from Douglas who hadn't wanted children in the first place. *Children are expensive and time consuming,* he'd said.

"They could also soil the carpet," she muttered bitterly.

Even now, as she remembered, she felt a pang of regret that she hadn't insisted they try again—instead giving in to his happiness without considering her own. There had always been the thought in the back of her mind that, in time, they might try again. She silently scolded herself for being such a fool. Why did it take half her life and a divorce to realize that Douglas was a selfish man, utterly content to be alone?

But was she?

Now that she'd reached the point in her life where she could do anything she wanted, why did she feel empty—as if life held no meaning? Her thoughts flickered to her parents. Both trial lawyers, they'd been delighted when she went to law school, and equally disappointed when she chose a lower profile in the legal profession. Though divorced now, two years after they married they had her. But who would she have when she was in her golden years?

Hell, she didn't even own a pet.

Kathryne forced her past aside. Nothing was to be gained pining over something that never was, and now could never be. If she were in the beginning stages of menopause, so be it. She'd discuss it with her trusted friend and doctor, and together, they would decide the best course of treatment, and after she finished her appointment, she'd stop by the florist and purchase a few live houseplants. And, when she got home, she'd check her lease and see if they allowed pets.

The door opened and her hopes of having someone to confide in crumbled. The man who entered appeared to be only a few years older than the new intern she'd hired last week. The doctor met her gaze and gave a brief smile and explained that Dr.

Anderson went home sick, apparently with the same flu Marcy had. But Kathryne found little comfort in the young man's explanation.

How, in God's green earth was she to ask this child-physician about menopause? She gave a weak smile, grateful that she hadn't had to remove any of her clothes.

CHAPTER TWO

Kathryne glanced at the prescriptions and two informative papers in her hand as she slipped into the back seat of the black, corporate Lincoln. The visit had gone a little better than she expected. She wasn't in menopause—not yet, as a simple little blood test confirmed, but her hormones were a little out of whack—probably due to stress.

The first sheet described the small pack of low estrogen birth control pills that would hopefully help her get back to feeling better. The second explained how a tiny little white pill would lessen the symptoms of acid reflux and heartburn.

No chocolate, no soda, no caffeine, no spicy or fried foods, and no alcohol.

What did that leave? Cold cereal with skim milk? Worse yet, the boyish doctor suggested that she might want to lose a few pounds, and lastly, he emphasized that she might want to consider changing professions to one which generated less stress, concluding that anxiety did a lot of things to the human body—like causing chest pains.

"Great, all I have to do is stop eating and change jobs," she muttered sarcastically as she turned the air conditioner controls to high. For a brief moment, her thoughts flashed to her father and the choice he'd made so long ago. Had he experienced the feelings she was experiencing now? Is that why he left the firm and moved back to New Mexico where he'd lived as a child? She instantly recalled his parting words. *It will be good for you,*

Kate. You'll be in charge. You're a responsible person—the perfect candidate to own and manage your own company.

"Why is it everybody knows what's best for me but me?" She flipped open her cell phone to call Helen. It was a courtesy she always extended—to check with Helen about taking time off.

But then she'd always checked with Douglas too. On rare occasions, he'd even take some time off, too, and they'd meet for an early dinner and sometimes a movie, but that was a long time ago, before their law firm had become so successful. Before they acquired the new offices and Douglas tried his hand at real estate investing.

But she soon suspected that her husband dabbled in more than real estate. He started spending more time at the office and became evasive when she questioned him about it. As a last resort, she finally hired a private detective to spy on him.

She inwardly hoped that she was being foolish, feeling guilty for what she'd done, until the detective gave her a pile of photos. The most hurtful: Douglas, half naked on the sofa she'd chosen for his office, with his secretary. A woman half her age.

Kathryne groaned. It seemed that lately everybody in the building was *half her age.* "Twenty-five years shot to hell," she muttered as she pressed the number that would speed dial the office. "Hi, it's me. Yes, I'm fine, but I think I'm going to take the rest of the day off." She paused, listening to Helen for a minute. "Doug called? Did he say what he wanted? Well, I guess if it was important, he would have tried to call my cell."

She listened for several minutes more, and then smiled. "No, I probably wouldn't have answered. I bet he was angry. He probably expected to use the company car to take his hussy to the airport."

She laughed with Helen to hide the hurt, then said goodbye and closed her phone as she checked her watch. "Ed," she said to the driver. "Take me to Alexandra's."

She flipped open her cell and quickly dialed another number. "Liz Barnwell, please. Yes, I'll hold." A moment later the phone clicked. "Hi, Liz, it's me. Hey, want a massage before our dinner date tonight? It'll be my treat."

Twenty minutes later, Kathryne lay on her stomach, with her chin resting on her forearms. A soft white towel covered most of her body. Her favorite masseuse, Richard, worked out the kinks between her shoulders. For a body-builder, he was not only gentle with his hands, he was eye-candy too and knew it. In fact, he had a great rapport with his female clients.

"This was a wonderful idea," her friend Liz moaned from the table where she was stretched out and being worked on by Richard's co-worker. "However, I've a feeling there's more to this *treat* than just being nice. You look tired. Has Doug been up to his old tricks?"

Kathryne opened one eye. "How'd you know?"

"Hmm, right there," Liz muttered, then spoke to Kathryne. "The man's a bastard. You shouldn't have let him keep his office in the same building. Besides that, the last time we had a massage together, he went away for a weekend with someone half his age—"

"Oh, please" Kathryne groaned. "Don't use that expression."

"What?" Liz cried in her Brooklyn-born accent.

"You know . . . *half his age*. It seems like that's everybody's favorite expression lately. And you guessed it—he's going away with another woman. You know his M O. And then he had the audacity to ask me to review a real estate contract in the same breath. I swear, he has nerve."

"Well, if you ask me," Richard interjected, "the man's a fool to let you go. Look at these buns, they're tight and firm as any twenty-year-old."

Kathryne lifted her head and gave the masseuse a sweet smile. "Thank you, Richard. You always know just what to say to get a big tip. However, just for the record, he didn't let me go. I let *him* go."

"Well, if you ask me," Liz interjected. "You should've let him go to another law firm. He's still getting to you, Kate. I knew it by your tone of voice over the phone." Liz rested her chin on her closed fist. "You know what I think you need?" She didn't give Kathryne time to answer. "You need a change . . . a vacation."

Kathryne raised a golden brow. "Have you been talking with my doctor?" She heaved a loud sigh. "I can't. I'm in the middle of a big project for an even bigger client of mine."

"Client, schmient," Liz countered. "You're working too hard, Kate. How many associates do you have? Ten? I'm sure one of the ten is capable of taking over your case load. My sister just got back from a darling bed and breakfast up north. I can't remember the name of it, but she said it was out of this world. A mountain retreat with a spa, aroma therapy, yoga . . . all the bells and whistles. Kind of pricey, but worth every penny."

"Sounds nice, but I—"

"You what?" Liz asked. "You know, hon, you can't take it with you. Besides, if you don't spend it, who will?"

Kathryne blanched a little at the firm look on her friend's face. Liz was right. There were no brothers or sisters, no children other than her nieces and nephews from Douglas's side, and their parents had already taken care of college needs. "It's just that—"

"You hate traveling alone?" Liz gave her an understanding nod. "You'll get used to it. Won't she, Richard?"

"I'm not so sure, Mrs. B. My guess is if she'd just circulate a little she wouldn't be alone for long."

"You're tip is as big as it's going to get," Kathryne countered. She glanced over at Liz. "Are you two in this together?" she asked skeptically. She looked at Richard. "Is she paying you to say nice things?"

Richard laughed and then patted Kathryne's behind. "Ms. Sheldon, just look in that mirror over there and tell me what you see."

Kathryne turned and stared at her image in the full-length mirrors mounted on the far wall. A million things swarmed in her thoughts—the doctor's advice—Liz's advice. There was something else, too, that she saw in the mirror—a woman, surrounded by friends yet feeling terribly alone, but also a woman who was optimistic, who loved adventures and surprises—the woman she used to be. Aware that Richard waited for her answer, and not wanting to vent her feelings of hopelessness, she groaned and buried her face in the towel on the table. "I see someone twice your age."

"How long has it been since you've taken a month off?" Liz asked, popping half a bacon-wrapped scallop into her mouth—the Monday night special at Murphy's Seafood Shack, one of Liz's favorite places. Since her husband was a chef, he didn't like to eat out very often, so Liz and Kathryne made a date for dinner each week. This week was Murphy's. Next week was still undecided.

Kathryne choked, put down her glass of wine, and dabbed her mouth with her napkin. She'd been sipping a glass of Riesling in their favorite restaurant, listening to Liz's suggestion about stress and relaxation, toying with the idea of taking a week off when her friend blurted out the absurd idea. "A month? I've never taken a whole month. You can't be serious."

Liz nodded emphatically, causing her dangling earrings to tinkle ever so softly. "Yes, honey. I am deadly serious. Look at yourself. You're a workaholic. Always have been. Been that way since your daddy gave you the company and took off to God knows where. If you ask me, you should have refused, but that's another story. Why, I can't remember when you last took a vacation. Can you?"

"West," Kathryne replied.

Liz frowned. "What? Are you trying to change the subject on me?"

Kathryne shook her head. "No, I know where my father went. And now I think I know why he left." She didn't give Liz time to respond—didn't feel like going into details. "He went to New Mexico. He wrote to me last summer. Wanted me to come for a visit, but I never got back to him. You know how it was between my dad and Doug."

Liz's expression changed from one of bewilderment to one of disgust. "That's nice, hon. Now as I was saying. I don't remember the last time you took some time off."

Kathryne poked at her salad. There was more truth to Liz's words than she cared to admit, and thinking of her dad just now sparked something deep down. "I took a few days off last month."

"That doesn't count. It was some kind of seminar . . . I don't remember what you told me, but seminars are not vacations." Liz took a sip of wine. "No wonder you're feeling shitty. Too bad you can't pass the baton on to a family member and go traveling, like your daddy did to you."

"Dad never cared for city life like Mom did." She took another sip of wine, smiling at Liz's impatient expression. "Look, Liz. I can't just take off on a whim. I've got clients—responsibility." *Consider changing professions to one that generates less stress.* She put down her glass, disturbed that Liz's advice emulated the doctor's.

"Yeah, sure," Liz responded, her Brooklyn accent thicker than usual as she lifted one skeptical brow, leaned over and patted Kathryne's hand. "What will they ever do without you?" she added sarcastically. "Especially if you're dead because you wouldn't take a lousy few weeks off to relax. You remember the word, don't you Kate? Ree-lax. It means to slo-ow down, have some fun and enjoy yourself."

Liz leaned back and stabbed another piece of scallop. "It's just like I said. You won't be able to spend all that money in your 401K if you're dead. You need a vacation."

"Maybe you're right."

Liz gave Kathryne a knowing glance. "Of course I'm right. I'll even plan it, if you want. I'll give you two weeks to clear your schedule. Then all you'll have to do is pack." Liz smiled a slow, secretive smile and then motioned for the waiter. "And don't pack until I tell you where you're going." Liz ordered another glass of wine.

"May I have some input?" Kathryne asked, leaning back against her chair, willing to let her friend have her way . . . at least for the time being.

"I suppose . . . if you insist." Liz picked up another bread stick and tore it in half. "After all, it's your vacation."

"I want to go west," Kathryne said, trying hard not to laugh at Liz's shocked expression.

"Out west . . . like cowboys-and-Indians out west?"

Kathryne nodded, already set on her destination, but unwilling to hurt her friend's feelings by not accepting her help. "Someplace where there are horses. I'd like to do some riding."

"Honey, upstate New York has horses. Dry and hot is bad for the complexion, and so is sand and dirt." Liz put down the bread, and then took her cell phone out of her purse and flipped it open. "Bobby, it's me, baby. Call Ruthie and ask her about that bed and breakfast she visited last month. Yeah, baby. Oh sure. Kate is going to take a little vacation." Liz was quiet for a moment, but her smile grew larger and her coffee-brown eyes softened. "Yeah, baby, I love you too. Kiss, kiss."

★ ★ ★ ★ ★

Kathryne sat in her office, staring out the window. Ever since Liz had mentioned the word vacation, she couldn't stop thinking about the summers she'd spent at her grandfather's ranch—the ranch her father left the firm and his career to reclaim.

If memory served, the ranch house itself was a huge place, three stories full of bedrooms and bathrooms and a kitchen bigger than any other she'd ever seen. Of course, she'd only been eight or nine years old, and to a child things seemed bigger. But nevertheless, ever since Liz suggested she take some time off, the memory of that ranch seemed to fill every waking moment. It did something else too. It had uncovered an old, fond memory about a trip she and Douglas had taken nearly ten years ago.

They'd spent the weekend at a quaint little bed and breakfast in Virginia. They'd had a superb time and had even talked about doing something like it when they retired. It had been a dream she'd put on the back burner, and like many other plans that never materialized, or that Doug wasn't exactly thrilled about, it was eventually forgotten.

Maybe it would be something her father might be interested in. If only she'd kept in touch over the years in spite of Doug. Was it too late to rekindle their relationship?

She was deep in thought when Helen knocked on her door. "Come in."

"You've been awfully quiet in here. Is everything all right?"

"Yes," Kathryne said with a thoughtful smile. "Everything's fine."

"That doesn't look like an *everything's fine* expression. It looks more like *I've got a crazy idea* expression."

"Maybe I do," Kathryne confirmed with a small laugh. She opened her desk drawer and pulled out a little note card. "My mother is somewhere in Europe with my aunts and uncles on one of those senior-anniversary tours they take. Here's the number of the travel agency they always use. See if you can track her down. I'd really appreciate it."

Helen looked at the number then nodded. "What do I do when I find her?"

"Have her give me a call."

Kathryne sat straight up in bed, slightly disoriented, wondering for a split second why she woke. The next instant she knew. *La Bamba* played on her cell phone in the next room. The clock on the bureau told her it was half past three. Tossing aside the covers, she hurried into the study and yanked the phone from its charger. "Hello? Mom? Yeah, I'm awake now. No, no, don't hang up—it's great to hear from you."

Kathryne padded into the kitchen and put a copper tea kettle on the burner. "Scotland tomorrow? That's great. Are you having a good time? Wonderful. No, nothing's wrong, I was just trying to remember where Granddad's ranch was. Taos . . . yes of course. You know what they say—the memory is the first to go." She gave a small laugh. "There were lots of trees and green mountains."

She retrieved a mug from the cupboard, and while holding the phone in the crook of her neck, took the lid off of a can of hot chocolate mix. She added a heaping tablespoon to the cup, and then filled it with hot water. "Yes, I realize Dad's there. That's part of the reason I called. Has Dad done anything with the ranch?" She took a sip, listening to her mother's explanation. "Are you serious? No, I had no idea. Well, yes, I guess it has been a long time. I suppose he fooled us both, didn't he?"

Kathryne sipped her chocolate, listening to her mother for several more minutes, recognizing the sound of her Uncle Dick's voice as he added something about their childhood home, as did her other two uncles.

"No, don't worry about my minutes. I've got plenty left.

Mom." Kathryne hesitated for a moment. "I'm aware that this might sound like I'm following in Daddy's footsteps, but how would you feel if I left the firm? Yes, I know I'm still young, but I've been thinking about stepping back—you know, doing something more . . . something different. No. Like you, I'd still keep my hand in the cookie jar. Well, now that you mention it, I was hoping to ask Dad's advice, but I've misplaced his number."

She hurriedly put down her cup and searched the drawer for a pen. "Yes, I'm ready." She wrote down a number. "I wish I could be as sure he'll take my call. We didn't exactly part on good terms."

She listened for several moments, smiling and feeling like a child while her mother scolded her. "Time changes things. Now that Doug and I are divorced, I've done a lot of soul-searching and realize that you and Dad are all I have. I will," she agreed. "I'll call him, and if he's willing, I'm going to New Mexico for a visit."

She yawned and then nodded slowly. "Yes, I suppose I'll be expected to attend, but I'm not exactly looking forward to it. Hopefully this ball will be my last. Yes, it's good to hear your voice too. Give everyone a kiss for me, and have a wonderful time . . . and Mom? Thanks."

Kathryne snapped her phone closed, clutching it to her chest for several moments. The sound of her mother's voice had been soothing, and even though the call roused her from a deep, dreamless sleep, it had been worth it. The news that her father had turned the ranch into a type of dude ranch was a shocker, especially since he seemed to prefer solitude.

But on the same note, at least he hadn't sold it. Her idea of a bed and breakfast slowly dwindled. Depending on how he received her call, she might suggest to him that they become partners—after all, he wasn't getting any younger.

Yawning again, she placed the phone back into the charger

and drank the last two sips of chocolate before returning to bed. Tomorrow, she'd call her father. Smiling, she snuggled down under the comforter and closed her eyes, hoping for happier dreams.

And, for the first time in a long time, she actually looked forward to going into the office in the morning.

John Hawkins pushed his dusty brown Stetson back off his forehead, and then took a bandana from his hip pocket to wipe the sweat from his brow. His employer, Henry "Hank" Sheldon, had left yesterday for a well deserved vacation in a place known for its abundant sun, sand, and ocean breezes.

While Henry was gone, John decided to mend the fence between Hank's dude ranch and his own smaller ranch in northern New Mexico. John had been working for most of the morning and still had several broken posts to replace.

Cattle were tough on fence, he knew, but he never minded hard work. To his way of thinking, hard work kept him healthy, and there were no dues to be paid to a gym. He walked over to his 1956 Ford pick-up truck and lifted an orange-colored, insulated jug out of the bed, filling a tin cup with a cold drink of water. Duke, his golden retriever, wagged his tail, raising his shaggy head in greeting from where he rested in the shade of the truck.

"Want a drink, fella?" John asked as he squatted down to rub the old dog's soft ears, letting him drink from the cup. A mountain blue jay called from the top of a nearby ponderosa pine, drawing John's attention. From his position on the ridge, John had a great view of the valley and the fifty or so head of cattle that dotted the grassy meadow below. His land bordered the Forestry Department's on the north, and the pine-scented breeze blew fresh and crisp down from the snow-capped Sangre de Cristo Mountains.

John stood, stretched a kink out of his back, and then tossed the cup in the truck bed. He was just about to string another strand of barbed wire when the sound of a vehicle approaching stopped him. With his hat shading his eyes from the sun, he quickly recognized the color of the car before he could see the driver as they raced down the dirt road. The car stopped on the road a hundred feet away from where John had parked his pick-up on the rougher terrain near the fence.

"Hey there, Johnny," Norman called as he jumped out of his baby-blue Thunderbird convertible. Duke got up and, with tail wagging, met Norman half way. "Oh, how's our baby, huh? You being good, Dukey?" Norman ruffled the dog's ears, then straightened up. "I almost didn't come. After all, it's my day off, and I just washed my car."

John leaned back against the front fender of his truck watching his best friend's approach. Norman, always high-strung and in a hurry—oblivious to where he was walking, stepped into a freshly deposited cow-pie, immediately cursing as he tried to wipe his beige-suede loafer clean on a clump of buffalo grass.

"Gosh damn it," Norman muttered. "I swear, Johnny. I don't know why you're never home to answer the phone. Always out here in the boonies. It must have something to do with your Native-American heritage," he added with a tinge of sarcasm as he raised his hands and made imaginary quote marks with his fingers. "*One with nature.* Well, I'm one with nature now. Just look at my car. It's covered in dust. I'll have to have it detailed . . . and now this."

Norman motioned for John to look at the green stain on the side of his shoe. "I just bought these. Look at this one. It's ruined."

"Just what color is that?" John asked with a sideways grin. "Beige?"

"Vanilla-cream," Norman grumbled, picking at the bits of

manure with a stick. "But no more," he exclaimed. "No, now it's cow-poop green."

John's grin widened at Norman's defeated expression. They'd known each other for nearly thirty years—were best friends and worked together for Hank.

Looking back, John ruminated that, without Norman, he'd have never met Ellie. Being Ellie's brother, Norman, with his heart of gold, had helped John deal with his grief when Ellie died of cancer last year after suffering with it for years.

"Out here," John drawled, "it's best to wear boots and watch where you're stepping. I would've thought you'd learned that by now." He ignored the disgusted look from Norman, aware that there was no malice directed at him. However, if a steer wandered up, John was pretty certain Norman would launch a rock at the poor beast.

"You need a haircut," Norman countered as he always did when they were having a friendly argument. "Long hair went out years ago."

"Yeah, like I care," John rebuked. "Didn't beige shoes go out years ago too?"

Instead of answering with one of his usual prompt comebacks, Norman held out an envelope.

"What's that?" John asked.

"This is a problem . . . one we need to address immediately."

John tugged off his gloves and laid them on the hood of the pick-up, then retrieved his reading glasses from his shirt pocket before accepting the envelope. He gave Norman a dark glance, noticing that the envelope had been opened. "Well, what does it say? Apparently you've already read it."

"Just read," Norman scolded, moving closer to look around John's shoulder. "Seems Marty has retired and sold the bank. But that's the least of our problems."

John glanced at Norman. "Do you mind?" he muttered. "I

can't see through your head."

Norman gave a snort. "Sorry, it's just that I'm terribly upset."

John grinned again. "You're always upset. Now back off and let me see what this says." He slid out a single piece of paper. "USIB and Associates of Baltimore have recently purchased your real estate contract . . . demand payment . . . thirty days?"

Norman toyed nervously with the gold chain around his neck. "What do they want from us, blood? Hell, it'd be a sight better if they did. We have blood. It's hard, cold cash we're short of."

John looked at his friend again, smiling slightly. Norman always used *we,* when the ranch was actually John's. Or at least it had been for a short time five years ago when he'd finally paid off his first mortgage. But that was before he'd had to refinance to pay some hefty medical bills when Ellie's cancer returned.

In many ways, Norman reminded him of his late wife, but Ellie was steady and had a good head when it came to most any crisis. Norman, on the other hand, constantly blew things out of proportion. As John read on, he dearly hoped this was one of those occasions.

But it was not to be, and when he finished, his chest tightened with an uneasy sense of urgency. When did it come to pass that a bank didn't hold a man's note anymore, selling it to some fancy corporation in some far off place like Baltimore?

"Well?" Norman's impatient tone invaded John's thoughts.

John folded the letter and stuffed it into the back pocket of his jeans. "I guess I'd better give them a call."

"I already did."

"Now, why doesn't that surprise me?" John muttered, tossing his tools into the back of his truck. "What'd they say?"

"I could only get a recording, but I left your name and phone number."

★ ★ ★ ★ ★

Kathryne heaved an impatient sigh, then put the phone back in the cradle at the same time Helen came in with a folder.

"Here's the Dickson contract for your signature." Helen put the folder on Kathryne's desk, then lifted her empty coffee cup, pausing before she got to the door. "Is there something bothering you . . . more than just being out of coffee?" Helen teased.

Kathryne forced a smile. "Last night my mother called and gave me my father's phone number in New Mexico. I was hoping to speak with him, but . . ." She gave a small laugh. "He's on vacation."

"If it's important, I'll be happy to see if I can hunt him down."

Kathryne shook her head. "If anyone could, you could, but it's nothing that can't wait."

CHAPTER THREE

John woke at his usual time and made a pot of coffee while the sun struggled to the top of the pines surrounding his ranch house. Dawn always brought with it a sense of newness, chasing away the memories of his life with Ellie—memories that over the years had become more and more depressing. It had been hard watching someone he loved die so slowly.

A gentle mountain breeze played with the branches of the ponderosas, swaying them gracefully back and forth, but John didn't notice. He was thinking about other things—the day he and Ellie got married and how, instead of a honeymoon, they put what they'd saved down on a rickety old log house and a small tract of land. In time, with lots of work and repairs, it became their mountain retreat, nestled among hundred-year-old pines.

Dear, sweet Ellie, how she tried to be the perfect wife. But soon after they were married, she discovered a lump in her left breast. They didn't know it at the time, but her bouts with cancer would steadily reoccur. He glanced around the cozy kitchen—not small, but rather a kitchen designed for lots of kids. Because of Ellie's sickness, their plans for a large family never materialized, nor could they qualify for adoption, but Ellie still made their modest house into a warm, comfortable home.

But it wasn't just the house. For John, it was the land—the land his ancestors had called their own. Land that made him feel he belonged.

He forced his memories aside, reaching for a pot-holder to lift the coffee pot off the burner. He'd just filled his cup with hot, fresh coffee when Norman came down the hall with Duke trailing after him. When Norman stayed at the ranch, Duke stayed with Norman, soaking up the extra attention and table scraps.

Norman's prematurely gray hair was tousled, and his light-blue terry robe hung haphazardly off one shoulder, exposing his blue-stripped flannel pajamas. His matching slippers made little scuff noises on the hardwood floor as he padded over to the tiled counter, pushing his gold-rimmed glasses up on his nose. "Coffee. I need coffee," Norman muttered.

John filled another cup and put it in Norman's outstretched hand. "Sleep well?"

Norman raised one brow. "Does it look like I slept well? No, I did not. I tossed and turned all night worrying. And then when I finally drifted off, that damned rooster of yours decided to crow his blasted lungs out. We should have chicken for dinner tonight. You kill him. I'll pluck him . . . no, on second thought, I'll kill him."

Norman took a sip of coffee, closed his eyes in bliss. "I love your coffee, John. It's strong enough to remove paint and unclog sinks." He opened one eye. "You're socks aren't in that pot are they?"

"Not my socks," John replied dryly, raising his cup in salute before taking a drink.

"Oh, don't tell me," Norman replied, playing along. "I'd rather not know which piece of your clothing gives your coffee that *special* flavor."

"Who said it's mine?" Chuckling, John turned and refilled his cup, enjoying himself. Most of the time, Norman stayed at his own apartment off the kitchen at Henry's lodge. Only on rare occasions did he choose to spend time at John's cabin, and now that he was here, making fun of the coffee, John realized what a good friend he had in Norman. "Want some breakfast?"

Swallowing another gulp of coffee, Norman nodded. "What do you have in mind?"

"Thick-sliced bacon, a couple of fried eggs and . . ." He held up a tubular can of biscuits. ". . . home-style buttermilk biscuits, and we'll have butter and strawberry jam. What else?"

"Well, gee, let me see if I can think outside your tightly sealed box. Sometimes, Johnny boy, in the outside world, people have half a grapefruit with a whole-wheat blueberry muffin, or bran cereal and soymilk and a glass of organic orange juice. Ever hear of cholesterol?" Norman shook his head. "You're so healthy, I doubt it. Anyway, how can you eat when we could lose the ranch?"

John pulled the skillet out of the drawer under the oven where he kept the pans. "I'm not going to lose the ranch. But if I do, I'd rather do it on a full stomach. Now, I'm making bacon and eggs. I've got some juice, but it's from concentrate, and I think there's some instant oatmeal in the cupboard. As for fruit, there are a couple of apples in the bin, but with just me around, I don't keep much fruit in the house. It spoils."

John paused a moment. "Let me take that back. There might be a couple of cans of peaches in the pantry."

John glanced at his friend who was already looking through the pantry on the other side of the kitchen, then added, "Next to the box of chocolate cookies and behind the pretzels. Now, how do you want your eggs?"

Norman mumbled something from inside the pantry.

"What? I can't hear you."

Norman poked out his head, a can of peaches in his hand. "I said bacon crisp and eggs over easy."

★ ★ ★ ★ ★

John put the phone back in the cradle and heaved a long, loud sigh. He'd left a message after breakfast, but a representative of USIB, a young woman by the sound of her voice, waited until nearly noon to return his call, and the news wasn't good.

Now Norman sat across from him, his expression so intense John almost felt like lying to ease his friend's distress. "Well, it's just like we thought. When Marty sold the bank, he sold my loan, and these new folks want six thousand up-front to catch up the payments. They're not interested in any extensions. The head honcho won't be back for a week, so she suggested I try back then."

Norman groaned and then leaned back in his chair, utterly defeated. "My God. Where are we going to get six thousand dollars?"

"That's the problem. I've only got about two hundred in the bank."

Norman's frown deepened as he stood and cleared the lunch dishes off the table. "I thought you were making regular payments?"

"I was until last year. Then when Ellie . . . got worse, and when the medical bills started adding up, and then the cost of the funeral, Marty let me make what I could afford. I've been trying to catch up, but cattle prices are down, and I just started making good money working for Hank. I guess I've been kind of short of the full payment for some time."

"Six thousand dollars short?" Norman cried, sitting back down across from John. "Why didn't you ask me? I could have helped."

John shoved away from the table. How could he tell his friend that he'd lost interest in the ranch since Ellie died? It went against his grain to admit defeat. It also went against his nature to confess that he didn't particularly care what happened anymore. He'd failed Ellie as a husband, failed to have enough in savings to cover her medical expenses, and now had no retirement—nothing to fall back on. "It's not your problem, Norm."

"John, you're my family. Let me help. I've got a little savings. It's yours if you need it. You know that. I've also got an exhibit coming up in June that'll net at least that much. Can they wait till June?"

"No." John went to the sink and looked out the window, too angry at his situation to see the beauty in the mountains beyond. "They want it all in thirty days, or they'll foreclose." He turned around to face his friend. "I already owe too much. I refuse to borrow more. Maybe it's time to face the music. Maybe it's time to sell. Henry's been after me to take one of the cabins over at the Silver Creek. Maybe I should."

Norman jumped up. "Johnny, don't say that. You love this place. I love this place. Don't let your pride get in the way. I'll transfer the funds on Monday."

"Norman, read my lips. No."

"Then there's got to be something we can do."

"I'm not so sure I want to stay here anymore." John walked over to the back door and took his hat from the hook, then shoved the screen door open, hating that he'd just lied to Norman about his true feelings for the ranch. "Duke, you coming?" The dog left Norman's side and bounded outside. "I gotta go finish repairing the fence."

John stood on the bluff that gave him a panoramic view of northern New Mexico. He'd finished the fence, driven back to the Silver Creek, and with the rest of the day off, decided to saddle up his gelding and take a ride. It felt good to be astride his horse—something he hadn't done in weeks.

He'd been too busy. Too busy helping Hank with running the resort, mending gates, repairing the horse pens, and teaching the kids—the job he liked most. Watching a child's eyes light up the first time he rode a horse made everything worthwhile.

The sky blazed with oranges and pinks as the sun settled between the distant peaks. It was a sight he never tired of, filling him with an inner peace. Many times when he was up here, he thought about his mother—how she taught him to love nature.

She had faced some tough times, raising a child alone. A full-blooded Navajo, she was disowned by many of them for sleeping with a white man, and as an Indian, she was scorned by the whites. But in spite of all her problems, she taught John to be strong in all things and to respect others, no matter their opinions.

His grandfather had taught him many things too. A World War II veteran, Charlie Silver-Hawk had been patient and wise—the one who'd taught him never to run from a fight, that it was always better to stand and face life's problems. *A man who faces death and defies it will never be afraid to live.*

John heaved a sigh, smiling at the memory of his grandfather's favorite expression. John had seen death and defied it in Vietnam, but when he had to stand by helplessly and watch Ellie face it, death took on a whole new meaning. Life was precious, and although things might get bad, he still had a lot to be thankful for—still had a lot of living to do.

A red-tailed hawk took flight from the top of a tall ponderosa, drawing John's gaze as it soared across the amber sky. The corners of John's mouth curved into a smile. Part of him wanted to think that seeing the hawk was a sign from his beloved ancestor. Maybe it was. Who was he to doubt Navajo folklore?

"Am I also to feel lost—hopeless—afraid of the unknown, Grandfather?" John murmured, watching the hawk soar effortless in the sky. "I'm lonely, and I'm angry that I did the right thing by my wife, but all the creditors seem to be aware of is my failure to make the full payments. They've got me backed into a corner, Grandfather. And for the first time in my life, I don't feel that I'm in control of my life. Some big-ass corporation back East is threatening to take my ranch, and I'm so angry, I'd like to burn the damned place down before giving it up."

Never be afraid to make a decision. Remember, Johnny, even a wrong decision is better than no decision at all. His grandfather's second favorite expression hit home. John had a decision to make.

At first it had seemed hopeless, but after riding up here, gazing out at the mountains, and talking with his Grandfather's spirit, he felt better and could make a clear-headed decision— one that would resolve his present financial situation and help him keep the land he loved. And, if he played his cards right, it could even provide a comfortable retirement. He mounted his horse and trotted down the path, anxious to talk it over with Norman.

"I can't believe it," Norman said with a disbelieving shake of his head. He dried his hands on the kitchen towel, then turned and leaned against the counter, shoving his hands into the pockets of Ellie's pink-flowered, ruffled-edged apron. "You did a land division twenty years ago?"

"Yup. I don't know why, but I thought if I ever needed to sell, it'd be easier to sell the house on five acres than it would to sell the whole hundred-acre parcel."

"Then you're really going to sell?"

John had a hard time keeping a straight face, but managed to remain as serious as he could for Norman's sake. And it was working too—as long as he didn't look at the apron. "It's really the best way," he said softly, trying his best to ignore the apron and the little-boy pout on his friend's face. "I'd rather Hank got the ranch than some developer."

Norman shook his head. "Johnny, you don't have to sell any

of it. Ellie loved this place. I love this place, and so do you. Don't let your pride get in the way. I can transfer the funds on Monday, and then you can forget all about your silly idea."

"Norman, you're repeating yourself. You know that's a sign of old age, don't you? Besides, you know I'm right. Land's been selling good around here. Hell, Hank's been nagging me for years to sell so he can expand the lodge."

"No, I don't know you're right . . . not for sure. There's got to be something else we can do."

John gave his friend an understanding smile. "I can lose it, or I can sell it to Hank. If I sell it, I'll still have most of the land, be able to pay all my bills, and have a few bucks to put in the bank. It won't be so bad living at the lodge till I fix up the old hunting shack. Besides, I'm over at the lodge most of the time anyway. Providing Hank buys it, we both know he won't sell it off to some developer for homes. If I remember correctly, he wanted to make this his family cabin for those folks who want the privacy of the mountains with all the conveniences of the lodge . . . like your good cooking."

Norman heaved a defeated sigh. "You could pay me back, John, later when—"

"Norm . . . I'm not so sure I want to stay here anymore." He walked over to the oven and opened the door. He had to change the subject before he rammed his fist into the wall in frustration. "Is that apple pie?"

"Dutch apple, but don't think you can change the subject so easily. Why? Why not stay here?"

Taking a patient breath, John put his hand on Norman's shoulder, biting back a chuckle when his fingers brushed the ruffled strap. "I'll talk to Henry when he gets back next week. In the meantime, I've picked up a little side job hauling a load of grass hay over to Albuquerque this weekend."

"Driving?" Norman cried incredulously as he shrugged away,

folding his arms over his chest. "You've got to be kidding."

"Trucking helped me pay for this place till I hooked up with Hank. It'll help me keep it until I can sell it."

"But, John, I'll never see you. And what about the animals . . . the horses?" Norman softly clapped his hands, a signal to Duke to lumber over. "And Dukey here. What will he do without you? He's old. He'll never understand."

"The cattle will be fine out grazing. As for the horses, I haven't decided what to do with them yet—maybe Hank will want them, but Duke will be fine with me."

Norman's face fell. "No, you can't take him. I mean . . . of course you can, but he's my friend too. I only get to see you on the weekends. I'll miss you both terribly. But it's worse than that. Do you realize what will happen to the ranch if you're not here to keep things in good order? It'll fall apart, and then we won't get a good price."

"Hell, Norm, who are we kidding? It's falling apart now." John went to the refrigerator, opened the door, and took out a beer.

"That will ruin your appetite."

An uncomfortable silence fell over the room until Norman turned and opened the cupboard and took out a pan. "I hate to say it, but all we have for dinner is leftovers." Norman shook his head. "Don't you ever go shopping?"

Choosing to appease his friend, John took a patient breath and then put the beer back. "I realize you're upset, but at least if I'm driving, I'll be able to make the payments. And during the week, after work, I can do the repairs."

"I suppose."

"Look," John began, trying to think of a way to cheer up Norman. "How long before the pie's ready?"

"Fifteen minutes," Norman replied with a disappointed sigh.

"But then it has to cool for at least an hour or the apples will run."

"Good." John headed toward the door to his bedroom. "That'll give me time to shower up. Take off that apron, and while the pie's cooling, we'll go into town and have supper. What do you say to that?"

Norman turned, still holding the pot, but his expression appeared brighter. "There's a new sushi bar I've been dying to try."

John stuck his head out the door. "Norm," he cautioned, shaking his head. "I don't eat bait."

CHAPTER FOUR

Norman followed the realtor to the door with a strained smile. "Well, let us know what you decide. You come highly recommended." The moment he closed the door, he leaned back against it with a long sigh. "My God, can this get any worse?"

"It's rather dingy. Isn't it? And it needs a lot of repairs," Norman repeated in a high, squeaky voice. Duke raised his head from his paws and cocked his head at the sound of Norman's voice. The old dog rose and lumbered over to Norman, who bent down, held Duke's head between his palms, and lifted the animal's snout to where it almost touched his own nose.

"I know, Dukey-boy. It needs some paint, but what did that crazy woman expect?" Norman straightened up when he heard the back door open and close. "Is that you, John?" he asked as he headed toward the kitchen.

"Yup. How'd it go?"

"Well, not too badly." Norman opened the refrigerator door and lifted out a large plastic pitcher. "Want some juice?"

"I'd rather have a beer," John replied, accepting a glass of grape juice instead. "What'd they say?"

"Juice is better for you," Norman said, filling a glass for himself. "In all honesty, I don't think she was impressed, but she'll list it. Let's just hope when Henry gets back he still wants it." Norman took a drink. "We've got to face it, John. Henry's our best hope. These days, folks just aren't interested in living in the mountains. They want amenities—big city amenities. You know, shopping malls and coffee shops . . . schools that aren't fifteen miles away."

"Shopping malls—cities?" John repeated. "Hell, that's no place to raise kids. Whatever happened to family walks, hiking, and fishing together?"

"Some folks don't have children . . . by choice."

John inwardly winced. He was childless, certainly not by choice, but by circumstance.

Norman heaved a long sigh. "Kids are just too expensive, and what with world hunger and over-population—both parents working to afford their dream home and pay for gas—kids get put on the back burner more often than not. Look at the kids who come here. Most of them are from broken homes or have parents who are just too busy to take the time to teach them how to hike or fish. That's what you're for. That's why they come to Silver Creek—to spend two weeks away from all the hustle and bustle of the city."

"Yeah, I guess," John said, putting the glass in the sink. He didn't like it, but there wasn't much he could do about it either. "I got another run into Albuquerque tomorrow. I'll be leaving before sunup."

"Good grief. Don't bang around. It's my sleep-in-day. While Henry's gone, I'm taking advantage of it. No guests, no cooking . . ." Norman stopped talking, gazing out the window with a frown. "However, it would be an opportunity to paint."

"Yeah, you could start early and paint the barn, then the fence—"

Norman's frown deepened. "The sunset . . . if I paint, it'll be to capture the sunset in oil, not the barn in latex."

John grinned. "Well, while you're capturing the sun, I'll be taking hay to Albuquerque. After road tax and fuel expenses, I should net a little over seven hundred for the two trips."

"Johnny, you need thousands, not hundreds." Norman heaved

another more impatient sigh then practically threw himself down on the kitchen chair.

"I know that, Norm, but this is a start. Hell, it's hay season, and we all know the valley is full of some of the best grass hay available."

"Maybe," Norman muttered, apparently not convinced. "Let's just hope Henry doesn't stay in Florida forever." He drummed his fingers on the table . . . the solid pine table that John had made. It was a beautiful piece, as were all of John creations, sanded and smooth, stained to bring out the grain, then coated with a tough poly-glaze that made the table glisten.

The chairs were comfortable too, sturdy and as finely made as the table. Norman shifted his weight, and then glanced at the nearly empty matching china hutch on the other wall. "How long did it take you to make that?"

"What?" John asked.

"The china cabinet and hutch. How long did it take you to make them?"

"Hell, I don't remember. A few days . . . a week maybe."

"How attached are you?" Norman asked, standing.

John followed him into the other room. "Not *too* attached, if I'm getting your meaning."

Norman glanced at his friend, pleased that he caught on to his idea. "You made these tables too," he muttered, then spun and faced John. "If I were to take them to my friend's studio in Taos and sell them, you'd be all right with that?"

"I suppose so. But, who'd buy used furniture?" John asked.

"Not *used*, Johnny, old-fashioned, hand-crafted, even *rustic* furniture." Norman turned, smiling. "I don't know why I didn't think of this sooner. What else have you got around here we could sell?"

John shrugged. "Well, why don't you have a look and then tell me, 'cause I'd just as soon get rid of it all. I've got a few things out in the barn too."

Norman's face brightened, and suddenly John felt as if he'd opened a can of worms. "What?"

"That's it, John. Between taking an occasional load of hay or whatever it is you haul on that thing, to Albuquerque, you could make a few pieces of furniture—furniture I could sell." Norman made a wide sweep with his arms. "Hell, we've got a whole forest out there. Our overhead shouldn't be too high."

John followed Norman's gaze, watching as his friend examined his lamps and even the gun rack over the rock fireplace. "Just what kinds of pieces do you want?"

Norman made another dramatic sweep with his arm. "These kind. Gun racks, coat racks, end tables, chairs." Norman hurried past John and over to the door that led to John's bedroom.

"Headboards and chests and . . ." Norman picked up wooden lamp that had a bear and its cub carved into the base. "This stuff is great. We should be able to get a small fortune for something like this." Excitement danced in Norman's eyes. "I don't know why I didn't see it sooner."

"You already said that," John muttered, looking at his overzealous friend. "What kind of money are you talking?"

Norman smiled. "Leave that part to me. I'm great with tourists. Sell it too cheap and they won't think it's authentic. Sell high and they appreciate it more. Trust me, I know. I had a painting, and I couldn't sell it for the life of me. Then one day, I just got so mad that I raised the price, and damned if some couple didn't come in from Chicago and buy it the very next day."

John had his doubts, but he knew better than to express them to Norman, especially when he was in one of his *I can do anything* moods. Although Norman had overcome his shyness with adulthood, his feelings were still easily hurt.

John glanced at the interior of his home, trying to see

something good in getting rid of all his belongings. With a heavy sigh, he went back to the kitchen and opened the pantry, calling over his shoulder. "How about I make some chili and beans for supper? There's some tortillas in the fridge."

Norman strolled in, his pleased smile still present. "No, no, no. I'll see to it. You go shower up. After supper, we can load your pick-up and take some of this stuff into Taos. We might as well get started, don't you agree? I'll be watching the shop on Sunday for my friend, and frankly, I'm a much better salesperson."

"I suppose," John muttered as he headed back to his room. "Don't go adding anything funny to the chili, either. Last time you tried putting in some carrots." John made an I-don't-trust-you face. "Like I wouldn't notice."

"You don't eat enough—"

John closed the door and leaned against it, grinning when he heard the word *vegetables* hollered from the kitchen.

His bedroom was large and had easily accommodated the wheelchair he'd rented in Ellie's last years. A huge four-poster, carved log, king-sized bed dominated the far wall with two matching bedside tables. He'd crafted them from smoothed logs, and he purposely left a few chisel marks on the surface to add that rustic appearance Norman had just been so excited about. The bench at the foot of the bed was also rustic, as were the eight-drawer dresser and six-drawer chest. The room itself was spacious, made more so with the double doors that opened outward to the porch and the two rockers he'd made so he and Ellie could sit outside in the warmer months and watch the sun set on the mountains.

Ellie never put up curtains, and the sicker she got, the more money got tight, and she'd said that she didn't want to spoil the view. And that nobody except the forest critters could see in anyway. But Ellie was gone now, and the house felt too big for one man and a dog. John sank down on the bed and tugged off his boots. It was times like this that he missed her most—missed talking to her—asking her opinion. He used to come in after doing chores, and they'd share supper and small talk and just spend time together. He glanced around the room once more, then shed his clothes and went into the adjoining bathroom to shave and shower . . . and forget.

Norman heard the water running, and then put back the pinto beans. Tonight he'd make something special. Fried potatoes with onions and bacon, and he dug around in the freezer and found a thick steak he could defrost in the microwave. He pulled out the bag of salad mix he'd brought over from the lodge and ripped it open.

Ten minutes later, the salad was made and the potatoes and onions were frying with some bacon. Norman had just put the steak in a red-hot iron skillet when Duke scratched at the door to be let in. Norman hurried over and opened the back door.

"Dukey, come in boy. Uncle Norm's making us some din-din, and there'll be a big juicy bone for you." He bent down and ruffled the dog's ears. "Don't you worry none. Uncle Norman will sell your daddy's stuff, and we'll use the money to pay that nasty old mortgage company. And your daddy won't have to go driving all over the country on the weekends, and he'll be able to play ball with you more often. But that's not the best part."

Norman ruffled Duke's ears. "We'll still get to see each other lots and lots."

"One of these days, that dog is going to up and talk back, and you're going to have a heart attack when he does," John teased, stepping into the kitchen in a clean pair of jeans and a towel draped over his shoulders. His hair was damp and loose from its usual braid, hanging halfway down his back.

Norman's cheeks went a little pink, but he quickly turned to wash his hands in the sink, and then picked up the dishcloth and wiped down the peach colored tile counters. "I was just explaining to Duke that with my great ideas, he won't have to worry about where he's going to live."

John laughed, then nodded toward the back door rug where Duke had stretched out for a nap. "I don't think he's overly concerned."

John dried his hair then went into his bedroom. "Smells good," he called out, "but it isn't chili."

Saturday morning John got up before daybreak, and after he dressed and braided his hair, securing it at his nape with a silver clasp, he made some coffee. He glanced around the kitchen, thankful he'd talked Norman out of hauling the kitchen table and chairs to town. If anyone was interested in them, Taos was only about an hour away, and they could come out and have a look. Meanwhile, he still needed a place to sit and eat.

If anyone could sell used furniture for top dollar, Norman could. Hell, the man was an artist in his own right and had lots of experience dealing with tourists. He could sell a three-legged horse to a jockey.

It had taken most of the night to convince Norman that he still wanted to sell the ranch. Only after he mentioned that he'd seen a nice house on the outskirts of town—a house they could share as roommates—did Norman finally agree to help. John wasn't sure if it was because they were such good friends or if it was the fact that Norman could be closer to Duke.

John finished his coffee, then shrugged on his jean jacket and took his Stetson off the hook by the back door. Duke got up from his usual place on the rug and followed him out to the big, red semi-tractor and fifty-three-foot flatbed. Duke rose up on his hind legs and placed his front paws on the first step.

"Don't worry, Duke," John said, bending to give the dog a boost. "Neither one of us is as young as we used to be, but we'll be just fine once we're behind the wheel." Once settled in the air-lift driver's seat, John slipped the key into the ignition. The big truck trembled before the 460 Detroit diesel engine growled to life.

Norman parked his car in the shade of a cottonwood, and then hurried toward the barn. If John's truck was missing, then he'd put his plan into action. He should've told John the truth—that the realtor didn't want any part of selling his house. But he couldn't. John didn't need any more bad news, and even though he hated the thought, Henry Sheldon wasn't due back for another two weeks, and they only had thirty days to sell.

A quick glance confirmed that he'd have the run of the place—just what he wanted. Norman practically raced back to his car where he retrieved his digital camera. If John found out what he planned, he'd have a lot of explaining to do. Anyway, there was no way to tell if the plan would even work.

Norman easily found the key under the rock by the back door and let himself in. "Gosh, John, how can you make such a mess in only one day?" he murmured as he straightened the kitchen towel and hung the dishcloth over the faucet to dry. He went into the living room, deciding he'd better do a little cleaning before snapping pictures. John was a good man, but housework wasn't one of his strong points.

In no time, Norman had dusted the remaining end table, the lampshade, and the rifles above the huge rock fireplace, wondering why John had rifles in the first place when he wasn't the type to gun down innocent animals. "Now all I need are a few pictures of this place," Norman mumbled as he lifted the camera to his eye.

Finished with the living room, Norman stepped out the front

door onto the porch. It was ten feet wide and wrapped around the entire house, offering a three-hundred and sixty-degree view of the mountains, valleys and grassy meadows that made this portion of New Mexico so breathtakingly beautiful. He lifted his camera and snapped a few shots.

"And they call our state a desert," Norman scoffed as he walked around to the west side—the side that jutted out over a small ravine. "Oh, this is great," he murmured, taking aim. He worked around the house, finally stepping up to the patio of the room John had added.

He'd become so intent on snapping pictures, he nearly stumbled over one of the two wooden rockers John had made—a fairly large one to hold John's tall frame, and one a little smaller for Ellie. Norman ran his hand along the back of Ellie's chair, remembering.

Slowly he sank down into his sister's chair, fighting back tears as he gazed out at the view. He missed Ellie and knew he'd miss this place, too. He loved it almost as much as John and Ellie loved it. Even before old man Sheldon put it up for sale, John had dreamed of owning it. It had been Ellie's dream too, and now, as with all things, the time to let go had come.

Norman rose and took one last snapshot of the scenic view, then took his cell phone from his pants pocket. "Hey, Ted. How are you? Oh, I'm fine, just fine. Say, Ted, do you still tinker around with computer graphic stuff? Oh, good, good. Would you consider helping me with a little real estate layout? Great. When can we get together?"

It had been a frustrating week for Kathryne. Liz had called every day, nagging her about their vacation, and apparently her father was still on his, as he hadn't returned any of the dozen messages she'd left. About the only thing that was going her way was that she'd lightened her schedule, relaying to Helen that she planned to take a vacation. She'd explain later. For now, she didn't want to divulge that she'd been thinking about leaving the firm for good.

In fact, ever since she'd talked with her mother, she'd been playing with the wild idea of packing up and moving to New Mexico—away from Douglas and his menagerie of women, away from the nine to five humdrums, and into something new and challenging, provided her father would speak to her. She'd been weighing the pros and cons off and on for days, concluding that her thoughts of a partnership were ludicrous.

She was also reminded of her opinion concerning her father's actions nearly twenty years ago. What had she told him? *Dad, you're reckless and irresponsible.* And apparently she wasn't the only one who'd disapproved. Her mother had wasted no time in filing for a divorce.

Even with the words *reckless and irresponsible* weighing heavily upon her shoulders, she'd privately drafted an agreement to have Dave Atkins, her senior partner, act as manager in her absence, just in case things didn't work out with dear old Dad. After all, this wasn't a decision to be made lightly. She'd experienced enough guilt in her life for making wrong decisions; she sure didn't want to jump into something she'd regret.

If, and she kept reminding herself that it was a very big *if,* she did take this quantum leap, what was the worst thing that could happen? She'd be happy? Would that be so bad?

Kathryne gave a little sigh. She'd get some more advice from someone who wasn't afraid to give it. She was just about to call Liz and run the idea past her best friend when the intercom beeped.

"Yes?"

"Liz is on the line."

"Gosh, is she psychic?" Kathryne muttered a moment before she lifted the receiver. "I was just going to call you."

"Good. Does that mean you're finally going to take that vacation we've been talking about?"

"Talking? I'd call it badgering, but yes, I'm ready, and I know exactly where I want to go."

After grumbling that reconciliations weren't considered real vacations, Liz gave up trying to persuade Kathryne to try her sister-in-law's favorite bed and breakfast. Relieved that their conversation had ended on a congenial note, Kathryne buzzed Helen. "I've decided to take my vacation, regardless that my father is still on his."

"Good. What do you want me to do?"

"Call my travel agent and get a first class ticket to Albuquerque. And I'll also need a small charter to Taos . . . providing they have an airport. It's been years since I've been there. And I'll need reservations at my dad's ranch. It's called the Silver Creek Lodge. If there's no airport, I'll need a rental."

"Consider it done."

This felt like a sound and rational plan, Kathryne mused. She'd visit first and then make her decision. She sat back with a very contented smile and then quickly pressed the button again. "Oh, and if I have to get a rental . . . make it an SUV."

"Feeling adventurous?" came Helen's voice.

"Yes," Kathryne said with a satisfied nod. "As a matter of fact, I am." She turned her swivel chair and moved the mouse of her computer to disengage the screen saver. She moved her mouse to an icon, and her search engine appeared.

Without hesitation, she typed the letters *T,A,O,S,* and then added the words, *New Mexico,* smiling when a website appeared. She opened the link to a beautiful mountain resort called Silver Creek Lodge.

"Wow, it's better than I would've thought," she murmured as she scanned the sight. Obviously her father had renovated, and as she clicked on *view the rooms,* she decided they were gorgeous.

Then she scrolled down to see the small notice. *Closed for the month of May while owner is on vacation.* "The whole month?" she muttered, wondering why anyone would do that.

Disappointed, Kathryne returned to the home page spotting the subtitle *real estate.*

"My gosh," she gasped, as she clicked through a few homes. "That's my grandfather's cabin." A moment later, Helen came in and Kathryne waved her over. "Hurry, come over here. My father was born in that cabin."

She leaned a little to the left so Helen could see it. "Look. It's exactly as I remembered . . . only better. Whoever owns it has added shutters and a hitching post before the front door."

"Are you kidding me? Your Dad was born there? Ouch."

"Yeah, can you imagine? No doctor, no epidural, just a midwife," Kathryne said, feeling more excited than she thought she'd be. "Look, that's new."

"It a barn."

"Oh, my gosh."

"What?" Helen asked, smiling.

"It's for sale by owner—John Hawkins, and it's a steal. Contact Norman . . ."

"But honey, you wouldn't really like it there. Be realistic. You're a city girl with a career. An independent, self-sufficient . . . control freak." Liz took a sip of red wine, shaking her head in disapproval as she placed the picture Kathryne had printed out down on the table.

Kathryne studied her friend for several moments. "Independent, self-sufficient," she repeated as she slid her knife through the grilled chicken breast. "I wish I were. But in reality I'm not. I've been emotionally dependent for so long, I've forgotten how to think for myself."

She held up the fork, looking at the meat. "I've always been in control. That part's true." She popped it in her mouth, chewed, and then swallowed, reaching for her wine. "But now . . . now I'm angry and frustrated because there's nothing I can do about my situation, and even if there were—"

"Oh, honey," Liz replied. "Some day you'll meet a nice man."

Kathryne shook her head. "No, you're not getting it. I don't want another man, nice or not." She took another sip of wine, then dabbed at the corner of her mouth. "You know the worse thing about all of this?"

Liz gave her a cautious glance. "I'm afraid to guess."

"It's my pride. Yes, that's it. Or maybe it's better described as my self-esteem." She cut another piece of meat. "I've always succeeded—graduated at the top of my class, took over Daddy's company in my late twenties, no major problems, nice apartment, nice car, nice life. I'm the one my co-workers come to when they have problems. I'm the one who listens and offers advice when they're contemplating a divorce. I reassure them that not everything goes as we plan and not to blame themselves."

"That's a good thing, right?"

"Yes . . . at least I always thought so. But no more. I'm a hypocrite, and I blame myself. It's hard to admit that I failed, that I couldn't keep my husband interested, and that he fell out of love so easily when I didn't."

Liz's sympathetic expression was expected. What she said next wasn't. "That bastard. You're better off without him. And, if you'd be happy somewhere in the boondocks working with your daddy or running a bed and breakfast, then I think you should do it."

Liz leaned over and placed her hand on Kathryne's. "I'll hate it, but I've got lots of air miles and unlimited long distance.

Now, where is that waiter? I need another glass of wine."

Kathryne's mouth dropped open for a split second, then she gave a disbelieving laugh. "There for a minute I thought you were going to talk me out of it."

Liz grimaced. "Oh, you silly, not after that speech you just gave. Do I look like an idiot? No, hon, if this is something you want, and God only knows you deserve it, then go for it." Liz smoothed the napkin resting on her lap. "Besides, now I'll have a reason to visit—what's the name of it?"

"The Silver Creek Lodge."

"Yeah, nice name." Liz gave a sly smile. "I'll get a discount, right?"

CHAPTER FIVE

Albuquerque International Airport looked exactly as Kathryne pictured it. The pueblo style design only heightened her excitement, as did the Native American art and sculptures adorning the interior of the spacious building. Before she collected her luggage, she decided to stroll through the nearest curio shop, pleased that she'd chosen to wear a pair of khaki slacks with a pale pink, lightweight sweater and comfortable cream-suede pumps.

She admired the rich-brown diamond design on the back of a wooden, jointed snake. Shifting the thin strap of her purse from her right shoulder to her left, she shook the snake, smiling when it moved as if it were alive.

"Can I help you find something?" the clerk asked.

"This is neat. It'll look great on my desk."

"I'll hold it for you while you browse."

Kathryne lifted a bottle of lotion marked *Desert Sage* and rubbed a little on her wrist, raising her dark brows. "Wow, this is different."

She dabbed a little behind her ear, and then put the tester-bottle back on the glass counter, turning to inspect an Indian doll.

"Where are you from?" The clerk asked while ringing up her purchases.

"Baltimore," said Kathryne, and then amended. "Actually, I

was born here, but then we moved to Baltimore when I was a baby."

The clerk handed Kathryne the paper sack. "A displaced native returning home to her roots. Staying long?"

"Maybe," Kathryne replied with a bright smile, eyeing a clear plastic, dome-shaped paperweight. "Is that what I think it is?"

The clerk nodded. "Yes, ma'am. That's a genuine Tarantula."

"So, how far is this place?" Kathryne asked the rental car clerk as she fastened her seatbelt then flipped open her compact to adjust the angle of her wide-brimmed, lemon-yellow straw hat.

The young man smiled. "Taos. It's at least four hours—"

"Four hours?" Kathryne heaved a quiet sigh. It had seemed a much shorter drive when she was a child. "I brought a map. Would you mind marking the shortest route?"

"No problem." The clerk took her map and drew a line along the roads that would get her safely to her destination and then handed it back.

Kathryne looked briefly at the map and then at the clerk, unable to see his eyes behind the dark sunglasses. "I'm sure there will be towns and restaurants along the way?"

"Yes, ma'am. It's a road well traveled."

She slipped on her own sunglasses then put the key into the Ford Explorer and threw the automatic transmission into drive. "This is going to be great," she murmured, feeling a little anxious. "I'm going to have all kinds of fun."

Three hours later, Kathryne leaned against the side of the SUV—her large straw hat shading her from the late afternoon sun. "Great. Just great. Now what?"

She walked to the back of the vehicle and opened the hatch. It was filled with luggage. After removing four suitcases and her laptop, she lifted out a small piece of carpet that was glued to a piece of pressboard. The spare was visible, but there was no sign of the jack.

"It's got to be here somewhere," she murmured. After a futile search, she went to the passenger's side to check the glove box for some instructions.

Thumbing through a few pages didn't help. She went to the back of the SUV and lifted out the small spare. Locating the jack was a different story. There was a small frame-like thing that held the tire, but it didn't look anything like what she thought a jack should look like. And if it was the jack, it sure didn't look sturdy enough to hold up the SUV.

The sound of approaching traffic caused her to look up. A large red semi-truck slowly approached, its air brakes hissing loudly as it came to a stop. Shading her eyes, Kathryne watched as a tall, slender man climbed out of the cab, then lifted down a big, yellow dog that immediately shook itself before he trotted toward her with its tongue hanging out the side of its mouth

The man's tanned features were obscured by dark glasses and a wide-brimmed cowboy hat with a silver band. He wore fairly tight blue jeans and a green plaid shirt with the sleeves rolled almost to the elbow. The sun glinted off the large, oval belt buckle that she suspected would be carved with his initials.

A cowboy. A real-life cowboy.

As he walked toward Kathryne, she got a glimpse of jet-black hair—long hair that was pulled back, neatly braided and secured with a sliver clasp. She was instantly reminded of the old expression, *tall, dark and handsome.* She also amended her first impression. Maybe not a cowboy. Maybe a Native American.

"Howdy," he said, smiling, exposing some great looking, perfectly white teeth. "You look like you could use some help."

"I sure could," Kathryne replied, bending to pet the dog. "My car has a flat tire."

The man glanced at the left rear tire. "I can see that." He

stepped closer, and she caught a slight trace of aftershave. "Excuse me, ma'am."

"Oh, ah . . . certainly." Kathryne stepped back out of the way, taking a position to his right, but staying behind him. Before he bent down to examine the tire, she figured he was at least six-two, maybe six-four, but then he had on brown cowboy boots. From the width of his shoulders and the way his jeans hugged his thighs, he probably worked out—a lot. With minimum effort, he lifted out the spare and leaned it against the bumper. A few minutes later, he had the jack together and knelt on one knee to slip it under the frame.

"I'll have this done in no time," he said in a deep, pleasing voice.

"I'd really appreciate that." While the man worked, she felt she should make small talk, "What's your dog's name?"

"Duke," the man said, flashing another friendly smile before turning back to the task.

Kathryne glanced at the man's backside, and then quickly looked away. Dear Lord, what if he'd caught her staring? Too quickly he finished, standing to dust off his hands on the back of his jeans before he repacked the mountain of luggage.

"This one's light," he said with a grin.

"It's empty," she said a little sheepishly. "When I'm on vacation, which isn't very often, I always take an empty suitcase so I can fill it with souvenirs."

"That's a great idea." An uncomfortable moment of silence passed before he spoke. "Well, that should take care of it, but when you get to where you're going, I'd have that tire fixed. These little spares aren't intended for much traveling." He gave the mountain of luggage another look, and when he turned back, he looked amused. "Or for carrying any kind of a load."

When the man turned to leave, Kathryne hurried to the driver's side of the SUV, grabbed her wallet, and took out a twenty-dollar bill. "Thank you so much."

The man put up his hand. "Whoa, now. I can't take that."

She held it out to him, wondering what color his eyes were behind those dark glasses, then immediately told herself she didn't care. "Please. It's the least I can do."

The man held up his hands. "You don't owe me anything. It was my pleasure to help."

"I-I would have never figured out the jack. Please, take this."

To her surprise he touched the brim of his hat—just like they did in the old western movies she'd seen on the late show. In spite of the turquoise wedding band on his finger, and in spite of her vow to give up men, her heart gave a silly little flutter.

"Nope, can't do it." He turned, and his dog trotted after him. "If you're going up to Taos, there's an old Chevron station near the edge of town that can fix that tire. Tell the owner John Hawkins said to treat you right."

John Hawkins. Kathryne's breath caught, but he was already too far away, and she didn't know what she'd say if she stopped him. *Hey, I want to buy your house?* Instead, she watched him lift the dog into the truck, then climb in behind it. The hiss of air releasing the breaks was rather startling as the big truck slowly rolled forward. She jumped when he gave the air-horn a quick pull, waving as he gradually gained momentum down the two-lane highway.

"Well," she said in a slightly shaky voice. "Nice to meet you, Mr. Hawkins." She put the bill back in her wallet and got into the car. And even though she tried not to do it, she thought about John Hawkins, the tight fit of his jeans and his long, black hair, while she extended the seatbelt over her chest and secured it.

She pulled out onto the road, and she couldn't help wondering if his hair were as soft and thick as it looked, but then she thought about his wedding ring, and all his attributes were reluctantly set aside. "Oh, well," she murmured softly, "I may be on a diet, but I can still look at the menu."

It was almost dark by the time Kathryne pulled into the driveway of the hotel Helen had booked for her stay. It was nice, but much to her dismay, it wasn't as nice as the Silver Creek Lodge.

"Can't say as I blame you, Dad," she remembered thinking when she'd discovered that the lodge was closed. She took a moment to admire the pueblo styling of the hotel—a style very popular in the area. A young Hispanic man came to collect her luggage, and then followed her inside where she signed in and received her key-card.

"This is nice," she murmured as they entered the lavish room.

Done in shades of gold and rust with smatterings of basil-green, the room was warm and most definitely inviting. No expense had been spared to make it as elegant as any to be found in larger cities. The only difference was the distinct Southwestern styles expressed in the rustic furnishings and colorful Navajo rugs. Two large paintings depicting ancient cave drawings hung on the wall over the bed.

"Real nice," Kathryne added. After the boy put the suitcases near the closet, she took the twenty-dollar bill out of her pocket and placed it in his hand. "Thank you."

Kicking off her shoes, she tested the pillow-topped mattress for comfort before she removed several items from her carry-on, disappearing into the spacious bathroom to place them on the counter. Back in the main suite, she found a menu and began to thumb through it at the same time she began to undress.

Most of what she saw she couldn't remember how to pronounce, but that was the least of her worries. Should she get it with or without *traditional New Mexican Hatch green chile?*

She pressed the button on the phone for room service at the same time she slipped on the thick white robe, which had been left on her pillow.

"Yes, is the kitchen still open? Good. What exactly are your nachos like? Tasty . . . a little spicy, and you recommend them," she repeated. "And you recommend the chicken and cheese enchilada with green chili? All right, I have the nachos and the enchiladas. That's all. Oh, wait a moment. I'd like a little extra of the traditional New Mexico Hatch green chile. Yes, I'm sure, thank you."

Thirty minutes later she sat at the table in the corner of her room with two plates before her—two large plates filled with food. They both looked delightful and smelled even better, but she'd had no idea nachos in New Mexico were a whole meal by themselves. She cut off a small piece of enchilada. Her smile faded as she quickly chewed, swallowed then reached for the bottle of Mexican beer she thought would go well with the local cuisine.

"My God," Kathryne gasped, waving her hand before her mouth. "This stuff is hotter than the blazes of hell." She ran into the bathroom, returning after a moment, patting her mouth with her napkin. "So, that's *Hatch* green chile. Interesting, but definitely an acquired taste," she muttered as she glanced at the nachos—nachos smothered in jalapeño peppers. She found a tiny one, placed it in the middle of a tortilla chip with cheese and refried beans and ground beef, then took a bite. This time she flew into the bathroom. After splashing cold water into her mouth, she came out, heaved a loud, disappointed sigh, and lifted the menu.

"Homemade *sopaipillas,* whatever they are, stuffed with French vanilla ice-cream, and covered with strawberries and whipped cream." A smile spread across her face. "Sounds harmless enough. Can't be hot—it has ice-cream."

She picked up the receiver, then hesitated remembering that she'd been told to lose weight. But a little voice inside said, *you're on vacation . . . enjoy yourself.*

"Yes, I'd like to order dessert." she replied ignoring the little voice's persistence. *You really shouldn't.*

"Hi there," Norman said as he looked up from the counter in his friend's shop where he was arranging some handmade Indian jewelry. A woman had just entered. She was tall with a medium build, and she had rich honey-blond hair curled under at the shoulders. She had on a pair of light moss-green slacks with a crisp white three-quarter-sleeved blouse. Her tan-leather sling purse matched a pair of sling-back, low-heeled pumps.

"You look like you'd enjoy a cup of piñon coffee."

"They make coffee from the trees around here?" the woman asked with a doubtful expression. "If it's anything like that stuff Mr. Hatch makes, I'll pass."

Norman laughed. "I assume you're not from around here and that you've tried some of our delightfully spicy Mexican food."

"I have, and remind me to tell Mr. Hatch if ever I meet him—"

"Hatch is a town in southern New Mexico, not a person."

"Really," she said, nodding. *Great, make a fool of yourself,* she chided.

Norman smiled, then filled a ceramic cup and handed it to her, immediately noticing her pleasant smile—a smile that lit up warm, green eyes. "There's sugar and cream over on the table."

"This hasn't got anything unusual in it, does it?" she asked.

"Oh no, certainly not, but we do have a way of roasting the beans with piñon nuts. Gives it a very rich, nutty flavor. If you like coffee, you'll just adore this."

He watched as she gave it a sniff then took a sip. "Good, huh?"

She smiled again, and if he were straight, he'd be in love. "Yes. Very." She walked over to the counter to admire a pair of gold earrings accented with small turquoise stones, then paused before the lamp John had made.

"Unique, don't you agree?" Norman said as he joined her. "Bet you won't see anything like that back East."

She turned with a surprised expression. "How'd you know?"

Norman grinned. "Well . . ." He held out his hand. "You can call me Norman, and you are?"

"Kathryne Wilcox . . ." She hesitated for a second, aware that she'd used her married name. To change it now would only make her look foolish, so she decided to let it ride. "However, my friends call me Kate," she added quickly.

"Charmed," Norman replied. "Now where was I . . . Oh, yes, there was one thing that gave you away—most of the locals don't wear Gucci pumps or carry handbags that cost more than their car payments." He laughed with her.

"You're a regular detective," Kathryne commented with apparent admiration.

"Not really, but we get a lot of tourists up here. Can I show you anything in particular?" He turned back to the counter. "I've got a darling hair brooch that would just look fabulous with that outfit."

"Have you lived here all your life?" she asked, sipping her coffee while she followed him over to the counter.

"Just about. Moved here when I was a boy . . . so I guess that makes it pretty much all my life." He slid open the glass door and lifted out an oval hair clip, inlaid with tiny turquoise stones.

"Really? Well, then I bet you could tell me where I might find the real estate agent handling the Hawkins ranch. His name is Norman, too."

Norman raised his grey brows. "May I inquire why you'd want to know about the Hawkins ranch?"

The attractive stranger smiled brightly, and an excited gleam lit-up her eyes. "Yes, you may. My grandfather used to own it. It was his first home after he and my grandmother were married. I had no idea it was for sale, but now that it is, I might be interested."

"Did you say your grandfather?" He nodded with her. "Ah, if that's the case, you're related to Henry . . . Henry Sheldon."

She smiled then. "Yes. He's my father."

When Norman couldn't find his voice, she added, "When I saw the pictures on the internet, I couldn't believe it."

Norman cleared his suddenly dry throat. "You-you saw the pictures?"

"Yes, and I was shocked to see it in such good condition after all these years."

"Shocked," Norman repeated, nodding like a Chihuahua statue on the back ledge of a fifty-six Chevy. "Yes, I'm sure you must have been." He took a calming breath, trying not to think of the way he and his friend had altered the pictures he'd taken. "Well, you'll be pleased to know that I'm the Norman handling the Hawkins ranch."

"You?" Kate leaned closer. "Your ad said there's a barn and the option of renting horses, or boarding horses? I can't remember."

"Yes, yes, indeed, but I have to confess, I didn't expect anyone to . . . Well, I didn't think anyone would want to see it this soon. You see, we . . . John . . . Mr. Hawkins only decided to sell a short time ago. I just put the web page up a few days ago. I wasn't expecting—"

"Is there a problem?" she asked, her excited smile fading into one of concern. "Is it sold?"

"No, not at all, it's just that the pictures don't . . . don't quite do it justice," he stammered, trying to think of a way to stall her. "You know how digital cameras are."

"No, not really. I'm not much of a photographer."

"Sometimes they make everything look a little better than they really are." Norman gave a small laugh. "I take all my personal photos that way . . . you know, to look better . . ." He cleared his throat again, wishing he'd told John what he'd done.

The woman wasn't daunted by his lack of enthusiasm. "I assure you, if it looks half as good as the pictures I saw, it'll still be great. How soon can we see it?"

"Good Lord," Kathryne muttered. Instead of the beautiful enhanced pictures she'd seen posted on the internet, the *real thing* appeared to be a startling contrast. It looked every bit its ninety-plus years old.

"I-I can explain," Norman stammered, turning in the passenger side of the rented SUV. "I should have told you, but you see, I just didn't know anyone would want to see it so soon." His shoulders slumped. "I'm so sorry I wasted your time. If you don't want to see inside, I'll understand. Hell, I'll even buy you a tank of gas."

"Ah, no. It's not too bad," Kathryne murmured. "It's kind of rustic, with its own special charm. I'm sure once it's torn down, I could rebuild."

Norman groaned. "I'm such a fool. Will you ever forgive me?"

"I was teasing." Kathryne undid her seatbelt and got out of the car, pausing again to gaze at the structure she'd visited so many times as a child. Shingles were missing from the roof, and it badly needed a fresh coat of paint, or stain, or whatever a person put on a log house.

The roses her grandmother had cared for so lovingly were gone, and there were lots of weeds, but all in all, it wasn't too bad, considering its age and the neglect after Granddad built the big house. She climbed the three steps to the front porch, aware that Norman followed. In her mind's eye, she saw herself and her grandfather sitting on a porch swing, singing *She'll Be Coming Around The Mountain* together.

"The swing's gone," she said softly, thankful her tone didn't betray the sudden burst of emotion that tightened her throat.

"The swing?" Norman asked. "I'm not sure I'm following you."

Kathryne turned and smiled. "No, I imagine you're not. You should have added one to your pictures. You added everything else." She walked over to the area before the large front window. "There used to be a porch swing right here." She hurried down a little farther. "And my grandmother hung her geraniums from these hooks. Look, they're still there."

"Yeah, I see them," Norman replied. "Wow, they must be ancient."

"Thanks," Kathryne said dryly. She shielded her eyes as she searched for something on the nearby ridge. "If my memory serves, you can see the big house. There it is. That's the house they built after my father was born. Uncle George was born there, as well as my Uncle David."

"Yeah, that's the Silver Creek Lodge, and compared to that this is really small."

"I guess that's why Gram wanted such a big house," Kathryne added, then turned and faced Norman. "How much?"

Norman looked shocked.

"What?"

Kathryne twirled around. "Although I don't approve of the deception, I love this place." When she stopped, she looked at Norman again. "How much?"

"D-don't you want to see inside first?" he asked with a worried frown.

"Not particularly," Kathryne replied, laughing at his anxious expression. "I don't see anything here that can't be fixed. In fact, I liked the picture with the added shutters. They really dressed it up. I'll probably add them, and green was a good choice. May I have a look at the barn? I think I saw some horses when we drove in."

Kathryne pushed aside the big door of the two-story barn and breathed in the scent of livestock. "Smell that," she said, as her head flooded with more memories.

Norman grimaced. "I sure do."

"It's not bad. It's just an *earthy* smell."

"More like a shitty smell," Norman muttered.

Kathryne laughed and strolled down the alley. There were eight stalls, three of them occupied on the right, and four empty on the left. One of the stalls on the left was filled with bales of green alfalfa and some bales of what she recognized as grass hay. A big bay gelding nickered a greeting, thrusting his head over the door to be petted. Kathryne instantly complied, barely able to hide her excitement as the huge animal nudged her hand. "Look at him. Isn't he sweet?"

"Sweet," Norman replied sarcastically. "And smelly."

"Very funny." Kathryne picked up some loose hay and gave each of the horses a little nibble. "I'm in love with this place," she murmured. "Is there more to see?"

Norman shrugged. "There's a chicken coop and a garage out back."

Kathryne followed him outside. A large, open-sided garage had been erected near one of the corrals, between some trees. By the recent tire tracks, it appeared that something very big had been driven out of it. A moment later it dawned on Kathryne that this is where John Hawkins kept his big red truck. She glanced around, spotting another smaller and definitely older pick-up truck. Fences and cross fences stood in the distance, making her wonder where the property lines were.

"Well, are you ready to go back to town?" Norman asked, returning her smile a little cautiously. "I've got some friends in real estate. I'm sure if you really want to live out here, they could find you a fabulous place."

"I don't want any other place, Norman. I want you to get hold of Mr. Hawkins and his wife—"

"John's wife died a little over a year ago. She'd been sick a long time, and . . . well, never mind, it's not important."

She felt so excited she missed the shadow that flickered across Norman's blue eyes. "I'm sorry to hear that. However, I'd like you to get in touch with Mr. Hawkins so we can talk about the terms. But before we go, I think I will take a look inside. I want to get some ideas for decorating."

"Sure." Norman lifted the mat and retrieved the key, slipping it into the lock. He pushed the door open, and then stood aside. "You know that the whole ranch isn't for sale, only the house, the barn, and five acres."

"That's not a problem. Five acres is more than enough." Kathryne stepped inside, feeling as if she'd slipped back in time. Fond memories of her childhood seemed to live in every corner of the old house. The inside was sparsely furnished with pieces similar to those in Norman's studio, but the emptiness didn't stop her from visualizing the house's potential.

The beamed ceiling and the wooden wainscot were all in sound condition. In contrast to the exterior, the interior wasn't so bad. All it really needed was a woman's touch, some painting of the dry-walled surfaces and some oil on the wood surfaces, but nothing much else.

For a moment she wondered why Mrs. Hawkins let it slip into such a state, but then she remembered what Norman had said. A widower wouldn't care if the floors weren't polished.

"What's your asking price?" She stepped out of the hall from her inspection of the other two bedrooms, keeping her emotions in check when Norman told her. With inflation, she'd expected a much higher price. "Fair enough. How soon can you have the papers ready?"

"S-soon? Ah, well, I've got to check with the owner first." Norman slipped his hand into his inside pocket and retrieved one of his cards, flipping it over to write on the back. "He's presently out of town. Do you have a cell?"

"Sure do. And I think he's back."

Norman swallowed hard. "He is?"

Kate nodded. "He changed a flat for me yesterday afternoon. He was going the same direction, so I assume he'll be home soon."

Norman returned her smile. "Oh yes, but he leaves every-day . . . back and forth . . . no particular schedule. I never know where he is." He shrugged his shoulders and raised his hands in a questioning gesture

"I'll wait." She walked to the worn leather sofa and sat down. A moment later she pulled out her checkbook and a pen. "This is earnest money to make sure you don't sell it to anyone else. I trust it's enough to convince Mr. Hawkins that I'm serious? Also, let him know I'm in no hurry for him to move his truck, or to move the horses. In fact, I might be interested in buying his animals too."

Norman took the check and glanced at it. "Yes," he croaked, then cleared his throat. "Why don't you give me your number? In the meantime I'll call John . . . Mr. Hawkins . . . and present your offer."

Chapter Six

Kathryne stepped inside her room at the hotel and leaned against the door, feeling as if she were a child again. Excited and thrilled, she felt all tingly just thinking about the old cabin. But then at the next moment, her excitement faded, replaced with anxiousness and doubt. Was her decision based on the fact that she needed a change in her life? Or did she just want to get away from Doug and all the things that constantly reminded her of him?

She heaved a sigh. Change had always been difficult for her, she admitted. Her fear of the unfamiliar was probably why she'd lived in the same apartment, in the same city, doing the same job for over twenty years.

Slipping off her shoes, she sat on the bed and reached for the phone. Perhaps if she shared her thoughts with her best friend, she'd feel better.

"Liz? Hi, it's me. Yes, I know I'm supposed to be on vacation, but I've got some wonderful news. No, I haven't met a man, and while we're on the topic, I wish you'd get it through your head that I'm done with men . . . finished." Kathryne smiled at Liz's retort, expecting one far worse.

"Well, the reason I called is I made an offer on my grandfather's old cabin and the five acres. Yes, I know it's sudden . . . no I haven't spoken with my father . . . of course I don't want to live with him. Living near him is different. I want my own place, but then, if you were here and could see the view you'd understand. There's a rocky ravine and in the distance. There's still snow on the mountain peaks. I've never seen anything so beautiful. I'm thinking I might take a correspondence course in photography."

The more details she gave to Liz, the more she began to let go of her trepidation. Even as she listened patiently while Liz went over all the reasons she should come home, Kathryne realized the move was what she wanted. "I know it looks like I might be making a hasty decision, but trust me. I'm not. It's beautiful. No, it's gorgeous."

She drew in a long deep breath. "And the smell. There are pines and wild flowers and . . . and it's just *too* beautiful to describe over the phone. I'll take some pictures the next time I'm out there and e-mail them to you."

Again she paused while Liz spoke.

"Yes, I know visiting and owning are two different things. Well, no, it needs a lot or repairs, but that's the best part." She pulled a pillow out from under the coverlet and placed it against the headboard, reclining back. "I can do most of them myself, and I'll hire a carpenter to help me with the rest. I'll be busy for weeks, maybe months, doing something exciting."

She nodded, expecting Liz to say what she said. "Yes, I know renovating the house won't last forever, but that's all right. I'm almost certain Dad can use my help with the lodge. So, you see, everything will be great. I'll have my own home, and I'll be able to work with my father again. It's a great plan, don't you think?"

Kathryne tried not to frown while Liz spoke. Couldn't her friend hear how happy she was? "Do I have doubts? Of course. But the one thing I'm sure of is that I need something different in my life right now. Why the rush? Because it's been a dream of mine for ages . . . a dream I almost forgot. After we had dinner that night, I started thinking about how I used to come here and spend my summers with Granddad and Gram, and then one thing led to another. And you know that I'm not happy anymore—and why the change. Didn't you tell me to go for it just a couple of days ago? I know I'm a little excited—"

She waited for a minute to let Liz finish. "All right, I'm *a lot* excited, but you've got to listen to me. Ever since Doug and I divorced, I've felt out of sorts . . . like there's something missing in my life. No, not a man," she said, shaking her head at her friend's persistence. "A purpose."

She rose, then crossed over to the window and looked at the distant mountain tops. "I'm aware that I have responsibilities back home, but I'm tired of doing the same thing every day. I'm tired of my life, and I want a change."

She walked back to the chair and sat down, toying with a pencil and small pad. "I don't want to come home. I don't want to accidentally run into Doug and have to pretend that it didn't bother me to see his new conquest hanging on his arm."

Kathryne took a breath, forcing back the urge to give into frustrated tears. "It's more than just Doug, it's me. I'm forty-four years old and have never done what *I* want to do. I know it sounds crazy, but thinking back, I believe I became a lawyer to please my parents. It was their dream that I take over the firm, not mine."

She heaved a loud sigh. "Don't misunderstand. I was pleased that they thought I was good enough to take over, but a small part of me didn't want it. In fact, now that I look back, what *I* really wanted never happened."

Again she paused, trying to stop her friend from saying what she didn't want to hear. "Yes, I do have it all, and yes, I want for nothing, but do you want to know what I really want?" Kathryne grinned. "No . . . I want . . . a dog! Or at least I want to have the option of getting one without someone telling me why I can't or what it might do on the rug! Oh, Liz. I know I must sound ungrateful, but down inside, I want some meaning in my life. I missed my chance at having children and deeply regret it. You joke around, but I know how much you love your son and his wife and how proud you are of his accomplishments. I've seen your expression when you're telling me how successful his restaurant is in Seattle—and your daughter and how she loves her teaching job. You're a proud mama and have every right to be one."

Kathryne smiled. By her friend's tone, Liz had begun to soften. "I can't change the past, but if there's one thing I've learned, it's to not take life for granted. I don't want to pass up this opportunity. This time, I'm making the decision I feel is right for me."

Kathryne leaned back in the chair, tucking a strand of hair behind her ear. "Maybe you're right. Maybe things would have been different if I had insisted that Doug and I try to have another baby. I don't know. It's too late to worry about now. I only know that right now, this feels right."

Kathryne felt her throat tighten as she listened to her best friend. "I know. I'm going to miss you too, but at least I'll be doing something I want to do, in a place that holds a lot of fond memories for me. This will be my dream, my choice, not my parents' or my husband's."

Kathryne tugged a tissue from the box, dabbing at her eyes a moment before laughing. "Yes, I promise. When I get a dog I'll name her after you."

John pulled his semi around behind the barn, and then shut the engine off. It had been a long day, and when he saw a light inside the house, he was glad that Norman had come for a visit. If his suspicions were correct, Norman would have something cooking, and the way John felt, it could even be organic and he'd eat it. His belly had been growling for the last hour.

He stepped down and caught Duke in his arms. The big dog's

feet had barely touched the grown when he scrambled toward the back door. John followed him up the steps and strode in, removing his hat as he greeted his friend. "Smells good. What is it?"

"Fresh roasted green chili, T-bone steaks, baked potatoes, garden salad—all organic of course, and real homemade biscuits, not the canned ones you're used to."

"Great, I could eat a horse. Left my lunch in the fridge by accident."

"*That* was your lunch?" Norman asked, feigning a shudder. "My God, it's a wonder you're not dead from clogged arteries or food poisoning."

John grinned and shook his head. "I'll be the first to admit it wasn't great, but it wasn't that bad either. I happen to like bologna."

"The bologna expired two days ago. I can only assume the Great Spirit is watching over you."

John opened the fridge and took out a beer, waiting for Norman to scold him. "Want a beer?" he teased intentionally.

"No, thank you, but you go right ahead. We're celebrating tonight."

John hesitated for a few suspicious moments, then twisted off the top and took a long drink, closing his eyes a moment to savor the taste and the icy temperature. "What are we celebrating? Did you win the lotto?"

"I've got to pre-heat the grill. I'll tell you while we're eating."

"Do I have time for a shower? I swear it was so windy in Albuquerque, it'd whip the hair off a cat. Sand was blowing everywhere. I'm still chewing grit."

"Then go shower, but don't take too long."

By the time John had shaved, the aroma of sizzling steak wafted through the open window and teased his nostrils. He thought about braiding his hair, but then decided it would dry faster if he just let it be. He glanced in the mirror, wondering for a brief moment if Norman was right and he should visit the barber and get it cut.

Part of him wanted to blend in with other men his age, but then there was that stubborn streak that made him keep it long. He was half Navajo, and damned proud of it, and surprisingly enough, there was only a tiny bit of grey at his temples.

He slipped on a clean shirt and tucked it into his jeans. He had just sat down and pulled on a pair of socks when Norman called him to the table. Grabbing his belt, he threaded it through the loops as he headed toward the kitchen.

"Damn, this looks good," John said. He took his seat across from his friend, and then reached for the steak sauce. He cut off a chunk of meat, and closing his eyes for a moment in pure delight, chewed slowly. After he swallowed, he cut another piece, holding it on the fork as he spoke. "Norman, no matter what I've ever said about some of the weird stuff you cook, you sure do know how to grill a steak."

"Why, thank you, John," Norman said, smiling. "I've got some good news." He pushed a check toward John.

"Now, Norm. I told you I couldn't take your—"

"John, just close your mouth and look."

John's dark brows snapped together as he picked up the check. The amount was unlike any he'd seen in a long time. "What's this?" he asked softly, still staring at the huge amount. "Kathryne Wilcox? This has a Baltimore address."

"I sold the house today," Norman said, barely able to contain his excitement. "That's the down payment. If everything goes well, and you still want to sell, she's prepared to have the remainder transferred to your account by the end of the week."

"Are you kidding me?" John asked.

"No. It's a cash deal. She accepted our price, no haggling,

and . . . are you ready for this? She wants to know if you'd be interested in selling the horses, and she says there's no hurry to move the truck. She also wants to know if you'd help her with a few repairs. She'll pay you twenty dollars an hour!" Norman practically screamed the last few words. He quickly picked up his glass of grape juice and held it up high. "Congratulations, Mr. Hawkins, after you pay off the mortgage, there will still be plenty left to invest, and of course I'll handle that for you if you'd like. John, my friend, now you won't have to drive that old hunk of junk again if you don't want to."

"Don't call my baby a hunk of junk." John tapped his glass to Norman's, barely able to comprehend everything that had just happened. He looked at the check again, then at Norman, then leaned back in his chair with relief. "Kathryne Wilcox. Well, I'll be damned." He quickly recovered, then jumped up out of his chair and grabbed Norman so fast Norman's chair fell over. "Norman, I could just kiss you!"

"Well," Norman croaked, barely able to breathe in the bear-hug John had him in. "I'd let you, but you're not my type."

John's smile faded just a little at the same time he let Norman go. "What about Hank?"

Norman frowned. "What about Hank? Oh, yes, Hank," he murmured, rubbing his chin. "I forgot about Hank."

"Yeah, I guess we both did," John added. "Before I accept this, we need to run it past him. I owe him that much."

Norman sank back down on his chair, heaving a loud sigh. "We should call him." Norman glanced at his watch. "It's getting late in Florida."

John hung up the phone with a bewildered look on his face. "Well, I'll be damned all over again," he muttered before turning to address Norman. "You won't believe this."

"Believe what?" Norman asked with a worried frown. "Tell

me, John. You know I hate surprises."

"Hank's in favor of the sale."

"You're kidding me, right?" Norman nodded anxiously.

"No. At first he sounded hurt that I'd put it up for sale without telling him, but after I explained that we didn't expect to sell, and after I mentioned the lady's name, he calmed right down. I could swear he even chuckled like something was going on."

"Good, good," Norman said. "Maybe he won't fire us after all."

"Fire us?" John questioned. "By the way he was talking, we might get raises."

Norman's head snapped up. "Raises? What are you talking about? Please John, you're killing me here. What did he say?"

"I'm telling you, Norm. Hank just didn't sound like himself. He was all giddy like, but that isn't the strangest part." John's frown matched Norman's. "He said to tell Mrs. Wilcox that he's looking forward to being her neighbor."

The little city of Taos appeared more exciting than Kathryne expected. It was full of art galleries and unique shops. After a day of shopping, she curled up on the sofa in her suite and began to read the local newspaper. If John W. Hawkins accepted her offer, in a month she'd be packing and getting ready for the biggest move of her life. She almost couldn't concentrate, her excitement felt so strong.

She came to the section that listed various types of livestock, reminding her of the horses she'd seen. One thought led to another, and soon she was looking in the yellow pages for a stable with saddle horses to rent. While thumbing through the pages, her gaze fell upon an advertisement for an old-fashioned saloon, offering good food, good drinks, and lots of country-western dancing on Friday and Saturday nights—ten percent off a meal with the printed coupon.

Western dancing? The thought wasn't unpleasant. It had been ages since she'd done a little boot scooting on a sawdust-covered floor. In fact, the last time she'd danced wearing anything but heels had to have been about thirty years ago, and it was a barn dance put on by one of the Taos town councilmen to celebrate the building of the new bank. And discounted food. That sounded good, too.

"My gosh," she muttered aloud as her memory raced on. She could almost hear the band and the laughter as if it had happened just a few moments ago. Smiling, she read on, noting that there would be a live band. What harm could it do? It wasn't as if she'd have to dance.

She wasn't exactly comfortable being on her own in public places, but she was fairly confident that she could make an appearance and not be bothered. She could just go and eat—enjoy the food, the drinks and the music and not be too conspicuous. It would be fun. She'd drink a beer and eat peanuts.

She noted the location, and then decided she'd need something more casual to wear so she'd blend in with the locals.

Kathryne's mind wasn't exactly on clothing as she looked through several racks of broomstick skirts with matching bolero jackets. She continued to think about the cabin and that as soon as the necessary papers transferring ownership of the ranch were signed, the plans she could put in motion. The fun would start—picking colors, choosing furnishings. She remembered the rustic tables in Norman's store and knew instantly that they'd be perfect.

She had held up a black satin women's western suit studded with red sequins in rose patterns, thinking with a grin that if Liz was here, she'd want the outfit for the Summer Ball.

The Summer Ball. Kathryne slowly put the suit back. For a

few blissful days, she'd forgotten all about the ball. Her good mood took a nosedive. Even though the ball was months away, there'd be no getting out of it. She and Douglas had hosted it for years. Even if she could get out of being hostess, as the senior partner, she'd be expected to attend. Her mother had already reminded her of her duty just a short time ago, but it had been easy to push it to the back of her mind with all the excitement of her pending home ownership.

Nevertheless, the thought of it now caused her stomach to tighten. This would be the first year in nearly twenty-five that she and Doug wouldn't be a couple.

Her mother and stepfather would be there, immaculate as ever, as would Liz and Bobby. Liz would be stunning. Damn her, she'd be stunning in a gunny sack. But it wasn't her parents or Liz or even her friend Helen that filled her with such uncertainty. Douglas would, no doubt, have a young, slinky blonde on his arm, showing her off to all their friends and co-workers, looking as happy as ever.

And there'd be no getting out of it. Like it or not, she, along with her parents, were still the owners of the firm.

Dad. Maybe she could talk her father into escorting her to the dance? She shook the thought away almost as fast as it popped into her mind. He had always hated the ball and hadn't attended one since he left the firm. Besides, what was she thinking? She wasn't even sure if he'd accept her back into his life.

Listlessly, she pulled out a deep green jacket trimmed with silver conchos and glanced at it, noticing a little *S* on the tag. "Small," she muttered, painfully reminded that she'd put on a few pounds since the divorce.

"That's definitely not your color," came Norman's voice, drawing her away from her gloomy thoughts. When she looked up, he smiled. "By your frown, you agree with me."

Kathryne returned his smile. "Yes, you're right. I've worn

enough skirts in my day to last a lifetime, and really," she said, scrunching up her nose, "this isn't me."

"It isn't anyone I know, either." Norman came over, took the garment and put it back on the rack. "What's the occasion?"

"Occasion?" she repeated, then quickly realized what he meant. "I need something to wear to the Last Chance Saloon on Friday night."

"Oh, that's a great place . . . so much fun. Or at least that's what I've heard. You'll absolutely love it." He crossed his arms over his chest and tapped his finger against his temple in thought a moment before his eyes brightened. "I know just the thing, but you'll have to trust me."

Kathryne followed him over to the far side of the shop where stacks and stacks of variously colored jeans were placed on what resembled large bookcases. Norman turned, folded his arms over his chest again and gave her the once over. His serious expression was comical, but she didn't dare laugh.

"Well?" she asked softly, curious to see what he'd choose.

"You've got great legs," he muttered, lifting his hand to rub his chin. He slowly walked around her. "Size eight?"

"Try ten." She heaved a long sigh. "Maybe even a twelve. It depends on the designer."

"You underestimate yourself. You don't have hips . . . I mean, like some women's hips. Yours are there. They just aren't as . . . obvious . . . more subtle." He turned and shuffled through several styles of pants, choosing two different pairs, both in black. "Subtle is good, but we should present your best side . . . if you know what I mean. The best part is your height. Men love long, leggy women. And your boobs. Not too big and not too small. A tailored blouse will really set them off."

Amused by his candid comments, Kathryne continued to follow him around the store as he chose a midnight blue western-styled shirt with black pearl snaps and the faintest black piping around the collar, yoke slit-pockets and cuffs. His final selection was a black silk scarf. "Try these, and I'll go get a black belt, then we'll find some black boots . . . stove tops I think, with a dogging heel. Didn't you mention that you wanted to do some horseback riding while you're visiting?"

"Yes, but I haven't the faintest clue what you're talking about."

Smiling, Norman turned her toward the dressing room. "I'll explain later, doll. Now scoot. I'm dying to see how you look."

A few moments later, Kathryne emerged fully clad in Norman's selections. "I hate to admit it, but it's been ages since I've done any country-western dancing. What's it like? A fast waltz? Rock and roll?"

"It isn't anything like that. It's kind of shuffling around, but then on some of the faster tunes, it's a blend of rock and roll and . . . and . . . more shuffling around, with a little something that could be called skipping."

He shrugged his shoulders. "I don't really know how to describe it, but don't worry. I'll just show you, and you'll catch on just fine. Besides, cowboys love to teach women how to dance. And trust me, sweetie pie, when I'm through, you'll have to beat them off with a stick."

"I'm not really interested in attracting men," Kathryne confirmed as she looked at her behind in the mirror, tickled to see how slim it looked. "I'm more interested in the food and music."

The boots were more comfortable than Kathryne expected, but she was almost sure she couldn't sit down in the jeans Norman made her buy. She would have chosen the larger size, but he insisted they'd stretch with a little wear. Skeptical at first about tucking her jeans into the high-top boots, she quickly realized it served a purpose. The jeans protected the soft skin of her calf from the leather finger-pulls sewn inside the boot.

By tucking the jeans inside the boots, the rich-blue phoenix design sewn on the shaft could be seen. The top of the boot ended just below her knee, and after Norman had explained that the boot got its name from the long, narrow, round chimney pipe attached to wood-burning stoves, she understood why Norman had referred to them as *stove-tops*.

She chose a more practical blue and white plaid cotton shirt and a little looser blue jeans too, convinced that she'd be more comfortable in them if she decided to get on a horse, which she hoped to do before her vacation ended.

"I can't believe you're going to be our neighbor," Norman commented as he slipped a CD into the player on the counter in his friend's shop the next day. "I'm so happy for us."

"I'm so sorry about your sister," Kathryne said as she put her hand on Norman's shoulder. "I had no idea you were Mr. Hawkins's brother-in-law. Both their names were on the contract, and I assumed—"

Norman smiled sadly. "It's all right. You had no way of knowing." He clasped her hand in his and then put his other hand on her hip. "All right, this is going to be fun. Just relax and follow my steps."

The beat of the music made it easy to follow Norman's lead. After the first few minutes, Kathryne had it down fairly well—enough to look up and ask Norman a question. "Why don't you go with me on Friday? Buying your dinner will be my way of saying thank you for finding me my dream home."

Norman glanced at her skeptically. "Are you serious? I was afraid that after you saw it, you'd sue me for fraud."

Kathryne laughed at his expression. "No, I'm serious. Let me buy you some supper. Besides, I hate eating alone, don't you?"

"I do," Norman said with an exaggerated nod. "I thought it

was just me, but now that I know you feel the same way, I'd be delighted to go with you." His smile faded. "Gosh, when we're through here, I'd better get something decent to wear."

The Last Chance Saloon was everything Kathryne hoped it would be. If she were going to make a new life in New Mexico, she might as well start enjoying herself. "Look at this place," she murmured to Norman as they stepped inside.

It was dark, but not too dark, filled with all kinds of people. The tables were covered with red and white checkered cloths, and the low-backed chairs looked just like the ones she'd seen in several western movies. There was a long, knotty-pine bar with leather-padded stools.

Behind the bar was a large painting of a naked lady, showing mostly her backside. The rest of the wall where the liquor bottles sat was mirrored. Much to her delight, there were several bowls of peanuts on top of the highly polished bar. Several customers nibbled them while enjoying a cold mug of beer.

Old fashioned kerosene lanterns adorned each table, offering a warm, mellow light, and the chandelier also had eight small lanterns placed on a wagon wheel and held to the thick-beamed ceiling by four stout chains. Among the pictures of John Wayne and Steve McQueen and Ronald Reagan, old ropes, bridles and bullwhips adorned the walls. Over a door near the back hung a sign reading, *Outhouse—His'n and Her'n.*

"Look, Kate. I bet you don't see that in Baltimore," Norman whispered as they were shown to a table. "The dance floor is covered in sawdust."

Three guitars, a set of drums and a violin were on the stage, but the musicians hadn't yet arrived. Just like Miss Kitty in *Gunsmoke* reruns, all the waitresses were dressed like dance hall girls with fish-net stockings, short frilly skirts and feathers in their hair.

Even the bartender look like he'd just stepped out of a Louie L'Amour novel, complete with handlebar moustache and his dark hair parted in the middle and slicked down on the sides.

"You look fabulous," Norman said with a proud grin as he held her chair while she sat.

"You look nice too," she quickly replied, trying hard not to smile at Norman's colorful outfit. He'd chosen a shirt with an American flag on the back and partially over his right sleeve, a red scarf neatly knotted around his neck, red jeans, and navy boots and belt, both with small flags inlaid in the leather.

"What's your pleasure?" the waitress asked.

Kathryne hesitated for a moment, and then said, "I'll have a beer."

"What kind?"

She glanced up at the waitress and then at Norman who took the cue and asked, "What's on tap, doll?"

"Sam Adams, Bud Light, Coors Light, Coors—"

"You like horses, so go for the Bud Light," he said to Kathryne.

"Then I'll have a Bud Light."

"And you?" the waitress asked patiently, smiling at Norman.

"Martini, no olive, extra onion, and a glass of water with lemon."

"Coming right up."

Kathryne waited until the waitress left then leaned toward Norman. "I thought we were going to drink beer and eat peanuts?"

Norman made a face. "Honey, peanuts? High in calories and lots of fat." He lifted the menu. "I wonder if the lettuce on their burgers is organic."

"Look at these names. My friend Liz would love this." Kathryne paused, and then put the menu aside. "I can't decide. What do you suggest?"

"Why don't you try the Buckaroo Barbecue Ribs, and I'll have the Roy Rogers Rib Eye and we'll each have a bite of the other's to see who has the best?"

A few minutes later the waitress brought their drinks, placing the martini before Norman. "Nice outfit."

"Why, thank you," he replied, obviously flattered.

Smiling, Kathryne shook her head. "Here we are in cowboy country and you order a martini . . . you could have at least had a whisky or something."

"Whisky? I don't drink whisky. Burns my throat."

"I'll have a whisky on the rocks," came a deep voice near the bar, behind Kathryne. Her eyes widened as she met Norman's.

"Did you hear that," she mouthed, then glanced over her shoulder to get a look at the man. She instantly recognized John Hawkins, and then quickly turned around. "It's him."

Kathryne took a sip of her beer, relieved that her back was to John, offering her some refuge as Norman looked past her, then stood.

"Johnny," Norman exclaimed in a loud voice. "Fancy meeting you here. Come over. I want you to meet someone."

Kathryne inwardly groaned and sank a little in her chair, straightening up the moment John Hawkins came into view.

"Look who's here," Norman said with a cheerful smile. "This is my friend, John Hawkins. John, this is my friend, Kate."

CHAPTER SEVEN

Kathryne looked up and smiled and at the same time held out her hand, slightly stunned. She'd expected John to have eyes as dark as his ebony hair, but they were a startling blue—gun metal blue—made even more interesting by his slightly high cheek bones.

His crimson-colored western shirt was opened at the neck, tucked in at the waist. The sleeves were fastened with pearl snaps that matched those down the front and on the two chest pockets. His blue jeans had been pressed, but unlike her, he wore the pants-legs over his black boots. He quickly put his small glass on the table then grasped her cold hand in his warm one. She swallowed, shocked by the jolt of pure pleasure the warmth of his touch caused.

"H-how nice to see you again . . . John." Against her better judgment, she motioned to the empty chair. "Please, join us."

"Come on, John. You have to join us," Norman encouraged.

"That's a mighty . . . colorful outfit you have there," John replied, taking the seat across from Kathryne's.

"Do you like it?" Norman motioned to Kathryne. "Kate invited me to join her for supper and I had nothing to wear."

John gave Norman a sideways grin. "You look . . . great, Norm." He glanced at Kathryne. "Patriotic is probably a better description, don't you think?" He smiled when she giggled an agreement. "So, how did you meet Norman?"

Kathryne blinked. "Didn't he tell you?"

95

"Tell me what?" John asked, taking another sip of his drink.

"I'm Kathryne Wilcox—actually my name is now Sheldon—" She stopped the moment he choked, hurrying to pat him on the back. "Are you all right?"

He nodded. "Yes," he said in a raspy voice. "You just took me by surprise, that's all." He cleared his throat. "I didn't quite understand what you said. There for a moment I thought you said Sheldon."

Kathryne nodded. "That's right. My name was Wilcox, but after my divorce, I chose to use my maiden name. I believe you know my father. Henry Sheldon."

John put down his drink. "I didn't make the connection— that is till now."

Norman lifted his glass. "Now that you know, let's celebrate."

John lifted his glass, his expression still a little guarded. "Ah . . . to new beginnings."

"New beginnings," Kathryne repeated.

"Hi, John," came a woman's voice. Kathryne looked up to see the waitress smiling down at them a moment before her eyes fastened on John.

"Hey, Julie, long time no see."

"Yeah, likewise. I heard a rumor that you sold part of your ranch?"

"Word gets out fast," he replied. "It's no rumor. This lady right here is going to be my neighbor."

Kathryne smiled a greeting, but apparently the waitress wasn't as happy about the sale as John.

"Are you ready to order?"

"I think we are," Norman said as he picked up the menu. "Ladies first."

By the time the plates were cleared from the table, the band members began to filter onto the stage.

"Do you dance?" John asked, taking a sip of the coffee he'd ordered.

Kathryne smiled sheepishly. "Yes, but ballroom dancing is much different. Norman was gracious enough to give me a little refresher course in country western, but I'm afraid I'll need more lessons to do it well."

Sounds of instruments being tuned drew Kathryne's attention away from the man wreaking havoc on her nerves. Much like the rest of the employees, three men were clad in cowboy attire, complete with ten-gallon hats, neck scarves and even authentic-looking six-shooters strapped on their hips.

The fourth man picked up the fiddle and was obviously a Native American, with his long black hair plaited in two braids and fastened with silver and turquoise tubular clips. Instead of boots he wore moccasins, and instead of jeans he wore fringed buckskins and a beaded leather band around his forehead. He glanced at John and nodded a greeting.

"Do you know him?"

"Yeah, he's a friend."

"John knows everyone, and everyone knows him," Norman replied, adding some cream to his coffee. "That's how it's been as long as I can remember."

The musicians started a new song, drowning out their conversation. The music was loud and lively, and soon several couples wandered onto the floor to dance. A moment later, Kathryne heard chair legs scrape. She didn't have to look up to know that John stood by her chair. When their eyes met, he offered his hand. "May I have this dance?"

"Ah . . . I—" Kathryne cast a frantic glance at Norman and then looked back at John. "I'm warning you," she said uneasily as she slowly stood, slipping her hand into his. Her heart leapt into her throat, and she silently prayed her palm wouldn't be sweaty. "I'm not a very good dancer . . . especially in cowboy boots."

His soft laugh did nothing to chase the butterflies out of her stomach. She became very aware of the wide grin on Norman's face as she passed by and wished for a moment that she hadn't been so eager to jump into this new adventure.

The twang of the music sounded pleasing, and as she tried not to watch the other dancers and their steps, John pulled her closer. He smiled, and this time she noticed a little twinkle in his eyes. "It's been a few years, but I promise not to step on your feet too much."

"And I'll try to stay off yours," she countered. His hands were warm, almost as warm as his smile, and as they mingled with the other couples, she suddenly felt completely at ease. "Tell me something," she teased. "Are those your initials on your buckle?"

"Yes, they are," John answered, and she knew by his expression he was amused that she'd noticed.

"JWH . . . what's the W for?"

"Well," John began, his mouth twitching as if he wanted to laugh. "My mother loved the old westerns and some of the old World War II movies. So when I was born she named me John Wayne Hawkins after the famous—"

"Movie star?" she added, and together they said, "John Wayne."

She laughed with him. "So you're a Native American with a cowboy name?" Kathryne realized too late that her attempt at humor might not be appreciated, and without looking up to gauge his reaction, she hurried to say. "I'm sorry. I'm always saying things I think are funny when actually they're—oh dear, did I hurt you?" she asked mortified that she'd practically stomped on his foot.

"Hey, relax," John said with a soft chuckle when her gaze met his. "I'll live, and the comment—it was a good one. And, it's pretty close to the money. My mother was a full-blooded Navajo, daughter of Charlie Silver-Hawk. My father was an Anglo. I think his name was Tim Johnson . . . I'm not real sure. It's been awhile since I've thought of him."

"Then how did you get the name Haw—ouch!"

They stopped again and this time John shook his head and laughed. "This is proving a lot more painful for you than it is for me. My feet are bigger."

He glanced at Kathryne, and she realized immediately she liked John Hawkins and his big feet. "Seems I can't talk and dance at the same time," he said, still smiling.

"Me either," she agreed.

"Anyway, my mother wanted me to have an Anglo name, but she wanted to honor my grandfather, so they came up with Hawkins." At that moment, they bumped into another couple who didn't seem too happy about the unexpected encounter. John made a polite apology, but their frowns didn't dissipate as they danced away.

"Maybe we'd better sit this one out," Kathryne offered, feeling a little clumsy.

"Don't worry about them," he said softly, so only she could hear. His warm breath tickled her ear, and when she pulled back and looked into his eyes, the twinkle was back and in full force. "Let's stop watching our feet and just hold on to each other, and everything will be fine."

And it was. In fact, he danced so well, she had no trouble following his steps. She found it easy to laugh at his jokes and enjoy the way he sang along with the music. The next tune was much more lively, and at one point he had tight hold of her and then the next moment he twirled her around, then reeled her in, grabbing her around the waist with a good-humored smile at her gasp. All too soon the music ended, and she became aware that she felt slightly flushed and a little breathless.

"That wasn't so bad, was it?" he asked, a bit winded himself. Again, a little shiver skittered spider-like down her spine.

Taking a deep breath, she gazed into his eyes. "No," she said smiling. "It wasn't bad at all."

Just when she thought they'd return to the table, the next dance started. "Shall we?" John asked. "After all, we're on a roll and it doesn't sound too fast. It'll give us time to catch our breaths. You know it's not good to rest right after a fast dance, don't you?"

"Really? Why not?"

"Well, if you were a horse and I put you in the barn after too much exercise, you'd colic." His smile was devilish. "I'm sure it's the same with people."

She laughed at his expression. "Well then, I guess we'd better get out there and cool down, if you're sure Norman won't mind."

"Norm won't mind a bit. He's a free spirit," John noted. "Most of the time he can find happiness in a rainy day, and then the next moment he'll turn the slightest little thing into a catastrophe. But the truth is, I don't know what I'd do without him. He's a good friend. He's also a darned good chef—works for your dad at the lodge."

John twirled Kathryne around again. This time she came back into his arms with a little more grace, subduing the gasp that jumped into her throat the moment her breasts made contact with his chest—a very broad, hard chest.

"What about you?" he asked. "Where do you find happiness?"

Kathryne found herself drawn into his gaze. "I-I thought I was happy being a lawyer, but then . . . then things changed. Now, I'm hoping to find it here, in my grandfather's old cabin," she replied honestly. "Did Norman tell you what I want to do with it?"

"Nope. He was too busy telling me that I need to think about taking a room at the lodge, but I'm thinking about fixing up the old hunting shack."

"The one on the ridge?" she asked, frowning in disbelief.

"Yup. That's the one."

"But it's old . . . older than the ranch, and . . . my gosh, is it livable?"

His grin widened. "Not according to Norman." He spun her around then pulled her back into his arms. "It needs a few repairs, but as long as the weather holds, I'll be fine. You've heard the old expression—home is where I hang my hat. I could live in a tent, for that matter."

"Don't you mean tepee?" she blurted out, feeling her cheeks warm the moment the words left her mouth. His laughter saved her from pure mortification.

"Yes, ma'am, tepee is a better choice," he said, his eyes sparkling with humor.

The music ended and this time, before he could make her dance another, she led him back to the table. "I need a cold drink," she said over her shoulder.

He motioned to the waitress, then held Kathryne's chair while she sat down. "What's your pleasure?"

"Just a glass of ice water," she replied. Once the music started, Kathryne glanced at the dancers, tapping her toe to the beat. Norman was among them, doing some kind of a line dance and looking as if he was thoroughly enjoying himself.

"Water for the lady, and I'll have a Coors." John glanced at the woman sitting across from him—the lamplight coloring her blond hair a coppery-gold. Damn, but she was a looker. He couldn't remember when he'd had so much fun. In fact, he couldn't remember the last time he'd been dancing.

He watched Kathryne watch the dancers, admiring her strong profile and the way her long fingers and perfectly manicured nails tapped against the table with the beat of the music. Though it was barely noticeable, there was a narrow indentation on the ring finger of her left hand, a proclamation that she'd worn a wedding band for many years.

"Here are your drinks," came the waitress's voice.

Kathryne turned back to the table with a smile that melted John's insides. He waited until they were served and the waitress had left before he asked, "How long are you staying in town?"

"At least another week. Then I've got some matters to settle back home."

He didn't understand why, but his good mood wavered ever so slightly. "Norman said you wanted me to do some repairs on the house?"

"Yes, if you'll agree? But if you work for my father, I certainly don't want to take you away from your duties at the lodge."

"It shouldn't be a problem. The lodge is closed for the month. I've got some previous job commitments, but my evening and weekends are my own." He took a drink of his beer. "So why does a fancy lawyer decide to relocate to New Mexico?"

"Corporate law is hardly fancy." She took a sip of water. "I guess New Mexico's in my blood. You see, I used to come up here every summer and help my grandfather. For years, that was the only time I thought about the place. Then my father came into my office one day and told me he was leaving—that he never liked living in Maryland, never really wanted to be a big-city lawyer, and was going home to the ranch."

"That sounds like Hank," John agreed.

"Well, I didn't think so at the time. I thought he sounded crazy. So did my mother. They were divorced shortly after."

"Hank said something about that, but he didn't elaborate."

"He didn't elaborate when he left either, and because I felt hurt that he didn't explain, and because my husband didn't care for my father, Dad and I lost contact with each other."

"So, now you're here to mend the fence?" John asked with a slight smile.

"I guess you could say that." She shrugged her shoulders. "It's difficult to *mend fences* with him gone. I'm hoping when he returns he'll forgive me. I said some pretty terrible things to him the last time we spoke. But then, I thought I was happy with my life and I guess I convinced myself that I didn't care what happened to him. It's an easy thing to do when you're nearly two-thousand miles apart."

"What changed your mind?"

"My divorce." She took a long drink of the icy-cold water. "It's amazing really," she began, playing with the corner of her napkin. "I felt very angry with my father and what he did, but then a month ago, I realized that he was right—that there's more to life."

She gave a slight smile. "I guess I've been a little down since the divorce, so my friend, Liz, suggested I take a vacation. We were talking about it when one thing led to another and well"—she shrugged her shoulders and grinned—"here I am."

"A vacation," he repeated, leaning back in his chair. "Now it makes sense."

"What does?" she asked with a perplexed frown.

"You being here." His smile turned serious. "You bought the cabin to make it your summer home?"

"Not exactly. I'm planning to move out here." She took another sip of water. "Lately, I've been spending too much time doing things that don't really make me happy."

"Buying old houses makes you happy?" he teased. Again her smile warmed, and he found it easy to return it.

"No, I'm not going to buy any more old houses . . . just yours." She met his gaze and he admired her brilliant-green eyes. Her smile widened. "If you're really planning to move into that rickety old shack, you and I are going to be neighbors too."

"Sounds good to me," he said. "Do you think you'll really be happy leaving the city life to put down stakes out here?" He shook his head. "This is about as far from the life you've known as the earth from the moon."

"Whew," Norman said breathlessly. "This place is a scream. Don't you just love it, Katie?" He sank down into his chair. "My God, I'm sweating like a pig." Norman picked up the dessert menu and began to fan his face. "I've got to rest."

"Then there's no use asking you for a dance?" John teased.

Norman gave John a stern look. "Kate's going to think you're serious, John. She doesn't know you've got a weird sense of humor."

"How about you, Kate? Shall we try it again?" John asked.

She would have refused, but that damned twinkle was back in those dark-blue eyes, *and* it was another line dance—the kind she secretly wanted to try the moment she noticed Norman doing it. She placed her hand in his. It was silly to be so shy. So what that she and Doug had been high school sweethearts and that she'd never really dated anyone else?

So what? She inwardly argued with herself through the next dance, the angel on her shoulder telling her she shouldn't be interested in finding another man; and the devil, who looked a lot like Liz, giving her hell for not trying to get to know John better.

Too soon, the evening was over. The band packing up their instruments and the tinkle of glasses being cleared from tables was the only music to be heard. Norman had given them some excuse and left before either one of them could respond, leaving them to their own devices.

A few couples lingered, speaking with the band members, but Kathryne hardly noticed. For the last hour, she and John had made small talk, exchanging life-stories about spouses, married life, their common likes and dislikes. She liked to cook. He could only cook eggs and bacon, and then only over easy and extra crisp.

They both liked horses and dogs, and both confessed that they would have enjoyed having children. John got a lot of pleasure from teaching the children who stayed at the lodge horsemanship skills. When he wasn't with the children, he had an endless list of repairs ranging from mending fences to fixing broken wheels on the hay-riding wagon. Neither one had any siblings, but unlike Kate, John never knew his father.

"Did you ever try to find him?" she asked, catching a small ice cube with her teeth before chewing it. "There's lots of agencies on the Internet that can help."

"Nope," he said flatly, shifting his gaze from his beer to meet hers. "I guess I've always felt that he did my mother an injustice, and a man who'd abandon his child wasn't the kind of man I needed to know."

Kathryne decided sometime during the conversation that she didn't need to think of John as a man on the prowl, but as a friend, and as soon as she made that discovery, she began to relax even more and really enjoy his company. When the lodge was closed, she learned he hauled hay into Albuquerque for several of the area's farmers. "So is it hard to learn how to drive a big truck?"

His grin was instant, maybe even a little arrogant. "Not really. You've just got to get used to ten gears instead of four. If you'd like, I could teach you."

She laughed. "Me?" she replied, shaking her head. "I can barely handle an automatic."

"My offer stands. When you're ready, just give me a call. The truck's always there. You probably saw the garage behind the barn." He took a drink and then leaned a little closer. "Why don't we trade a little work for letting me keep the truck and the horses on your property? I'll make a few repairs, and you won't have to pay for them."

"The barter system . . . sounds good, but I've got a couple of conditions."

"I'm not sure I like that crafty gleam in your eyes," he countered.

"I'll pay for the materials and, like you said, we'll trade for labor."

"Deal," he replied.

"Not so fast. There's more." Her eyes narrowed. "I also get to ride the horses once in awhile."

"Do you know how to ride?"

"I think it's like riding a bike. Once you do it, you never forget."

He hesitated for a moment, then nodded. "That's what I thought about dancing, but it didn't work out that way."

They both laughed. "Hopefully I'll ride better than I danced," she said.

"Well, why don't you come on up tomorrow, and we'll take a little trail ride. You can get to know my horses, and I could show you some of the country."

"Why, that would be wonderful," she exclaimed, excited about the prospect of getting on a horse again after so many years. "Will Norman be there too?"

"Most likely. However, I've got to warn you. Getting Norman on a horse," he grimaced, "It *ain't* pretty." He glanced at his watch. "Damn, It's nearly two. They're going to close this place down, and I've got to get up early." He stood and offered his hand before escorting her toward the door. "I haven't danced that many dances in years. I've got a feeling I'll be needing Ben Gay tonight."

★ ★ ★ ★ ★

The next morning while Kathryne dressed, the phone rang. Secretly, she hoped it was John, but then blushed at her silly thought as she quickly slipped on her jeans and zipped them up. How could the man call if she didn't give him her room number? And, why didn't she think to do so?

She sat on the edge of the bed and lifted the receiver. "Liz! Hey, how are you?" She nodded complacently. "Yes, I was out late. I'm sorry I missed your call. I went to a saloon. Yeah, a real saloon with a live band. I ate Buckaroo Barbecue Ribs and drank beer and danced. Even a line dance."

Kathryne's smile widened. "I am telling you everything. I went with Norman the real estate agent-slash-artist-slash-chef, and while we were there, I met John Hawkins, the man who owns the cabin I'm buying." She shook her head, laughing at her friend's comments. "Well, he's tall and has this gorgeous long black hair—"

She shifted her position on the bed, sitting with her legs crossed and leaning her elbows on her knees. "That's right. It's long and black—maybe a few grey hairs, but they weren't really noticeable. Did he kiss me good night? My gosh, Liz, we've only just met. One moment I'm trying to answer your question, and the next you're asking me if we kissed. I swear, you've got a one track mind."

Kathryne rose and picked up her watch from the bedside table near the phone. "I'm telling you again that I like being single. John is nice, but I don't think he's really my type." She shook her head. "Breathing is your type. Yes, as a matter of fact, I'm going out to his place in a little while . . . now Liz, stop. I'm trying to tell you, but you keep interrupting. We're mature adults. We ate together, danced a little. Talked a little—"

She paused, slowly shaking her head in disbelief. "How can you consider horseback riding a date? I know you're rolling your eyes, so please stop jumping to conclusions." She held the phone in the crook of her neck while she fastened her watch around her wrist. "What do you mean, I've been alone too long? Four months. That's not too long. In fact, it's not near long enough. No, I'm not attracted to him—at least not in the way you're implying. John and I are just friends . . . two people doing business together. He's like . . . a client, nothing more. You can certainly understand that. I've had dinner with many of my male clients . . . and we certainly didn't kiss each other afterwards."

After glancing at her watch, Kathryne heaved a patient sigh. She had plenty of time, and in a special way it felt fun talking about John—made her feel like she was in high school again, sharing her latest crush with her best girlfriend.

"Yes, I'm listening. I just don't like what I'm hearing. Yeah, well, I'm sorry I disappointed you. Somehow I just didn't get the urge to put a lip-lock on the guy . . . no, he didn't try—not that I'd let him if he did. The man's a gentleman, pure and simple, and I respect him for that. Besides, it's not like we were on a date or anything. We merely ran into each other at a restaurant. I was with Norman—"

This time Kathryne rolled her eyes. "Norman is the sweetest man I've met in a long time. No. He's not the kind of man that's particularly interested in women. That's right. Good grief, Liz, you should have been a lawyer. You can fire off more questions faster than any trial lawyer I know."

She laughed at Liz's retort. "I told you, Norman works for my Dad, and so does John. Norman's a chef. John teaches kids how to ride while their parents enjoy their vacations. You know, hay rides, trail rides, things families do together. If you're through drilling me, I've got to finish getting dressed. John invited Norman and me out to the ranch for a ride and lunch. It's not a date. Now goodbye." Kathryne placed the phone in the rocker laughing at Liz's parting words.

"Sounds like a date to me."

CHAPTER EIGHT

"Hey, Helen, is Kate in?" Douglas asked striding past Helen's desk. She watched him open the door to Kathryne's office without knocking, look inside, and then return his gaze to hers.

"No," she said, and then pretended interest in a contract on her desk. She felt his presence but refused to take the bait. Instead she continued to ignore him until he rested his hip on her desk, catching the edge of the contract and preventing her from turning the page.

"You're looking great. Been working out?"

She gave him a *get lost* glance, tugged the file from under his hip and stood to leave, but he caught her arm. "Where's Kate?"

Helen glared at him for a moment. "On vacation. Now may I get back to work?" She pulled her arm free, turned to the lateral file cabinet, and placed the contract inside.

"Where'd she go?"

"Mr. Wilcox," Helen began with a sigh. "I'm not at liberty to tell you. Apparently she didn't feel the need to disclose her whereabouts to you, so for me to divulge that information could jeopardize my position here."

His laughter caused her to look up.

"Did I say something funny?"

He stood, shaking his head. "Damn, but she's got you trained." He stepped a little closer, and she felt his gaze slip from her face to linger on her breasts. "If she calls in, ask her to give me a call, will you? I stumbled onto something that might

110

interest her."

He strode from the room before she collected herself enough to think of a smart retort.

Doug paused outside Kathryne's office door and then stormed toward his own office. He didn't like being ignored. He'd gotten a brief on the contract he'd sent over, but some intern named Ron had done it, not his ex-wife. He stopped in his tracks, and then went back to Kathryne's office. "Helen?"

"Yes, Mr. Wilcox?" she answered, not bothering to look up from her work.

"If it's not too much trouble, would you mind finding Ron and ask him to stop by my office? I want to speak to him about some inquiries he made for Kathryne."

"Yes, Mr. Wilcox."

Her tone awakened his temper and he almost said something, but decided against it. He closed the door and started down the hall, muttering under his breath. "Bitch."

"Here's the mail," Vicky said, placing it on Doug's desk, pleased that he'd hired her as his personal secretary, even if he didn't treat her as nicely as she thought he should. It was one thing to play around after work, but she took her new position and responsibilities seriously and had hoped he would too. "There's a young man waiting to see you. His said his name is Rod."

"Ron," Doug corrected, catching Vicky's wrist. "You're going to have to get the names right if we want to make good impressions, got it?" He pulled her down and kissed her, oblivious to the fact that he'd hurt her feelings.

"Doug," she murmured when he released her. Pouting, she rubbed her wrist. "I don't think we should be so . . . so personal when we're working."

He grinned, then began to sort through the stack of envelopes on his desk. "I don't pay you to think, Vic, I pay you to get the names right. Now, have Ron come in and remember to offer him something to drink."

"I already did," she muttered as she walked away.

Doug didn't have to wait too long. A few moments later, a young man stepped into his office. "Mr. Wilcox, you wanted to see me?"

"Yes, thank you for coming." Doug stood and offered his hand. "I don't believe we've met."

Ron returned the handshake. "No, sir . . . well, not really, sir. Mrs. Wilcox . . . I mean Ms. Sheldon hired me right before the divorce."

"Ah, I see." Doug motioned for the young man to take a seat. "I asked you here because you've left several messages regarding a parcel of land in New Mexico."

Ron frowned and shook his head. "I'm sure I would have remembered calling you. There must be some mistake."

"No, I'm sure there's no mistake. You left your name, Kathryne's name, and a phone number where I could reach you."

"USIB?" Ron exclaimed. "You're USIB?"

Doug nodded, smiling. "That's me. It's a catchy name, don't you think? Stands for *you sell I buy.*"

"But *you* begins with . . ." Ron's cheeks brightened with color. "I didn't realize you'd started another company. Ms. Sheldon asked me to investigate—"

"Kathryne's interested in this property?" Doug leaned back in his chair. "I had no idea." He fastened his gaze back on Ron, watching the young man fidget as if he'd revealed something he shouldn't have.

Ron straightened a little in his chair and cleared his throat. "If I may ask, Mr. Wilcox, what's your interest in this parcel?"

"My company bought the mortgage. It's in foreclosure . . . or at least it will be in a couple of weeks." He didn't bother explaining that he had already had a developer interested, and by foreclosing he could more than triple his investment

"I hardly think it will go that far," Ron replied, adjusting his tie. "As we speak, I've reason to believe that you—USIB should receive payment in a matter of days."

By the time Kathryne and Norman let their horses follow John's the last hundred feet toward the ranch house, she could barely hide her pain. She'd forgotten all about being saddle sore when she was a child, remembering only the hours of fun she'd spent on the back of a horse. She glanced at Norman, who gave her a murderous look.

"How are you doing?" she asked softly.

Norman's lips thinned. "Fine, doll . . . just fine. Of course I'll never be able to walk again, and most likely I'll have to stand in the shower to pee, but other than that, I'm just great . . . terrific."

Kathryne stood up a little in the stirrups, trying to ease the ache in her knees and hips. She silently offered a prayer that she'd be able to dismount without falling. As it was, she was sure her legs were numb from the knees down.

But that wasn't the worst part. The new jeans she'd bought for the occasion had a little rivet in exactly the same place as her tail-bone, and she was sure they had worn a hole in her skin.

"We'll get in the hot tub at the hotel," she whispered, offering Norman a sympathetic smile. "You can be my guest."

"Hot tub? I need a freaking ambulance!"

"Shusssh, he'll hear you," Kathryne hissed. She glanced at John's back before turning to Norman. "This is my fault. We'll go to the spa if they're open and have a massage, too. My treat."

Norman muttered something Kathryne didn't hear, but there wasn't time to ask him to repeat himself. They were at the house. John swung down from his mount with the agility of a large cat and tossed his reins over the rail—but Norman wasn't so graceful. He groaned loudly as he eased himself out of the saddle, clutching the horn until his foot hit the ground. He paused there a moment or two, and then carefully lifted his left foot out of the stirrup.

"Thank God," Norman moaned aloud. "I didn't think I was going to make it. Now I know why the cowboys on all the old westerns were always yelling ay, yi, yi, yi. It was probably the only way they could voice their pain in public." Norman glanced over at Kate. "Forgive me for the outburst. I don't ride well." He leaned against his horse. "Are you all right?" he added.

"Sure. Maybe a little sore, but I think we all had a good time. Right?"

Norman glared at Kathryne, then at John. "You actually enjoy this?" He staggered over to the rail, placing both hands on the balustrade to drag himself up the steps. "I'll make us Bloody Marys on the rocks." He groaned again, once for each step. "On second thought, I'm going to save the rocks and put them in a baggie, wrap a towel around it, and tie it to my butt."

Absorbed in Norman's conversation, Kathryne didn't realize she was still on her horse until John stood beside her. "Ready?" he asked.

"Ah . . . I can manage," she said quickly . . . too quickly. She stood in the left stirrup, dragging her right leg over the horse's rump, stifling a groan as it seemed forever before the tip of her boot touched the ground. After she kicked her left foot free, she paused beside her mount a moment, not sure if her wobbly legs would support her weight but determined not to let John see her distress. "Wow," she said, taking a step and then another.

"You sure you're all right?" John asked, his dark brows drawn together.

She forced a smile. "Oh, sure. Just a little stiff—been a long time since I've ridden, that's all." She walked awkwardly to the hitching post and tied the reins next to where John had tied his.

"Well, if it's any consolation, I think you did fine for a city slicker."

When she turned to challenge him, he grinned, and at the same time she saw that mischievous twinkle in his eyes. It was hard to know exactly what he was thinking, but she decided she liked being teased.

John Hawkins was a sweet guy—the kind of man who'd never last a moment in a big city like Baltimore. He'd hate the confinement of tall buildings and lots of people. But that didn't matter. He'd probably never leave New Mexico. And darned if he wasn't one hell of a handsome man, with that jet-black hair and those midnight-blue eyes.

A crazy idea flashed in the back of her mind—the Summer Ball—John in a tux—a western cut tux with his silver belt buckle and new black boots. *Why don't we trade a little work for letting me keep the truck and the horses on your property?* She blinked to break the spell, and then smiled.

"Come on, country boy," she muttered, holding out her hand. "Help me up these steps. I want . . . no I *need* a Bloody Mary before Norman drinks them all." She put her hand on her behind and rubbed. "Do you have any of the Ben-Gay left?"

Holding a Scotch on the rocks in his hand, Doug stood at the window in his office staring out over the city lights, silently cursing himself for being so stupid. He should have fought the damned pre-nuptial. But Kathryne had caught him with his pants down—literally—and like a fool, he'd been so wrapped up in his own wants, he never saw it coming. If he had, he would have been more careful.

One moment Kathryne seemed perfectly content, the next she was tossing a divorce decree at him, and with it, two dozen expensive shirts, cut into pieces. Now she hardly spoke to him at all. If only he'd been more careful, things wouldn't have gotten so terribly out of control. He'd had everything in the palm of his hand. Now he wondered if it had all been worth it. Although he hated to admit it, he missed her.

He'd be the first to admit that he also missed the financial independence and the security she offered, but mostly he missed the stimulating conversations they used to have on a variety of different topics. *If you want a good debate, have it with a lawyer,* he mused.

Vicky was great in bed, did stuff to him Kathryne might have thought vulgar, but he found himself thinking more and more that Vicky was the typical blonde, air-headed and lucky to form complete sentences. Did she even have a degree? He wondered.

He raked his fingers through his hair, and then turned back to his desk. Four hours ago, Vicky had brought in the mail shortly before a meeting with Kathryne's junior partner. During the meeting he'd learned that the woman he'd spent most of his life with expressed interest in the parcel he'd hoped to obtain through foreclosure.

The information had puzzled him at first, and then he'd remembered a nearly forgotten suggestion—that when they retired, Kathryne thought they should open a bed and breakfast somewhere in the mountains.

He'd never given her retirement dream any merit, but tonight he almost wished it had become a reality—a place to escape the hustle and bustle of the city—a place where he and Kathryne might be able to reconcile their differences.

Douglas sat down in his plush office chair with a loud, tired sigh. He picked up the money order he'd received and looked at it again. An hour ago he'd opened a hand-addressed envelope postmarked in Taos, New Mexico. When he pulled out a folded letter, the very last thing he expected floated down and landed face up on his desk—a money order for six thousand dollars.

He had quickly read the letter, then in a fit of anger, crumpled it and threw it across the room. Since that time, he'd been struggling with his conscience.

Lost in thought, he jumped when the phone rang. "Hello?" he said flatly. "Yeah, Vicky, I know it's late. I had a few things to catch up on." He swiveled his chair to stare out the window at the city's lights. "Yeah, I'm sorry dinner's ruined . . . no, I love your cooking . . . no, no Vicky, don't cry. I'm on my way, and if you want, I'll stop at Earl's and bring your favorite. Yeah. Sure . . . I love you too."

Doug turned back to his desk and put the phone back in the cradle. He drummed his fingers on the polished surface for several minutes then stood, picked up the money order, and put it through the shredder.

Two days later, after Kathryne could walk without hurting, and clad in a crisp white shirt, blue jeans, and boots, she slowly strolled down the street doing a little window-shopping when she heard the deep rumble of a large engine. She shaded her eyes with her hand, watching while John slowed, pulling the big truck to a hissing halt in the street across from her.

"Howdy," he called from the open window.

"Hi," she shouted over the rumble of the engine.

The prospect of getting a ride in such a huge vehicle persuaded Kathryne to cross the street. John opened the door and stepped down, telling Duke to stay when the dog jumped up on the seat and looked as if he wanted to be lifted down.

"How are you doing?" he asked, pushing his cowboy hat off his forehead.

She returned his smile. "I'm fully recovered, and it only took two days of total bed rest."

His laughter came easily. "Shopping?"

"Not really. Just browsing." She glanced up a Duke, who immediately started wagging his tail. "He likes it up there, doesn't he?"

John glanced at his dog. "Yup. He's a good traveler." He turned, shoving his hands into his back pockets. "Ever been in a tractor?"

"A tractor? I thought they were called semis."

"The trailer attached to the tractor is called that, but the truck itself is technically a tractor. Most drivers just call them big trucks or big rigs."

Kathryne looked up at the huge red truck. "I'll say it's big. May I look inside?"

"Sure, but let me shut her down first." A moment later, he motioned for her to approach. "I'll tell you how to climb in." He pointed to the rail inside by the driver's seat he'd just vacated. "Grab that and the door handle there, and come on up. I'll keep Duke from getting in the way."

Much to her surprise, he was standing inside the cab, holding Duke's collar. When she was halfway up, he grabbed her hand and pulled her into the driver's seat. The interior was a smaller version of the huge motor-home she'd seen at her mother's house.

"Sit and I'll tell you what you're looking at." Gauge by gauge he explained all their uses and why they were important, ending with the air gauges. "Well, are you ready for a ride?" he asked.

"Oh, I don't know if I should. I told Norman I'd meet him at his friend's shop—"

"I'll call him and tell him you're going to be late." John flipped open his cell phone. "Hey, Norm. Kate's with me. I'm going to take her for a little ride in Red. Yeah, I'll drop her off at the shop in about an hour."

John stepped back and motioned to the passenger seat. "Well, what do you say? We won't be gone too long."

"As long as Norman doesn't mind, I guess I'll go." She got

up from the driver's seat and slipped into the comfortable leather passenger's chair. While she found the seatbelt, snapping it into place, she was already making plans to call Liz and tell her all about her day. "My gosh, I had no idea these were so roomy inside."

"Let me get this baby off these city streets, and then I'll give you the grand tour." John started up the engine and threw it into third, easing out into traffic. "The one thing you've got to remember driving something this big is that it's not as easy to see the cars behind you. That's why we have all these mirrors."

It was noisy inside, especially with the window down, but Kathryne didn't care. She rather liked sitting up high, being able to see over all the other cars. Not that there were many, but the few that were in front of them didn't block her view of the road ahead. In a few short minutes they were on the highway, leaving town.

She recognized some of the homes as they drove by, aware that they were heading toward the ranch. She was just about to confirm their destination when John slowed down and turned onto a wide dirt road, rolling to a stop. He pulled out a rather large yellow button positioned above a large red button. As soon he pulled it out, a whoosh of air sounded, and they stopped.

"This," he began, "is the brake. The yellow one is the parking brake, the red one affects the trailer. But I'm bob-tailing right now, so I don't need to do anything with it." He wiggled the long gear shift stick, and it also made a small hissing noise. "We're in neutral, so I can let up on the clutch."

"What would happen if you took your foot off the clutch and we weren't in neutral?"

He gave her a devilish grin. "Let's see." He suppressed the clutch, shifted to first, and then released the clutch. The big truck seemed to jump, then stalled, swaying from side to side much more forcefully than she prepared for.

"Wow, I shudder to think what would happen if we'd been in a higher gear."

"It'd be about the same. You see, there are ten gears forward, and two in reverse. We were in first, commonly called grandma." He paused as if he were searching for the right words. "It might be easier if I give you a mile-per hour ratio to the gears."

And he did, and even though she didn't think anything like this would be interesting, it was. Or at least, John made it sound interesting. She had watched him intently as he went through the gears, secretly wondering what it would feel like to drive such a monster.

Not only would it be a challenge, but the stories she could tell around the water cooler would be worth every intimidating moment. So when John asked her if she wanted to drive, she gave him an eager nod. "I can't hurt anything, can I?"

"Nope," he said, smiling. "Only my pride if you're good."

"We'll be lucky if I get it out of first."

"Well, don't go making it look too easy now," he replied, making sure they were in neutral before moving out of the driver's seat. "I've got to protect my reputation."

With room to stand, Kathryne glanced at Duke, who had his head resting on his paws on the twin-sized bunk in the back. Kathryne looked around, surprised to see a small refrigerator, much like the one she had in her office, under a roomy shelf. There was a small closet on the opposite side and a small television in the cupboard above it. "This seems to have all the comforts of home," she said as she took her place behind the large steering wheel.

"A lot of drivers spend two or three weeks at a time in these rigs—some even longer. They need those comforts. I've got a friend who has a shower in his."

John sat on the passenger's side, drawing the seatbelt across his chest. "Old Red here is equipped with satellite radio and a CD player, and there's room for a small microwave in back, but I never found the need for a truck with a shower. I guess I like coming home at night."

He motioned for her to look at the pedals on the floor. "You probably know this, but the long one is the accelerator, the one next to it is the brake, and the one on the far left is the clutch."

"Just pretend that I know nothing about driving," Kathryne insisted, then turned and smiled. "Because I haven't a clue how to drive a standard—especially one this big."

"It's easy. Trust me, you'll do just fine." He motioned around the area. "We're on a dirt road, no one's around and there's no traffic. You're going to be double clutching—"

"Double clutching?"

He nodded patiently. "Yup. In once to get it out of gear, in the second time to get it into gear. It's easier than it sounds. There are a couple of things to remember before we start. See this gauge? It's called a tachometer. In cars, especially automatics, it's mostly for show, but it's very important when driving a tractor. On Red, you'll want to keep it between fourteen and sixteen hundred revolutions per minute. This is the window that will make shifting easy, otherwise it'll bind on you or you'll miss a gear and have to go for gear recovery—which is something we don't want to worry about today."

His smile reinforced her determination to do it right the first time. She had no desire to go for *gear recovery,* nor did she want to know the details of what would happen if she didn't *recover* the gear.

"Are you ready to start?" His voice broke into her anxious thoughts, and for a moment she wondered if she were about to make a fool of herself. But as quickly as the thought came, she banished it with sheer determination.

She wasn't dependant anymore.

She could be or do anything she wanted, and right now, she wanted to drive a very big truck down the road.

"Step on the clutch and hold it, then start the engine, but don't let up on the clutch till I tell you."

She did exactly as he said.

"Take firm hold of the stick and pull it down toward your hip. You'll feel it click in. If it sticks, give it a little gas and it should slip right in. Good, now—no, don't let up—"

Too late, she moved her foot off the clutch. Old Red jumped then shook, and then died what felt like a violent death.

She gave a little giggle then glanced over at John, not really knowing what to expect. Would he be angry, impatient as Doug would have been in his place? Much to her surprise, John's expression was neither. Mostly amused. *No,* she amended silently. *Very amused with a tinge of arrogance.*

"You've got to kill it a few times to get the feel."

"Good, because I doubt that'll be the last time." She went through the steps again, suppressing the clutch, pushing in the brake, shifting, giving it a little gas, easing up on the clutch . . . spurting, shaking, and then the bone wrenching halt.

"Try again," John encouraged.

How sweet, she thought, certain that Doug would have been screaming at her by now. She tried to do everything right, but again she stalled out.

"It's all right, just takes some getting used to. Try again."

By the fifth try, Kathryne actually managed to go about thirty feet before she let out the clutch too fast and it stalled. While John explained the technical reason she was having so much difficulty, she calmly rubbed her left quadriceps. Pushing in the clutch and holding it had started to become painful, and the last thing she needed right now was a muscle cramp.

John finished, then relaxed back in his seat. "Let's go again," he replied with an encouraging smile.

"Won't all this stopping and starting hurt the engine?" she asked, hoping he'd take over.

"You've got to learn. Might as well be now."

CHAPTER NINE

Thirty minutes later, Kathryne pulled onto the highway, shifting out of fourth, easily into fifth, then sixth, and on up until they were cruising at a comfortable forty-five miles per hour. When they got closer to town, she slowed down to the speed limit, heading for Norman's shop to show him what she'd accomplished.

"Can I toot the horn?" she asked as she began to slow down even more. She cast a quick glance over at John, who nodded.

"Don't use the one on the steering column," he said with an ornery grin, "reach up there and give that cord a couple of short tugs."

She complied, flinching at the blast of sound that seemed to ricochet off the building's walls. She cast a nervous glance over at John, who chuckled at her expression. "That's the air horn. No use blowing your horn if it can't be heard."

"He's sure been blowing his own horn around here. Especially since Ms. Sheldon's been gone," Helen said to Ron as they sat across from each other, sharing a cup of coffee on their break in the building's cafeteria. "I used to wonder what Ms. Sheldon ever saw in Mr. Wilcox. And just between you and me, I'm glad she left him. As long as I've known him, he's never treated her right."

"I don't doubt it, but I do think we should let her know that her ex-husband is the lien holder on the property she's interested in. Have you heard from her lately?"

"No," Helen replied. "And I hate to call her. This is the first vacation she's had in years. Do you think it could wait?"

Ron shrugged his shoulders. "I think it probably could. He said something about the foreclosure taking place by the end of the month, but it's only the nineteenth."

Helen stood. "Well, we've still got the rest of this week and all of next."

"But I really think she needs to know before the thirty-first."

"I promise I'll tell her the moment she's back. Do you think Doug would try and stop her from buying the ranch?" Helen asked.

"Who knows? Was the divorce friendly or not?"

"Not."

A slender blonde came into the room just as Helen and Ron were leaving. Ron turned, nearly bumping into Helen. "Put your eyes back in your head," she said teasingly.

"Who is she? Do you know her?" Ron asked.

"Not personally, but I know she's Doug's latest conquest."

Ron frowned. "You're kidding. The man's old enough to be her father."

Helen shrugged. "I don't think she cares."

Ron's frown deepened. "What does that mean?"

"It means, some women like what a man can give her, and very often the older he is, the more he has to give."

"I should have known," Ron said shaking his head. "I suppose, someday, I'll be able to get a good looking woman like that, but for now, I'm not making enough."

"You're not old enough either." Helen stopped and put her hands on her hips. "Besides, that's not the only way to pick up a woman, Ronald. Sometimes just being a nice guy works too."

It was a gorgeous morning, cool enough to make the hot coffee taste good, but warm enough to not miss a jacket. John had called early in the morning and invited Kathryne up to listen to her ideas about the repairs she wanted done around the ranch house. Thirty minutes later, she was on her way, thinking about all the wonderful things she wanted to do to her grandfather's old home. As she turned off onto the graveled road leading up to the cabin, her thoughts turned to John.

In spite of herself, she was beginning to really like him. He was kind, funny, and patient. Never once did he ridicule or affirm his superiority when she was learning how to drive the big truck, even though she knew he drove better.

There'd been a few times when she grew anxious, waiting for the proverbial shoe to drop, but John never took advantage of her ignorance. *Not knowin, is a hell of a lot different than just not trying,* he'd told her. And although she'd suspected he said it to make an impression, she soon realized that was the way John viewed things. The term, *what you see is what you get,* fit John to a tee.

She envied his honesty. If only she could let her guard down, relax, and just enjoy day-to-day life, but she didn't dare. Not yet, not since being hurt so deeply—and maybe not ever. Only time would tell. Being single wasn't so bad—was it?

She turned to the left at the fork in the road, but before she entered the winding, graveled road that led to John's driveway, she pulled down the visor and checked her hair and make-up in the mirror. A moment later she pushed the mirror back up and popped another breath mint into her mouth. With everything else she had to worry about, she didn't want to worry about morning-breath, even though she'd brushed her teeth when she'd showered.

John stood on the front porch, leaning on the handrail, holding a coffee mug. The sunlight glistened off his hair, and by the way several strands blew gently in the breeze, she could tell it was only tied back, not braided.

On any other man, the style would look silly, but on John it added to his unusual good looks. He had on a light blue, plaid western shirt, tucked into well-worn faded blue jeans, and as always, his silver-buckled belt and scuffed brown boots.

The moment he saw her, he raised his hand in greeting. He left the mug on the rail and came down to open her door. "Good morning," he said with a friendly smile. "Hungry?"

Helen drummed her fingernails on the top of the desk, listening to the phone ring in Kathryne's room. She'd already left a message on the cell phone but decided to play it safe and called the lobby. "Hello? Yes, I'd like to leave a message for Ms. Kathryne Sheldon. Yes, I'll hold." A few moments later, she hung up, wondering if she and Ron were just being too suspicious.

Kathryne sat across from John at the kitchen table holding a mug of steaming hot coffee. He'd made bacon and eggs over easy and opened a can of biscuits, but it didn't matter if the biscuits weren't home made. They had been served, straight from the oven, hot and crusty, and as she ate her second one smothered in butter and honey, she couldn't remember when breakfast had tasted so good.

The only time she got breakfast back home was when she stopped and bought some. Doug had wanted to get a cook and a housekeeper, but since they were hardly ever home, Kathryne didn't see the need.

"Breakfast was wonderful," Kathryne said, placing her fork on the empty plate. "You're going to have to teach me to cook just like you taught me to drive."

"You were a natural when it came to driving Red," John stated, taking a drink of his coffee. "I hardly had to do anything at all." He pushed away from the table and began to clear the dishes, telling her to stay put. "And as far as the horseback riding goes, you're just not used to it. You had good form. In fact, you looked damned good on a horse. I think Apache liked you, too."

"Remind me to tell him I'm flattered," she teased, taking the last sip of her coffee. She rose and carried her cup to the sink. "Well, do you mind if I take another look at your home before we start listing the things I want to do?"

"Not at all. Do you want some paper to make some notes?"

She shrugged. "I guess it wouldn't hurt. There's not that much that needs to be done immediately. I just wanted one last look before I leave in a week."

"Damn, time sure flies," he said, squeezing a little soap into the sink. "There's some paper in my desk in the other room. Help yourself while I wash up these few dishes."

"No dishwasher?"

He shook his head. "No need. How long can it take to wash a few dishes? Besides, that's how my mother and I caught up on the day's events. She would wash and I'd dry, chattering the whole time."

"Then let me dry." She reached for the towel, but John snatched it away. "I've got other plans for you, now get."

"Really? What kind of plans?" she asked with a little mixture of excitement and trepidation. He must have sensed her feelings, as a slow, seductive smile spread across his face.

"Nothing too serious, I promise." He turned back and ran a wet, soapy cloth around a plate.

A little startled by her reaction to his teasing, she went into his bedroom and sat down at his desk. A rustic wooden frame held a five-by-seven picture of John and a woman. Kathryne picked it up for a better look. It couldn't have been taken more than a few years ago because John looked exactly the same.

The woman next to him appeared tiny and had long brown

hair. She resembled Norman, was thin, and looked . . . ill. It showed in her face, especially in her sad brown eyes.

She put the picture back on the desk, noticing another of an old Navajo man with long. Grey hair that hung over his shoulders. He had a red kerchief tied around his forehead and a matching red shirt tucked into faded blue jeans. He also wore a buckskin vest with leather fringe, and he had on a silver belt buckle just like John's.

Kathryne looked one last time at the pictures, and then hurried upstairs, wondering why the pictures of John's family made her miss her own so badly.

John's plan turned out to be another horseback ride, and this time Kathryne was much more relaxed, letting Apache follow John's horse up the narrow trail. They'd shared some small talk about installing a dishwasher and a clothes dryer to replace the line John had strung between two trees in the backyard.

Too soon, the trail snaked upward, thwarting any more conversation. Fifteen minutes later, they broke out of the trees and entered a large grassy, flowered-filled meadow. "Wow," Kathryne murmured. "This is beautiful."

The meadow stretched out for several hundred feet, offering a panoramic view of the Santa Fe and Carson National Forests. John stepped a little closer and pointed toward the distant mountains. "Over there—the one with all the snow and trying to hide behind those clouds is Truchas Peak, the tallest in New Mexico at a little over thirteen thousand feet. And that one there is Santa Fe Baldy. Both are part of the Rocky Mountain chain."

Squirrels chattered and scolded about the intrusion as they scampered up and down the tall Ponderosa pines. Purple, yellow, and white wildflowers bobbed up and down in the late morning breeze, adding to the picturesque scene. White puffy clouds rose like mounds of whipped cream in a deep blue sky. "I don't think I've ever seen such a blue sky," she said, aware that John had dismounted and stood by the shoulder of her horse.

"It's nice up here, isn't it?"

She looked down at him and smiled. "Very nice."

"Want to stretch your legs for a few?"

His warm hands slipped around her waist as she stepped down, and when she turned, he smiled but didn't let her go. His gaze fused with hers, and she knew if she stayed still he'd kiss her. Her heart leapt into her mouth.

Should she turn and pretend an interest in the view? It was only when she realized that her hand rested passively on his chest, did she feel the warmth of a blush creep up her neck, aware it tinged her cheeks with pink.

His soft laughter drew her away from her momentary embarrassment. "It's been a long time for me too, and for a few minutes I was thinking of not trying. But now that I've kind of started things . . . well, I reckon it's up to you now."

"Up to me?" she said, her voice barely above a whisper. She felt like a girl waiting for her first kiss.

"I've never kissed a woman when she didn't want it," he confirmed softly. She would have looked away, but he gently caught her chin between his thumb and forefinger then gently kissed her on the forehead. "Maybe next time," he said, and then gave her Apache's reins. "Come with me. There's a pretty good view from those rocks over there."

They walked side by side, leading the horses, and when Kathryne's heart slowed down to its normal pace, she stopped to pluck a flower or two, tucking them in Apache's bridle while the big horse bent his head and stole several mouthfuls of lush mountain grass.

"When you're done making him look pretty," came John's

deep voice, "let me show you how to tie him so if he spooks or sets back on the reins, they won't break."

When she caught up to him, John flipped the leather strap loosely over a stout branch, then wrapped it over itself, and even though she paid close attention, she had no idea how he did it. On her second try, he brushed her hands aside and finished the job for her, placing his warm hand on her shoulder. The faint scent of his aftershave wafted over her. "We'll practice that when you get back."

His dark gaze fused with hers again, but this time, other than her breath catching a little in her throat, she was able to keep from blushing. She expected him to try again, and to be honest, hoped he would. She mentally braced herself for it, but then he simply smiled and started up the hill, turning on the rock to offer his hand.

"It's not too steep," he said, reaching out. "After we get past this part."

She slipped her hand into his, and allowed him to pull her up to where he stood. Then she followed him, the rocks acting like steps until they reached the top. The panoramic view before her took her breath away.

She followed his gaze as he pointed to several things, explaining in which direction they were looking and why it was significant, but she had stopped listening, choosing instead to study the man who so resembled this rugged, yet beautiful country.

She wasn't sure when it happened, would never tell a living soul that it had, but Kathryne suddenly knew with crystal clarity that she could be happy with someone like John—and if he tried to kiss her again, she'd gladly kiss him back.

"Are you listening to me?" he asked, raising one dark, skeptical brow, at the same time he grinned knowingly.

"A-absolutely," she lied, feeling the warmth of another blush creep up her neck. She took a step away so he wouldn't notice. "It's just so beautiful—endless. I wish I didn't have to leave." A shadow flickered across his vivid eyes. "Did I say something wrong?" she asked.

He pushed his hat off his forehead, then knelt down on one knee and plucked a yellow flower. "Nothing's wrong. I'll just miss spending time with you, that's all." He held out the solitary flower, reminding her of a child giving his teacher an apple, kind of shy, yet sweet.

She accepted the flower, meeting his gaze. "I'll be back soon, and then you'll wish I stayed away longer."

"Never," he said, standing. He took a step closer, and he was so tall, she had to tip her head to look into his vivid eyes. "I've enjoyed every minute we've spent together."

"You say that now, but just wait until I ask for your help with the repairs. Some of my employees have nicknamed me *Attila the Hun*, you know. I'm a regular task-master."

"I'll remember that," he replied, but his smile didn't lessen the shadow still flickering in his eyes. "Just don't get back to the city and decide to stay."

Slowly he bent his head and she closed her eyes expecting his kiss, and at the same time, feeling a little foolish that the prospect had terrified her. It was a soft gentle kiss that was so exquisitely sweet it shook her to the core. As his lips moved over hers, she slipped her arms around his waist, losing a little of herself in his protective embrace.

When he pulled away, he smiled again, and the delightful twinkle was back in his gaze. Before he let her go, he lightly dragged his knuckles across her cheek, and then kissed the tip of her nose. "It's a good thing that I've got a job starting Monday."

"Why is that?" she asked, knowing that he'd paused just for that reason.

"Well, when a man's busy, he thinks about work and not stuff he shouldn't concern himself with."

"And what are you concerned about?" she asked, too curious to care that she might be prying.

"Mostly I'm concerned that I'm already missing you more than I should."

"Are you sure?" Kathryne asked, sinking down on the bed in her hotel room. As she listened to Helen, she gave an angry sigh and slowly shook her head. "Sometimes I'd like to strangle that man with my bare hands." Another sigh. "Well, he's in for a surprise. I'm sure by now, John—Mr. Hawkins has sent the amount necessary to stop the foreclosure. USIB . . . and what did you say that stupid name stands for?"

She began to pace, giving a disgusted laugh. "Couldn't he come up with anything better. Good grief, *you sell, I buy?* That name was probably given to him by one of his highly intelligent girlfriends."

She laughed with Helen, but it didn't make her feel any better. Just when she was starting to feel like someone different, she learned that Doug had his fingers in the pie. Well, she'd make sure John paid the delinquency, and then there'd be nothing to worry about.

"No, my father isn't due home for another two days." Kathryne sank down on the bedside. "I've got something to tell you, Helen, and I might as well tell you now. I'm not just interested in the property Doug's after. I bought it. Yes, that's right. That's why I know Doug can't foreclose."

Kathryne toyed with the telephone cord. "It's beautiful, and it's close to my dad, and I know I'll be happy here. I've taken some pictures, and now that you know, I'll e-mail them to you. You'll love them."

She smiled at Helen's response. "No, I haven't met a man.

Well, that's not exactly true. I've met the owner, John Hawkins, and he's very nice." The smile widened. "Well, we went dancing and then horseback riding . . . twice, but that's about the extent of it."

Kathryne gave a defeated sigh. "Have you been speaking with Liz? Well, it sounds like it. And as a matter of fact, his kiss is great. No, it's better than that. It's absolutely wonderful. If I were to put a name on it, I'd have to call it a knee-weakening kiss. And make sure you tell Liz about it too. It'll kill her to think you were the first to find out."

She laughed at Helen's comments. "Oh, yeah. It put Doug's to shame," she confirmed with a satisfied nod. She listened for several moments, tucking a strand of hair behind her ear. "No, I'm glad you called. Tell everyone 'hi' for me . . . and thanks, Helen, for being such a good friend. Tell Ron I appreciate his loyalty. I'll see you soon, bye."

Kathryne tried to call John, but there was no answer and no message machine. "Who *doesn't* have a machine these days?" she grumbled, then shook her head. "John."

With nothing to do, she went down to the pool and took a swim. Even while sunbathing pool-side, the scenery was breathtakingly beautiful, but then she decided she'd become biased. She'd grown to love New Mexico and loved the idea of starting a new life in such an enchanting place.

Enchanting, she mused. From pristine mountains to wind-swept deserts, New Mexico was most definitely enchanting. Rising, she went back to her room, pleased to see the message light blinking on the bedside phone.

Kathryne glanced at the digital camera on the seat—the one she'd stopped and bought so she could e-mail pictures to Helen and Liz. As she turned up the winding dirt road, she recalled his deep, teasing voice on his message. "Hey, it's me, John. That job I told you about will take me out of town for a while, and I was hoping we could get together before I leave. Call me."

And she did, immediately. "John, it's me, and I've got a little proposition for you." She smiled when she heard his soft laughter before he asked her what kind of proposition, sounding way too agreeable. She eagerly suggested that he let her stay at the cabin while he was gone. "You won't have to ask Norman to feed the animals. I'll take care of Duke and feed the horses."

She'd nearly jumped off the bed the moment he agreed, stating that *he'd owe her one for sure.*

"Wonderful," she exclaimed. An instant later she envisioned him in that black, western-cut tux. Now, she was on her way up to the cabin—invited for dinner, and asked to spend the night—in the guest room, of course—to allow her to give up her room at the hotel earlier.

"What time are you leaving? Gosh, that is early, and they have to be fed right away. Well, I guess it does make sense," she'd replied reluctantly. "All right, I'll see you at six tonight."

Kathryne was precisely on time. She had only just glanced at her watch when she saw John standing on the front porch. The moment his gaze met hers, a wide grin spread over his features. "Hey," he mouthed, then stepped down to the drive and opened her door. "This is great," he said aloud, placing a quick kiss on her cheek the moment she exited the car. "These are for you." He held out a small bouquet. "They're kind of pathetic, but it's all I could find on such short notice."

Kathryne glanced at him in amused wonder as she accepted the tiny bunch of daisies, bluebells and Indian Paint Brushes, tied together with a garbage bag twisty. "They're beautiful," she said softly, touched by his thoughtfulness, "But if we keep this up, there won't be any left in the meadow."

He laughed, then glanced over at her car. "Did you bring your bags?"

"Yes, they're in the back." She handed him the keys. "Are you sure you feel like having a houseguest?"

"Absolutely." He grabbed her suitcases, placed them on the ground, and closed the hatch. "I was expecting more than three."

She grinned. "I sent some back—decided I didn't need so many dresses, and my laptop is on the front seat."

"Ah, about the laptop. I'm afraid I don't have the connections you're going to need to access the Internet, but the lodge has them. Norman has a room over there, and I'm sure he'd be happy to let you in to use it."

She glanced around. "It's so beautiful here, I doubt I'll be using my computer much. However," she began with a wide smile. She lifted out the camera. "Look at what I bought." When he came closer she held it so he could see. "It's digital with ninety-five shots—more if I reduce the resolution. I'm going to take some pictures and send them back to my friends in Baltimore."

"Well, let's put these inside and have some supper."

"Sounds great," she replied, following him into the cabin and instantly feeling at home. "So," she began, "what are you taking to Florida?"

"I have no idea. All I know is I'll be hauling a fifty-three footer filled with dry freight as a favor to a friend of mine in Albuquerque. He's an owner-operator who's got to have a little minor surgery." John shrugged. "The pay is good, and like I said, he's a friend, and who can refuse a friend in need?"

"Are you taking Red?" she asked.

"No, she's staying at the ranch this trip. I'll be using my friend's truck, splitting the costs and the reward." He paused at the foot of the stairs. "I'll take these up. You can put your purse and computer over there on the table, and if you feel like washing up before dinner, you can use my bathroom through there."

"No thanks, I'm fine." She strolled closer to the kitchen. "Something sure smells good."

John paused at the top of the stairs. "I'll be sure to tell Norman you said so. He was fussing in my kitchen all afternoon."

Kathryne raised her reddish brows. "Will he be joining us?"

"Nope," came John's answer as he disappeared around the corner. "It'll just be the two of us for a change."

The meal tasted fabulous. Kathryne had found a small vase for the flowers, and Norman had seen to everything else including a white tablecloth, china and silver obviously from the Lodge, and two long taper candles. He'd also prepared beef tips in a savory wine sauce on a bed of fluffy rice with asparagus tips and a crisp garden salad. And on the table was a bottle of red wine and two crystal glasses.

"Norman gave me strict orders on how a gentleman serves a lady, so if I make any mistakes, I'd appreciate it if you wouldn't tell him." John opened the wine and filled both their glasses.

"I promise," she replied, taking a sip. "This is good, very good."

"Really?" he asked, placing the bottle back on the table. He picked up his glass and took a sip, trying hard not to grimace. "If you say so," he added reluctantly. "I guess it's an acquired taste. Mind if I have a beer?"

Afterwards, while Kathryne cleared the table, John put on a pot of coffee, warning her that sometimes his coffee turned out a little strong, and if she wanted, Norman had brought a selection of teas.

"I'll try your coffee. After such a delicious meal and two glasses of wine, I'm feeling adventurous."

When he placed a cup on the table, she added. "They've got

machines out now that have pre-measured pods. Makes a perfect cup every time."

"*One* perfect cup at a time?" By his expression, he found her statement amusing.

She smiled, realizing that he probably drank at least four cups a day. He placed a little silver pot of cream and one with sugar on the table, then returned with two small plates containing a thin slice of cheesecake topped with strawberries, whipped cream and a little bit of chocolate syrup drizzled on top. When she glanced at him with a quizzical expression, he said, "Norman."

Kathryne added a small spoonful of sugar and a liberal splash of cream to her coffee before taking a sip and then raising her eyebrows. "Wow, this is a little strong. You might want to get one of those machines and try it. They have several different blends of coffee, too. Like vanilla and hazel nut, Columbian, and decaf."

"Decaf?" he asked as he sat down across from her. "Do you think I'm jittery?" His relaxed posture and smile contradicted his question.

"No, I wouldn't say jittery, exactly."

His eyes began to twinkle. "Then what would you call me?"

Kathryne picked up her fork and paused as if she were searching for just the right word. "I'd call you sweet, and kind, and considerate, and full of energy."

John's dark brows snapped together at the same time he slid his fork through the dessert.

She found herself studying his profile, liking what she saw. "What?" she asked, concerned that she'd said something wrong. "Seriously, you're a very nice person."

"Kind and considerate?" he repeated, making a face while he chewed and swallowed. Slowly, purposely he took a sip of coffee. "I was hoping you'd say I was devilishly handsome or irresistibly sexy." He dabbed the corners of his mouth with his napkin. "Norman's a *very nice person.*"

Kathryne grabbed her napkin, forcing herself to swallow before she choked and embarrassed herself. "John, you could have waited another minute before you said that. Of course you're irresistibly sexy." She matched his mischievous expression. "If it makes you happy to hear it, I'll say it. But in the meantime, nice isn't so bad, especially given my jaded opinion of men."

"Jaded?" He paused, drawing his brows together again and nodding, as if he knew something she didn't.

"What now." She narrowed her eyes. "Tell me before I die of curiosity."

"It's the dark water." His grin always left her wondering what exactly he was thinking, regardless of his words.

She matched his concerned frown. "Dark water?"

"Yeah. You can't see what lies beneath dark water, right?"

"Right," she replied cautiously.

"It could be good, but most likely it'll be bad—dangerous, even harmful. The name Douglas means dark water."

He nodded again, as if he'd just given her justification for her ex-husband's bad behavior. "On the other hand, John means God is good, but I'm sure in Navajo it probably means clear water." He grinned and shrugged as if to say, *look at me.* "There's nothing sinister or mysterious beneath this *handsome* exterior."

"And just where did you learn that, Chief Clear Water?"

He laughed, picked up his fork and sliced another piece of cheesecake. "I made up the last part, but I found the first part in a baby-name book."

Kathryne couldn't resist. "Let me get this straight. You, a big, *handsome, sexy,* truck-driving rancher reads books on baby names in his spare time?"

He chewed then swallowed. "Your point?" he countered.

She laughed at his expression. "Nothing, I guess. It's just that I figured you'd read things like *Diesel Mechanics* or *Farm and Ranch.*"

He lifted his cup and took another drink of coffee. "Those are good. Diesels need to be taken seriously if you want to get where you're going. And books on planting crops and breeding cattle are interesting, but let's not overlook the fact that babies need names too."

Kathryne held up her hands. "I surrender. Never again will I question your choice of reading material. I promise."

CHAPTER TEN

The next morning, Kathryne woke when the door closed and the engine of John's old pick-up grumbled to life. A quick glance at the clock told her it was only half past six, but she felt rested, having gone to bed early to make up for lost sleep. A smile inched its way across her face as she stretched then slipped out of bed and shrugged on her robe.

She learned last night while enjoying a great dinner and dessert that John would probably be gone longer than he expected—at least a week. It wasn't bad news, as the added days would give her plenty of time to explore and make plans, but she'd have to call Helen and let her know to reschedule her appointments.

She hurried down to the kitchen, finding a note from John telling her that he'd already fed the horses and the chickens. Also on the note were feeding instructions, in case she forgot what they'd talked about the night before.

Five minutes later she had a pot of hot water boiling. With a mug of tea in one hand, she opened the door and stepped outside for a few minutes of quiet reprieve, leaning against the rail on the covered porch overlooking the rocky ravine. Duke followed her out and rested beside her, his big shaggy head nestled between his front paws, watching her as if she'd always been part of his family.

After a few minutes of enjoying the peace and quiet while sipping her tea, she went inside, emerging thirty minutes later clad in blue jeans, t-shirt, work boots, work gloves, and a western style straw hat. A loose fitting denim shirt slightly rolled at the sleeves acted as a light jacket. Regardless of the warmer season, higher elevations brought cooler temperatures.

Before she headed toward the barn, she placed a clear glass pitcher on the rail in the sun, then dropped in two super-large tea bags she'd found in the pantry. Sun tea, she decided, would taste good later. She'd called a Taos florist earlier and had a potted plant sent to Norman. A little thank you for helping her find the right clothes for the jobs she intended to do.

Her first task? The barn.

Her plan? Clean out the horse stalls before John got back.

She smiled as she hurried down the steps catching a familiar scent on the breeze. Norman had been right. The pens smelled a little shitty, but soon, very soon, the place would be back to being *earthy*.

Two hours later, with her hat resting on the back of her head and her gloves on the ground beside her, Kathryne sat in the shade of a large cottonwood, sipping an ice-cold bottle of beer. She'd stopped for a glass of tea, but it was warm and there were no ice-cubes in the small freezer. *So much for the tea,* she'd mumbled searching the refrigerator. That's when she spotted the six-pack of beer.

In between sips, she inspected the new blister at the base of her thumb on her right hand, imagining how much bigger it would have been if she hadn't been wearing the leather gloves.

Worse than the blister, her back ached. Worse than her back aching, she'd only cleaned one stall and an adjoining pen. And, worse than that, she smelled like manure, and no wonder. There were bits of the stuff clinging to her boots and dried bits of it dusting the bottom hem of her jeans. If Liz could only see her now.

She smelled so bad that she had to shoo away several flies.

However bad she smelled, she felt good. There were eight little piles of manure spread out behind the barn where she had deposited eight wheelbarrow loads. Eight times, she had to shoo away Apache, open the gate, and try to maneuver the wheelbarrow out the half-door before he could squeeze past.

Three times she made it; two times she accidentally dumped the manure right at the door, and once Apache got out and moseyed around the other stalls, reaching over the rail to grab a bite of hay from the stack while she emptied the damned wheelbarrow. The next six times went without incident, accomplished by catching Apache, putting his halter on, and tying him outside to the hitching post.

Kathryne glanced at her watch, dismayed to see a dark ring of dirt around her wrist. She'd worked up a sweat, but didn't realize how dusty it had become, or how hot. She'd shed her denim shirt, discovering that hard work kept a body warm.

She dragged the back of her hand across her forehead, heaving a tired sigh. It was only noon. She had three more stalls to do, but she was bushed and her blister had begun to hurt.

She finished the beer, and then stood, groaning a little as her back protested. If she quit now, she could always finish tomorrow. However, if she kept going, she might be able to work out the stiffness in her back. She tugged on her gloves, telling herself that she'd better try to use her left hand a little more as she headed back into the barn to clean Sunny's stall.

This time, she haltered Sunny right away, tying the mare to a tree before getting started.

By the time Kathryne finished Sunny's pen, it was late afternoon. She was stiff, dirty, and hungry. Too tired to cook, she found a can of tuna and mixed it with a little salad she found in a bag in the back of the fridge. After she added a little dressing that had just expired that day, she ate, pleased that it tasted better than it looked. She had started to climb the stairs to take a hot, relaxing bath when she remembered she had to feed John's animals.

"The horses get half alfalfa and half grass," she reaffirmed as she wearily entered the barn. "And half a coffee can full of oats."

Still somewhat cheerful, she broke a bale of hay and loosened four individual flakes, one for each horse. Pretending that they were her horses, she picked up the first tightly packed flake and carried it over to Apache's feeder with a big smile and a few kind words for her favorite horse. Before she could drop it in, Apache reached over and grabbed a big bite, shaking it loose from the flake. Kathryne ducked, but a shower of hay rained down on her head, down her sweat-sticky back, and down her front, into the small space between her breasts and her bra.

"Damn it," she muttered, spitting out the little pieces that had blown into her mouth. Apache reached over for a second bite, but this time she pulled back, threatening him with a fierce glare.

"Get back," she ordered through clenched teeth. To her total amazement, he obeyed. Cautiously she tossed the hay into the feeder, stepping back immediately. This time she avoided the fallout when he took a huge mouthful, shaking it loose before he chewed.

The next three flakes were deposited much in the same manner—a firm order to stand back, the toss, and the hasty retreat, but still, by the time she'd finished adding the oats to the feeders, she itched all over. Her neck itched from the bits of hay, as did her back and her front. Her arms itched too. She leaned forward and tried to shake the bits of hay out of her bra, but they didn't budge, holding tightly to her sweat-dampened skin.

"Crap," she muttered, shifting uncomfortably. She found the

bag of chicken feed, and following John's instructions, filled the empty, three pound coffee can to overflowing.

The moment she stepped into the coop on the west side of the barn, she was besieged by a flock of white and red feathered hens, squawking and flapping their wings in an effort to be the first to eat.

"Get back," Kathryne hollered, trying the same command she'd used on the horses, but to no avail. She pressed back against the closed door. "Get Back!" she said a little louder, a little more desperately. Chickens surrounded her, clucking and pecking at her pants, scratching the toes of her boots.

Frantically, she flung a handful of chicken feed across the pen, sagging with relief when they immediately dashed toward it. *That wasn't so bad,* Kathryne told herself as she poured the contents of the can into the small tin feeders around the coop. Finished, she dusted off her hands.

"Tomorrow there had better be some eggs, girls, or I'm going to have to call a production meeting." She gave a satisfied smile, and then stepped out the door, scratching a little at the hay stuck under her collar.

By seven o'clock, Kathryne closed her eyes and eased back into the hot bath, sighing contentedly. Yet in the back of her mind, she longed for one of Richard's massages. She winced a little as the two blisters on her hands made first contact with the water, but they were only a small part of her pain. She hurt in more places than she thought she had, but she quickly decided it was a good hurt.

She chuckled. Was there such a thing as a *good hurt?* If there was, this was it. Good hurts were aches and pains caused by honest, fulfilling work that gave instant gratification. She'd only learned this today when she took a moment to admire the two clean stalls and pens.

And while she had lingered, thinking how wonderful they looked, Apache had lifted his tail and thanked her in his own special way—with a fresh pile of manure.

She sank a little deeper into the hot water, leaning back and wetting her hair. After she lathered it with sweetly scented shampoo, she piled it on top her head so she could soap the rest of her body. When she glanced at the water she grimaced. It was a brownish color filled with little bits of floating green hay.

She pulled herself into a sitting position, then quickly pulled the plug. After it drained, she turned on the water and reclined back again. It took a few moments to realize it wasn't as hot as it should have been. Drawing herself up, she put her hand under the faucet.

"Damn," she muttered, shutting off the cold, only to find that the hot was only tepid. She was out of hot water. Disappointed that she wouldn't be able to soak longer, she gave a disgruntled sigh and then quickly rinsed, making a mental note to have a larger hot-water heater installed.

She stood, stepped out of the tub, and dried off. She shrugged on her terry robe, wrapped her hair in a towel and went in search of the aspirin and Ben-Gay that John said were in the medicine cabinet.

Kathryne sat straight up in bed, disoriented at first, then remembered she was at the cabin, in one of the two spare bedrooms. She felt certain she'd heard something. It was still dark, but some kind of noise had awakened her. Wincing when she moved, she glanced at her illuminated travel clock. It was four in the morning.

She quickly noted that Duke still slept on the bed beside her. He hadn't even lifted his head or opened an eye. If Duke wasn't bothered, then surely there was nothing to worry about. She'd locked up the house the night before and all the windows were latched.

But still, she felt a little nervous. Sleeping alone in a strange house was a whole lot different than sleeping alone in a secure apartment, complete with a motion-detecting alarm, not to mention a doorman to stop anyone who didn't belong in the building.

Slowly she reclined, sending little shards of pain to her overused muscles. She had just got comfortable when she heard it again. She sat up, swinging stiff legs over the side of the bed, feet slipping into slippers and her shoulders crying out in pain as she shrugged on her robe. She went to the window and opened the wooden blinds. The sun wasn't visible, but the sky was beginning to turn an orange-pinkish-purple over the distant mountaintops.

Kathryne glanced around, looking for something to protect herself if need be, just as she heard the noise again. This time Duke raised his head, looking at her with a curious expression.

"A rooster?" she muttered to the drowsy dog as enlightenment struck. "Your master actually has a rooster?"

Kathryne glanced in the mirror above the sink where she'd just finished brushing her teeth. Her cheeks seemed rosier, and there was a definite touch of sunburn on the bridge of her nose. Her hair, which she'd done nothing to the previous night, had curled in several different directions, but instead of reaching for the curling iron, she pulled it back and put on one of the colorful cloth-coated rubber bands she'd bought in town.

She donned a clean pair of jeans, realizing why Norman had insisted that she have at least two pair, and slipped on another clean v-necked tee. Carrying her socks, she went downstairs. She'd left her boots by the back door, thinking that they were too dirty to wear into the house.

Duke lumbered down with her, sitting by the door once they entered the kitchen.

"Want out?" Having a dog of her own would be great, she mused, opening the door after she ruffled the soft fur around his neck. Much to her dismay, only one boot sat on the porch. Frowning, she stepped outside to have a better look, spotting the other boot lying in the dew drenched grass, several yards from where she felt certain she'd left it the night before.

Tiptoeing, she hurried over to it, wondering at the tiny scratch marks on the soft leather inside the top. She set it down by its mate, then went back inside and dried her feet on the braided rug.

While she sat to put on her socks, she decided a little breakfast would do, but after searching the pantry, she couldn't find much more than an open box of sugarcoated corn flakes. She filled a bowl and went to the refrigerator for milk, but the carton was nearly empty and didn't smell too fresh.

"I wasn't that hungry anyway," she muttered, popping a few dry flakes into her mouth. She searched the pantry and spotted a small can of peaches. Once opened, the cereal tasted pretty good topped with peaches and some of the juice.

The air was clean and crisp when Kathryne sat down on the back porch step to pull on her boots. Today, she'd drive to town, get a few groceries, then come back and finish mucking the stalls.

She found her purse, car keys, and then called Duke, who placed his front paws on the seat then looked at her to as if to ask for help.

"This car isn't as big as Red," she muttered, grunting as she hoisted the dog into the car, and then rolled down the passenger-side window so he could hang out his head.

Fifteen minutes later, just before she turned onto the pavement, she remembered she hadn't fed the animals.

"Shoot," she grumbled as she slapped the steering wheel. She made a hasty U-turn and headed back up the graveled road. The moment she arrived, she left Duke in the car with the windows down. "I'll be back in a few."

When she entered the barn, she began to fill the feed cans, and pull apart the flakes of hay with a more determined attitude than she'd had the day before. This time, she'd be ready for Apache's sneaky, snack attack.

An hour later, she pulled to a stop in the parking lot of a local farmer's market.

"Are you going to be all right if I leave the windows down?" Kathryne asked the dog. He just looked at her with his tongue hanging out and his bushy tail thumping against the back of the seat.

"Sure you are," she confirmed, rubbing his ears. She slipped out of the SUV and went inside. The market was filled with fresh produce, fruits, and much more, and the combined smells were delightful. She had only just added a head of lettuce and some plump red tomatoes to her little cart when Norman came in. She waved, happy to see a familiar face.

"Well, hello, doll," he said as he hurried toward her. "How are you doing at the cabin? When John called me and told me I didn't have to feed, I did a little happy dance." Norman leaned a little closer. "Apache and I don't always see eye-to-eye, if you know what I mean. The rascal's so sneaky. He gets hay all over me."

Kathryne laughed. "Believe me, I know, but there's a trick I've learned. It's called the *toss and run*. I walk over to his stall, toss the hay over the side, and then run."

"That's a good one. Does it work?"

"So far. Now if I could only find a way to keep that darned rooster from crowing all morning, I could blissfully sleep in."

She laughed at Norman's expression.

"He's bothering you too?" Norman cried. "I thought he just hated me. John doesn't seem to mind him, but then he gets up at the crack of dawn anyway. As for myself, I'd love to wring his scrawny neck. Getting up before noon should be a sin."

"Why don't you?" Kathryne smiled evilly.

"Why don't I what?"

"Wring his neck. I'll help."

Norman gave a defeated sigh. "I'd like to, but I'm . . . *chicken!*" He laughed at his own joke. "Get it? I'm chicken?"

Kathryne nodded her head, trying hard not to laugh. "I got it." She turned and placed a yellow bell pepper in a small plastic bag before adding it to her cart. "Are you doing anything for supper tonight?"

Norman strolled with her, picking up a cantaloupe and sniffing it, before placing it in her cart. "Nope. Why? Want to go out for dinner?"

"Thank you, but no. According to John, Dad's supposed to be home tonight. I thought I'd invite him over and make supper as a kind of ice-breaking thing."

"That's a wonderful idea. Want some help?"

"Would you?" Kathryne asked, feeling a little guilty by the way she led Norman to volunteer to help her with the cooking. "The meal you prepared the other night was so good, I thought I'd sent to Baltimore for it."

"That good?" Norman exclaimed. "I'm so flattered." He paused for a moment then narrowed his eyes. "I've been cooking for your Dad for years. I know just what kind of food he likes."

"Really? Then it sounds like I've nothing to worry about," Kathryne replied with a cheerful smile.

"Sweetie, I'm so used to John and his steak and potatoes, anything different would be a welcomed change. But, seriously,

150

dear old Dad loves salads, and I like anything organic, so you decide if you want fish, pork, or poultry"—he winked and she knew he was referring to the rooster—"or beef, and then all we'll have to do is choose the wine."

"What's Dad's favorite meal?"

"Well, steak if you choose beef. Chicken—roasted with rosemary and basil, baked halibut with lemon-pepper sauce—"

"Stop. I'm starting to drool," Kathryne teased. "The fish sounds divine, but where do we get fresh fish in Taos?"

Norman raised brows. "In the frozen section. Where else?"

On the way home, Kathryne thought about her father and wondered if she was expecting too much. After all, it had been years since they had spoken. Could she expect a warm reception or a cool one? She glanced at her watch. There was plenty of time to worry about it while she finished some chores.

After she put away the groceries, she changed into her work clothes and headed toward the barn. Several hours later, she hung up the rake and leaned the shovel against the barn wall. She was hot, tired, and dirty, but compared to being cooped up in an office, mucking stalls wasn't so bad. She tugged off her gloves, wincing at the popped blisters on her hands—the price she'd been willing to pay to get the job done.

She glanced around. By the looks of Apache and Sunny's stalls, picking up manure was going be a daily chore. Tomorrow she'd feed early, and then, after she picked up the new piles of horse *apples,* she'd sweep out the tack room and dust off John's saddles.

She was certain when John returned, he wouldn't be sorry he agreed to her proposal. In fact, she mused with a sly grin, he might be even more indebted to her, and perhaps a little more willing to accept another proposition. She quickly checked her watch as she hurried toward the cabin. There was just enough time to take a shower and do her hair before Norman showed up to help with dinner.

"I hope the two of you are hungry." Norman opened the oven door, checking on the halibut. "This is just about done."

Kathryne glanced at her father and smiled. "I don't know about you, but I sure am." In truth, her stomach felt as if a swarm of butterflies had taken up residence. The strange feeling had plagued her the moment she realized she was about to see her father for the first time in nearly twenty years.

She'd made the salad ahead of time, using all organic ingredients and even going so far as to mix olive oil and red-wine vinegar to make her mother's dressing recipe. Although John didn't have many dishes, she and Norman managed to find a glass bowl in which she could arrange the colorful vegetables in a very appealing manner.

"It was really sweet of you to bring some wine," she said to her father.

"It's not often that I get to share a good bottle with someone who knows about wine . . . besides Norman," he added.

Kathryne decided that Henry Sheldon looked pretty much the same as he did from the picture he'd sent at Christmas five years ago—a little more grey, but then he appeared very tan from his vacation in Florida—a trip she'd just recently learned he'd been planning for years.

While her father and Norman chatted, she remembered that the Christmas picture had been accompanied by a letter that, at the time, she almost didn't read. A letter filled with details of a lodge to be used for vacationers in the summer and hunters in the winter. She clearly remembered Doug's comment that he thought it was a foolish endeavor.

Only now, after seeing the beauty of New Mexico with an open mind and hopeful eyes, did she understand its appeal—

understand why her father had left the firm for such a faraway place. She gave a little sigh, content to be in the company of her dad and good friend, Norman. She discovered something else sitting in a cozy kitchen that would soon be hers. She no longer doubted her decision to stay.

Norman served them, then took the seat closet to hers, patting her hand as if he'd read her mind. "So, you two," Norman began with great enthusiasm. "How many years has it been?"

"Let's just put it this way," her father said. "Too many to count. But that doesn't matter. What matters is Kate is here, and I couldn't be happier."

Kathryne felt a little embarrassed and reached for her wine to take a sip. When she looked at her Dad, he smiled, and suddenly she knew with all her heart she'd made the right decision to rekindle their relationship. "Did Norman tell you on the way over that I'm going to be your new neighbor?" She made a wide sweep of the kitchen. "I'm buying this . . . this cabin and five acres."

Her smile increased when her father grinned. "I know," he admitted. "I knew the day you gave Norman the binder. John called me. He's like that. Always making sure nobody's feathers get ruffled."

Norman looked first at Kathryne and then at her father. "Isn't that just fabulous? Kate's going to be your next door neighbor." He immediately raised his wine glass. "A toast. A toast to friends, family, and neighbors."

Hank followed suit, but Kathryne didn't budge.

"Let me get this straight," she said firmly. Her gaze left his to impale Norman. "You and John knew that my dad was happy about the sale, and you didn't think I'd be interested in knowing that little piece of information?"

Norman nearly choked on his wine, dabbing his chin with his napkin as he placed the glass on the table. "Yes . . . yes, I thought you might. But before you get all riled up, I didn't see the problem."

"Apparently," she grumbled, placing her napkin on the table.

Hank suddenly realized she was getting up to leave. "Wait a moment, honey. There's nothing to get so upset about. I'm sure John and Norman didn't realize that you and I hadn't spoken in a while."

"Twenty years is *a while?*" she asked, with more calm than she felt. "You have no idea how I worried about it. Would you be angry? Would you be happy?"

"I'm happy, see?" Her father turned and gave her an exaggerated smile.

Kathryne didn't smile back at first. "Very funny."

Hank reached across the table and put his hand over hers. "Seriously, I'm delighted."

Kathryne gave him a sideways glance. "That's good, because it's too late. John and I have already signed the purchase agreement."

Norman reached over and took her hand, gently squeezing it. "Tell her, Hank," Norman said, nodding toward Kathryne and smiling. "Tell her you're absolutely delighted that she's going to be your neighbor and that you want her to become your partner."

Her father gave Norman a dark look, and then turned his gaze to Kathryne's. "Kate. I kind of wanted to tell you myself, but since the cats are out of the bag, it's true. I want you to be my partner."

She gave him a skeptical glance. "In what?"

He laughed and shook his head. "Nothing you won't just love to do. I want you to help me with the lodge. In fact, if you say yes, it's more than I could have hoped for."

"All right then, yes." She smiled at his expression. "Why are you looking so shocked? Didn't you just ask me to be your partner a few seconds ago?"

"Yeah, Hank, you did. I heard you," Norman added.

"Yes, but I didn't expect you to make a decision without sleeping on it for a while."

Kathryne gave a soft laugh. "I've been doing that lately . . . making hasty decisions. But so far even after I've had a good night's rest, I'm still happy with them." She stretched out her hand. "I've heard that in these parts," she began with a teasing smile, "a handshake is as good as a written contract." Her father instantly took her hand and gave it a vigorous shake. "Partners?" she asked.

"Partners," Hank repeated.

"That's wonderful," Norman exclaimed. "Partners. Isn't that wonderful Kate? You and your dad, partners." He hurriedly refilled their glasses, then stood with his glass raised. "A toast," he exclaimed. "A toast—"

The sound of glasses tinkling together roused Duke. He strolled into the kitchen and then flopped down by the back door and gave a loud yawn, drawing everyone's attention. Her father put his napkin on the table and scooted his chair back. "Well, it's getting late, and I've been up since dawn, Florida time. I think I'll head over to the lodge and catch up on some sleep."

"Not so fast." Kathryne rose and followed her father to the door. "Now I have a favor to ask of you."

He grinned, then glanced at Norman. "Uh-oh. This doesn't sound good, does it?"

"Gee, I don't know, Hank. Whatever she asks, I wouldn't do anything till you sleep on it," Norman teased, looking contrite the moment Kathryne narrowed her eyes. "Just kidding, Kate," he hastily added.

"Well," Kathryne began, turning her gaze to her father's. "I'd like for you to attend the Summer Ball this year. Since it's going to be my last as senior partner, I'd like to dance with my father."

"Well, I guess I could do that, since it's just this one time."

Much to her delight, her father opened his arms, and she couldn't resist. She turned into them and wrapped her arms around his waist as his arms closed around her. "Partners," he murmured close to her ear. "Just like old times . . . only better."

Soon Norman was there, wrapping his arms around them both. "Isn't this just wonderful? It's like we're all destined to be family."

Kathryne lay awake for a long time after going to bed that night. The years she and her father had spent apart seemed to melt away. And even though there were a few moments when she wanted to climb over the table and confront him about it, everything had worked out in the end, partly due to Norman.

She really liked Norman and his crazy ideas and sense of humor, but over the course of the evening, she discovered something else she liked. Norman was a truly compassionate person. He cared about her father's wellbeing, and she knew he cared about hers too.

After her father had left and they'd sat talking over a cup of hot tea, Norman had shared memories of the time he'd met John and then how they'd become best friends, John a little more reluctant than he to strike up a friendship. "But nevertheless," Norman had stated with true conviction, "John and I were destined to be family."

Yawning, Kathryne rolled over and wrapped her arm around Duke, who grunted and stretched blissfully but never opened his eyes. She snuggled a little closer to the dog repeating Norman's words. "We're all destined to be family."

CHAPTER ELEVEN

Kathryne looked blurry-eyed at the lighted face of her little travel clock. It was four a.m., and that damned rooster was somewhere close by. She rose slowly, not having got enough rest the previous night. She'd laid awake thinking about her conversation with her father, and just when she'd finally fallen into a deep restful sleep, something had knocked over the trash can, jarring her awake. After that happened, it was difficult to relax. She'd even found a poker by the fireplace and looked around a bit, but couldn't find a reason for the disturbance.

The rooster crowed again, then again. Perhaps if she tossed some chicken feed around, he'd busy himself with breakfast, and she could go back to sleep? She was just tugging on her robe when the bedside phone rang. Hesitant to pick it up, she finally lifted the receiver and gave a sleepy, "Hello?"

"Good morning," came John's familiar voice. "Did Herbert wake you?"

"Herbert?" Kathryne mumbled, still not fully awake.

"The rooster."

Kathryne reclined on the bed, the receiver pressed to her ear. "That's not exactly what I named him," she said, smiling at John's soft laughter. When he asked her about it, she simply told him she couldn't use words like that over the phone.

"So, have you been doing all right?" he asked, and she knew he was fishing around, wondering how she was getting along with all the animals.

"I'm doing well," she replied. "The horses are great; Duke is great; and I think after this morning Herbert will be doing better too." She listened intently, and then laughed. "No, I'm not going to wring his neck. I think I'll just put a little food out at night so when he wakes, he'll eat instead of crow."

"Then make sure you bring in your boots," she heard him say.

She sat up, remembering that just the other night one of her boots had been carried out into the grass. "Why?"

"Rachel."

"Rachel who?" she countered, drawing her brows together.

"Rachel . . . my pet raccoon. She's nocturnal—"

"Noc—what?"

"Nocturnal. She sleeps during the day and roams around at night. She'll find a way to eat the chicken feed and probably hide a little in your boots if you leave them out."

Kathryne took the phone away from her ear and glared at it a moment before placing it back. "You could have told me about Rachel a little sooner," she snapped, slightly annoyed to learn that there'd been no reason for her to be terrified last night. She felt guilty when John apologized, relaxing back against the pillows. "It's just that I thought someone was trying to break in last night, and . . . oh well, now that I know it's only Rachel, I'm sure I'll sleep much better. I suppose I should have known it was nothing. Duke never opened an eye."

"What?" she asked, sitting up again. "Are you serious? He never gets up, no matter what?"

John's phone call had completely revived Kathryne, and after she showered, dressed, and came downstairs, she decided against breakfast and had two cups of coffee instead. John had a little note taped to the inside of the door where he kept the coffee can, addressed to Norman and containing instructions on how to brew a pot of coffee.

Following it to the letter, Kathryne took a sip when it finished perking on the stove. It wasn't anything fancy, not like those she had at her favorite coffee house back in Baltimore, but it tasted good, strong and really hot. For a moment she missed the city but realized she'd probably have bouts of homesickness from time to time.

She went to the fridge and found the small carton of fat-free, lactose-free rice milk Norman had insisted she try, explaining that dairy wasn't always the best choice.

"Babies and baby animals need milk. Not grown-ups," he had warned.

By the time she'd finished her second cup, she was eager to start on the tack room. She noticed that the floors in the house needed a good scrubbing too, and if she wanted to get everything done before the end of the week, she'd better get to it.

Kathryne stood, pressing her hands against the small of her back. She'd been on her hands and knees most of the day, but the end result had been worth every backbreaking moment. The wood floors gleamed. Even the banister glistened in the late afternoon light streaming in through the open doors and windows.

The wooden mantle above the rock fireplace glowed as well. In fact, every piece of wood, whether furniture or fixture, had been scrubbed with a special preservative soap designed to enhance the natural beauty of the wood grain. And it did. And even though she hurt all over, she felt accomplished. The instructions on the box had said that it only needed to be done every six months. By then, she affirmed, she'd be completely recovered.

Too tired to be hungry, she decided against making dinner

and went outside to feed the animals. She eyed several new piles of manure with disdain, and with sheer stubbornness reached for the rake and shovel.

She'd be damned if John came home and found the stalls messy. Not after all she'd done, and certainly not when she was trying so hard to be the perfect country girl. What had Norman said when he'd stopped by that morning? John would be impressed?

"That's Norman's crazy talk," she muttered, slipping into Apache's stall. "I'm not doing this to impress John."

But the little voice in her head, asked. *"Aren't you?"*

Regardless how many times Kathryne told herself she was just being silly, she worked a little harder with each passing day; pulling weeds, raking leaves, and tending the long neglected rose bushes. She rearranged the rocks outlining the flower bed, and even made a trip into Taos to find a nursery where she could buy some bedding plants.

A little while later, the soil had been prepared and the petunias looked a little sparse, but she knew they'd spread in a week or so. She had purchased two moss pots filled to overflowing with geraniums, and standing on a chair, she managed to place them on the two hooks left by her grandmother.

When she went in to change her clothes so she could go to town to get a few more supplies, she realized just how hard she'd been working. The jeans she'd worn to the restaurant several weeks ago were now a little loose, causing her to take a notch up on her belt. Pleased beyond measure, she decided the first stop would be to the clothing store to buy a smaller size.

The moment she got home, she went into John's room and to the large mirror to inspect her new figure. Much to her surprise, she looked better—different. Her face was tanned, as were her arms, and they looked firmer. She lifted her arm and did a muscle-man pose. But then, on closer inspection, her smile faded.

Almost immediately she realized she had a tan line, and it wasn't on her legs or her back like it would have been if she went swimming. It was on her hands. Apparently, her gloves had not only saved her hands from serious damage on several occasions, but they had also protected her from the sun. They were several shades lighter than her arms.

Frantically she tore off her short-sleeved shirt, gasping at the line across her upper arms. She spun, and using a hand mirror to help, she lifted her hair and looked at the back of her neck. "Oh, no," she moaned, trying to picture herself in a sleeveless evening gown. "I've got a farmer's tan."

She knew without looking that her legs would be as white as her hands, if not whiter, but then a long dress would conceal them. But that didn't ease her concern. Liz would have a perfect tan—either with a spray or by visiting the tanning salon every day, but Kathryne had never enjoyed the booths, usually burning before she could reach the golden color everyone wanted.

Heaving a disgruntled sigh, she slipped on her shirt and then smoothed several strands of sun-bleached tendrils back into her ponytail. "Oh, well, there's still nearly eight weeks before the ball," she muttered. "I can get something sprayed on."

"And just what would you spray on yourself? You look fine to me."

Kathryne jumped at the sound of John's deep voice. "How long have you been standing there?" she asked, inwardly wincing at the breathy sound of her voice. She tried to look stern, but the moment he grinned, she couldn't stay mad. After all, she stood in his bedroom, and by rights, she had no business being there.

"Well, if you must know," she said, "I was looking at my tan.

You have a bigger mirror, and I noticed that in the short time I've been here, I've managed to get a tan, but not altogether in the right places."

John's eyes began to twinkle, and she knew without asking what he was thinking. "Maybe those places don't need much sun."

She gave him another firm look and held up her hands, wiggling her fingers. "I meant my hands. See? They're white. I've been wearing gloves, and now I look like a freak. Half dark and half white."

Again he grinned, and she felt her heart do a little somersault. "I've had that feeling most of my life, but I got over it."

She tried hard not to, but she laughed when he did. "Damn it John, I wish you'd stop making those comments. In my profession, saying the wrong thing can get you sued."

"What do you get if you say the right thing?" He came a little closer, standing behind her as his gaze met hers in the mirror. "I'm sorry, it's just that you set yourself up so perfectly, and it makes your eyes light up, and you've got these cute little dimples. I like making you laugh."

He turned her to face him. "You've got a great laugh and a beautiful smile." He held her at arm's length. "And if I didn't know better, I'd say you've lost a few pounds. You look downright skinny."

"Skinny? Don't be silly." Somewhat startled at the jolt of desire that coursed through her when his warm fingers closed around her upper arms, she twirled out of his grasp. "I've got to go feed the horses. You look like you could use a shower and a shave."

She hurried to the door before she had time to question her reasons for leaving so quickly when actually she wanted to wrap her arms around him and give him a proper welcome home. "If you'd like, I'll make some breakfast when I get back."

He nodded, but there was no doubt by his expression that food wasn't exactly what he was hungry for. "Sounds good."

"All right," she said, mortified by the breathy sound of her voice. She practically ran from the room before she made a fool of herself and flung herself into his arms.

John let the hot water flow over his head. He'd shaved and then stepped into the large shower to wash away the hours of being behind the wheel. He felt a little tired, and if Kathryne wasn't in his home he'd probably be thinking about a nap, but sleep was the last thing on his mind now. A grin spread across his face as he remembered watching her.

Had her hair always been that color—the color of ready-to-harvest wheat, or was it just his imagination? He wasn't sure, but hadn't her features become more animated? Her eyes more vibrant?

He picked up the shampoo and squeezed a liberal amount in his palm, soaping his hair. For a brief moment, he wished he'd had it cut, wondering if a woman like Kathryne would appreciate a more professional look. God only knew he couldn't compete with the men she must know, but he could at the very least look a little more civilized.

He'd seen something else in her eyes when she'd met his gaze in the mirror. Something that he didn't want to see.

"The woman's afraid," he muttered, but knew instinctively he wasn't the cause. *I'd like to meet the jackass who hurt her,* he thought as he stood under the water, letting it run over his head and face.

By the time he finished dressing, he could smell the first faint whiffs of bacon frying in a pan. His stomach grumbled as he tried to get most of the wetness out of his hair with a dry towel. With another towel wrapped tightly around his hips, he glanced at his reflection and frowned.

Bare-chested, he looked every bit the savage warrior. His hair hung over his shoulders, reminding him of the pictures he'd seen of his great-grandfather when he was a young man and considered a great warrior. His grandfather Charlie had been proud of his locks too, displaying them adorned with beads and silver. But at the moment, John wasn't seeing the gentle man most folks thought him to be, but only the savage, and he wished he had a pair of scissors.

Kathryne leaned back against the kitchen wall, taking a moment to catch her breath—the breath that had been driven from her chest when she got a glimpse of John, half-dressed, staring at his reflection in the mirror. And that hair—long and thick and black as night.

The kind of hair a woman could get lost in. The kind of hair that could make her forget to be so civilized—the kind of hair that could bring out a savage passion. She gave a little laugh, surprised by her rampant thoughts.

Thankful he'd been so intent on whatever he was looking at that he didn't see her, she'd quietly backed out before he noticed. She took another calming breath, ashamed of herself and where she'd let her imagination roam. Yet, on the same note, slightly pleased that her suspicions were correct.

John Wayne Hawkins was a fine specimen of a man. All the way from the tip of his strong, angular nose, to his bare chest, flat tummy and . . . and . . . she stopped herself, feeling the heat of a blush creep up her neck.

"Breakfast," she called after she had regained her composure. "Come and get it while it's hot." Still smiling, she added softly. "Who's hotter, John or this bacon?"

Her hand shook a little as she placed several strips on each of the empty plates. If he came out without his shirt, God help her, she'd probably start drooling.

"That hit the spot," John said as he leaned back against his chair. "And if I didn't know better, you found the instructions I left for Norman on how to make coffee."

She matched his grin, both because he was fully dressed and her dilemma was over, and because he had the kind of smile that made a person want to smile back. "Yes, and I have to confess, at first I thought the coffee was a"—she raised her hand and gave a flat wave—"a little strong, but now that I've gotten used to it, I like it this way."

She stood and began to clear off the table. "I've also found out that if you put the leftovers on the ant hills, it'll kill them better than bug spray."

"Don't let Norman know that. He'll swear I'm trying to kill him. He's been after me to try that decaf stuff, and just between you and me and this table, I like my coffee with a little kick to it." He took another sip then carried the mug to the sink. "Since you cooked, I'll clean."

"How about we do what my grandparents did after they had supper?"

He gave her a sideways glance. "And that was?" he asked skeptically.

"When Gramps washed, Gram dried."

John feigned a look of utter relief. "All right, that'll work. I thought you were talking about going outside, holding hands, maybe sharing a little kiss, and sitting on the swing—the one I don't have."

"You're terrible," she scolded, trying not to laugh at his expression.

"Well," he teased, "from the size of their family, they apparently did a little more than just dishes together."

"John," she chided.

"What?"

"Don't give me an innocent look. You turn every conversation into a battle of wits with sexual innuendos so plentiful that if an editor for *Playboy* was within earshot, he'd be asking for literary rights."

John's hands were in the sink of soapy water, but that didn't stop him from leaning closer and placing a quick kiss on her mouth. "I love it when you use those big words. I find it . . . arousing."

"Just wash the dishes, all right?" She reached for a rinsed plate, but he moved it aside, catching her hand in his. "Damn it, girl, what have you been doing?"

"Why do you ask?" She followed his gaze to her palm, catching her breath when his thumb caressed the healing blisters. There wasn't any pain, just the most delightful sensation she'd ever felt.

A wave of apprehension washed through her. This couldn't be happening. It was too soon. She'd sworn off men, and she wasn't ready to start a relationship. But then he did it again, and all thoughts of resistance vanished. Then a comforting thought crept into her mind. She didn't have to marry the man; she could enjoy his company and keep her heart separate.

"I bet these hurt." He lifted his head, his gaze locking with hers. "You shouldn't have worked so hard. All I wanted you to do was feed the—"

She stopped his words by placing her fingertips against his mouth—a mistake the moment she touched him. A jolt of liquid fire raced down her spine and pooled between her legs. *Simply a sexual attraction,* she told herself. *Perfectly normal for a woman my age.*

Then he did it again.

Dear God in heaven, she silently scolded, feeling like a silly schoolgirl on her first date—all tingly and weak. At first she thought to jerk her fingers away, but then realized it would look as if their touching had meant something . . . and it didn't, did it? She slowly pulled away. "I wanted to clean the stalls. I'm not a child. I can make my own decisions," she defended needlessly. "Besides, it was worth the effort. My jeans aren't as tight as they were."

He made a point of looking at her butt. "They look pretty tight to me."

Secretly thrilled with his comment, she pretended to be insulted and threw the small dish towel in his face, trying hard not to smile. "You can do the dishes by yourself, John Hawkins."

She would have left, but he gently grabbed her arm. When she gazed into his eyes, she lost the urge to leave. All she wanted stood before her. Hers for the taking.

Without a word, he bent his head and kissed her—the kind of kiss she'd read about in several of her romance novels. The kind of kiss that made her feel soft and feminine and wanted, all at the same time. The kind of kiss most women only dream about and never receive.

Slowly, she leaned into him, slipping her arms around his neck, kissing him back. Not the type of kiss she'd become used to giving to Doug, but a kiss that felt good on her lips and in other places too. And she knew John liked it by the way he groaned ever so softly, deep in his throat, a second before they parted.

"Wow," John said quietly as his hands slipped down to rest on her hips, and a smile slowly spread across his face.

Kathryne took a half step back. "I-ah, I'd better go let Duke in. He's been out for a while."

"Sure," John replied in the deep, sexy voice she was growing to adore. "I'll just finish up here."

Did he need some time to recover too? Kathryne wondered.

She went outside and leaned on the railing, letting the summer breeze cool her down. For some unexplainable reason, John's ornery expression had brought a flush to her cheeks. A flush she knew had nothing to do with menopause. Even if she tried to deny it, she was sexually attracted to him. And it felt good. She hadn't felt sexy for a very long time.

With the thought came a defensive shrug. *So what? Why be sexy if I'm content being alone?* She focused on the view, but only for a moment. *Am I content?* She wondered. *Or am I just afraid I don't have what it takes to keep a man satisfied?*

She heaved a sigh. Women were supposed to be attracted to the opposite sex. It was the way of nature. *Sex is sex, nothing more. It's fun and it feels good. Commitment is different. Commitment is something I'm not interested in right now.* She gave a satisfied nod. *Maybe all I want is some good, old fashioned, noncommittal sex.*

Lost in her thoughts, she didn't hear John's footfalls until he was standing next to her, looking at the same beautiful view, and appearing as relaxed as Duke after his morning walk.

"I don't think this place has ever looked so good," John said, leaning on the rail next to her. "Even when Ellie wasn't sick, she wasn't much of a housekeeper."

He was quiet for a long time, and Kathryne noticed a deep and lingering sadness in John's eyes. She met his gaze with a small smile when he finally looked her way.

"Your grandmother knew how to clean. I remember when I first saw this place. The floors and the banister and all that stuff were clean and shiny, just like they are now. She'd be proud of you."

Kathryne cast a quick glance at John, pleased that he'd noticed the inside of the house. "Do you think she would?"

His smiled washed over her. "I'm certain of it." He turned his gaze back toward the mountains. "I was sorry to hear about her death. She was a good woman."

"She lived a long and fruitful life," Kathryne said, feeling the unexplainable need to offer this man some measure of comfort. "I'd say I'm sorry you have to sell, but it would be a lie. I'm happy here."

Their eyes met for several moments, and then John looked away. "It's best this way," he said. "Sacrifice a few to save the many."

Kathryne frowned. "Sacrifice the few? I don't understand. Did you get that from a movie?" They both grinned.

"Maybe, but when Ellie got sick, I'd paid enough off on the property to ask that your grandfather deed me the house and five acres. It wasn't something anyone else would have done, but he did for me." John looked at Kathryne. "I could have sold it, when in reality it wasn't entirely mine. I still owed him plenty."

"He probably trusted you. Gramps was always a good judge of character." A brief memory flashed in the back of Kathryne's mind. The day she introduced Doug to her failing grandparent, proud of the handsome man she was going to marry. The old man had caught her arm before she could leave and looked deeply into her eyes. *"Some men aren't what they appear to be on the outside, Katie. You've got to look past his appearance and see what lies in his heart."*

"Well, I can tell you this. If he hadn't done that for me, I couldn't have sold you the ranch. You can't sell what you don't own."

John took a long, deep breath and let it out slowly. "I don't know how I knew, but after the doctors told Ellie she had cancer, I knew it would wind up killing her. I didn't want it to be that way, but"—he tapped his chest—"inside I knew it was only a matter of time."

Once again he was silent for a long time, but she sensed he wasn't through. "And as it turned out, I was right. We thought they got it all, then she got sick again, and again, and finally this last time, they told us there was nothing more they could do."

He laced his fingers together and stared at them for several moments. "It's hard to watch someone you love die. But the really strange part is that twenty years went by in a blink. One moment we were happy newlyweds planning a big family, and the next all our dreams were shattered. Ellie was too sick to have kids, and too sick to adopt, so all we had was each other."

"I'm sorry, John. It must have been very difficult for the both of you."

"Worse for her than me," he said. "She changed after she found out she couldn't have children. I guess it affects women a little differently than men."

Kathryne gave a disbelieving laugh. "I guess," she replied tightly.

John frowned. "Did I say something I shouldn't have?" She would have left, but he caught her and made her face him. "Kate, I'm sorry. I suppose it sounded as if I made it Ellie's fault, but that's not what I meant. I just meant that she wanted children so badly, not being able to have them affected her more than me 'cause I was grateful for just having her."

Kathryne gazed into his eyes, feeling terrible that she'd jumped to conclusions. "I'm the one who should apologize," she murmured. "There for a minute you sounded like Doug."

"Sometimes talking about it helps," John said, lifting her chin with his knuckle. "I'm confident that when you feel like telling me, you will." He brushed the back of his hand across her cheek. "What do you say we forget about work today and focus a little on relaxation?"

"What do you have in mind?" she asked, relieved that he didn't pressure her to talk.

"Well, we could fire up old Red and take her up to that peak over there." He pointed to the mountain. "I know a little place where we could have a picnic and spend a little time getting to know each other. What do you say to that?"

Kathryne felt her melancholy vanish. "Can I drive?"

John pulled a quarter out of his pocket. "I'll flip you for it."

It was way past noon by the time John had packed the truck with a *few essentials* he said they'd need for the trip.

"Trip?" Kathryne had questioned when he tossed an extra flake to the horses. "Just how long are we going to be gone?"

"Not long," he replied with an innocent shrug that instantly put her on her guard. "Why don't you go and sit down while I pack us some food."

Reluctantly she agreed, surprised that as she sat in the rocker, the easy motion nearly put her to sleep. She jumped when John placed his hand on her shoulder and told her it was time to leave.

Sixty minutes later, Kathryne sat back in the comfortable seat, watching as the cedar and scrub oak turned into a thick pine forest, speckled with blue spruce and piñon, as well as the tall, stately ponderosas.

Several rocky formations added a kind of majesty to the scene as the road turned into what she would have described as a paved cow path. But John didn't seem bothered by the narrow road, or the steep drop-offs they passed. He put Red into low and slowly climbed to the top. A moment later, he pulled out the yellow button, and they stopped. "Well, we're here."

Kathryne looked out the front window and realized why John had stopped. There was no more road, just a steal guardrail. It appeared as if the whole world lay before them—miles and miles of open space, distant hills, some crossed with tiny lines that she knew had to be roads, both paved and dirt.

"My gosh," she breathed, looking around. "Is that Taos over there?"

"Yup," he said, then pointed out several more landmarks, explaining each until she had a fairly good idea where they were, where the lodge and cabin were, and just how far they'd come. "It isn't far." John smiled. "It's just *up.*"

"I'll say," she replied. "Straight up."

He laughed, then got up and retrieved a basket from the bunk. "Hungry?"

"As a matter of fact, I am. What's in there?" Kathryne followed him outside. The fresh smell of the mountains was one she'd never tire of she decided as they walked a short distance away from the small parking lot. In a secluded spot, she helped John spread the blanket under an ancient spruce.

"Well, while you were napping in the rocker, I was cooking." He lifted the lid, exposing a plastic tub filled with fried chicken.

"Oh, yes," she replied with a sly smile. "Tell me this is Herbert."

John's shocked expression only added to her feelings of contentment. "It's from a box I got in the freezer section at the grocery store," he said flatly.

Their dinner tasted wonderful; especially when John retrieved two cans of root beer soda from the little fridge in the truck. "Here," he said. He scooted back to rest against the trunk of the tree and patted the place next to him. "Come, sit and enjoy the view. In a little while the sun will be setting between those two peaks."

"Truchas Peak," she added to show him she remembered the name. She accepted the can of soda, and then scooted over to sit close to him. "Dinner, a cold drink and"—she motioned toward the horizon—"a seat with a view. What more could a girl ask for?"

"I think we've got it covered. Let's kick off our boots and get more comfortable." He put his arm around her and shifted his position so her back was supported by his chest, his arms wrapped casually around her. "If I remember correctly, your granddad said they had four kids."

"Six to be precise. There's my dad, his two sisters and three brothers—all except Dad are somewhere in Scotland this very moment enjoying their annual family vacation with my Mom."

"Damn. No wonder they needed such a big house." He took a sip of his soda. "And you're an only child."

"That's right. I always wanted siblings, but I guess my mother enjoyed her career too much to consider it. I asked her once if I was an accident, and she only smiled and patted me on the head."

"Uh-oh, sounds like you got your answer."

She turned and raised one fair brow. "Regardless, they never made me *feel* like an accident."

"Well, when handed lemons, make lemonade." He grunted when her elbow made contact with his ribs. Grinning, he bent his head and kissed her. It was a quick kiss, but completely satisfying, making her forget the remark that sprang to mind. She looked at him for several moments. His eyes sparkled like dark sapphires, and she sensed he still had more to say when she settled back against his chest.

"With your folks coming from such a large family, and having you and all, didn't they pester you for grandchildren?"

Kathryne turned and looked up at John for another moment before she shifted back to her former position, resting against his chest watching the sunset. "I almost had a baby . . . but I guess it just wasn't meant to be."

"What happened?"

"I lost her."

John turned her, brushing his knuckles against her cheek. "I'm sorry, Kate. It must have been terrible for you."

The compassion in his eyes melted some of the ice around her heart. "I remember it like it was yesterday." She gave a sad smile. "The doctor kept telling me to stay focused, that it would all be over soon." She sighed and her smile faded. "I was eight months along."

"Did you have a lot of pain?" John asked, and she knew by the way he tightened his hold of her hand he was offering her his strength and at the same time encouraging her to talk. He'd said before that talking always made things better, and here with the glorious sunset shining on the mountain peaks, snuggled in his arms, she believed him.

"No." She shook her head. "It was terrible, but it wasn't because of pain—there wasn't any. The spinal injection they gave me saw to that. From the waist down I felt nothing but a little pressure. It was my heart that hurt."

"If you don't want to, you don't have to tell me anymore," John said softly, kissing her temple.

She lifted her head and gazed into his eyes—eyes filled with compassion and concern and something more—was it love, or did she just want to see it so badly, she imagined it?

"I remember being angry—angry that everyone kept calling my baby *it*. We'd chosen names. At least I had. Doug wasn't into the prospect of being a parent like I was. Kimberly for a girl, and James for a boy, to be determined after . . ." she paused, swallowing back the tears, glad it was growing dark and John couldn't see them. "*It* was a girl, and even though she never drew a breath, she was my perfect little angel."

John tipped her back a little and kissed her again. A soft, gentle kiss, and when he pulled back, he gazed deeply into her eyes, his warm fingers holding her chin. "I bet she was beautiful . . . just like her momma."

Kathryne wrapped her arms around his neck. There were no more words, just holding and caressing, a joining that made her forget her past and think only of the present—of John and his strength—a strength he shared with her.

She no longer felt alone. She no longer felt unsure. She felt good and special, finding her own strength more powerful when fueled by his. But most of all, she felt sexy and desirable—a feeling she didn't think she'd ever feel again.

Then she'd met John.

And the sex was great too.

It must have been the sun shining into the cab of the truck that slowly woke Kathryne. She was on her side, totally naked in the spoon position with John's right arm around her waist. She never imagined that sleeping in the sleeper-berth of a semi-tractor could be so cozy or so comfortable. Twice they'd made love, and never in her life had she thought it could be so satisfying.

Carefully, keeping the blanket over her bare shoulder, she turned to face him—placing a soft kiss on his warm lips. Smiling, she watched as he slowly opened his eyes.

"Good morning," she whispered.

A lazy smile spread across his handsome features. "Good morning." He kissed her back. "What time is it?"

Kathryne rolled onto her back, retrieved her watch from the small, bedside counter, and glanced at it. "Almost six."

"Got anything pressing to do?" he asked in a sleepy voice, rolling her back so he could hold her again. She snuggled close, gleaning his warmth. He kissed her throat, then her exposed shoulder.

"No," she breathed as shivers of delight skittered down her spine. "But don't forget, we've got horses and chickens to feed."

More kisses, and then his calloused palm slipped underneath the blanket, skimmed across her belly, smoothed over her hip, then to the small of her back, causing her to shiver with a nearly unbearable anticipation. Slowly, deliberately, he rolled on top of her, bracing his weight above her like he had night before. Long, ebony hair fell over a muscular shoulder, tickling her neck. His gaze was hooded yet intense, overflowing with a sexual magnetism that matched his self-confident smile as he said, "Herbert can wait."

CHAPTER TWELVE

Kathryne stretched between the satin sheets in her apartment, feeling absolutely exquisite. She no longer felt dumpy or angry or even jealous. She felt good—confident—and more importantly, sexy. She'd proven it to herself when she'd tossed her pajamas aside, choosing to sleep entirely in the buff as John had asked her to do the three days they'd spent at the cabin together.

There was a little added pleasure she'd hardly expected. Yesterday, when she arrived home after the long flight from New Mexico, her bathroom scale had confirmed what she suspected. In the two weeks she stayed at the cabin doing chores, she'd lost a little over ten pounds—and that was weighing in the late afternoon. She'd keep the pounds off too, by making sure there was time in her busy schedule for a vigorous workout every afternoon.

The only thing that could make her feel better lived two thousand miles away, probably watching the sunrise with a cup of hot, strong coffee in his hand. John Wayne Hawkins had expertly chased away all her buried feelings of inadequacy. She didn't even care if her first day back at work was awful. Nothing mattered except that the sooner she could close all her cases, the sooner she could catch a flight back to the man who did wonderful things to her.

Noncommittal sex was everything she'd hoped it would be . . . and more.

She rose, passing by her full-length mirror with a slight, approving smile. A month ago she'd dreaded the Summer Ball—now she could hardly wait to attend. John had agreed to act as her escort, saying he'd cut his hair for the event. Now all she had to do was let her dad know he was off the hook.

She went into the bathroom and turned on the shower, remembering what a difficult time she'd had explaining that she loved his hair long and if he cut it, she'd shave her head bald. After that threat, she recalled, he dropped all talk of haircuts.

After she showered and applied a few subtle touches of make-up to hide the suntan on her nose, she called Helen. "Hi, yes, I missed you too. Hey, I want you to keep it light—"

She held the phone in the crook of her neck and slipped on a pair of navy-blue, pinstriped trousers, but they were too loose. "I should have known you would," she added, pleased that Helen was a woman of foresight. "All right, see you in about an hour."

She tucked in the white silk blouse, and then decided she'd have to poke another hole in the belt. She put on a pair of small silver engraved concho-style earrings and a matching bracelet she'd bought at the shop Norman watched for his friend. She pondered putting her hair back in a ponytail so she could wear the sliver clip, but decided to leave it down and loose instead. Slinging her purse over her shoulder, she headed to the office.

"Wow," Helen said, covering her heart with her hand the moment Kathryne stepped into her office. "My God, girl, you look wonderful."

Kathryne flashed a bright smile. "Why, thank you."

Helen rose from her chair, walking around Kathryne. "What was this place? A health spa? You've lost inches, and you're so tanned and, my God, did you put highlights in your hair?"

Kathryne shook her head. "Just the sun," she replied, trying hard to keep a straight face. "You'll never guess what I learned how to do."

"What?" Helen's features grew animated. "You went hang-gliding!"

"Better. I drove an eighteen wheeler!"

Helen's mouth dropped open. "A truck?"

"Not just a truck, a huge truck. A bright red truck that has a refrigerator and a television and a bed with another bed that folds up or down depending on whether or not two people need to sleep at the same time. And shelves and two comfortable captain-style chairs, and most of all, it had ten gears forward and two in reverse."

"You drove a standard?"

Kathryne gave a very satisfied nod. "And I had to double clutch each time I changed gears."

Helen burst out laughing, "That's terrific. And all this time, I thought you only knew how to sit in the back seat of your company car." She shook her head then giggled again. "Who taught you how to do this amazing feat?"

"That, my dear, is going to remain my little secret for awhile." Still smiling, she pulled out the wooden snake. "Look at this. Isn't it neat? I thought it would look good on the corner of the reception table."

"Yeah, neat."

Kathryne reached back into the tote and pulled out a small white package. "I brought this for you." She watched Helen's eyes light up when she opened the box. "They're hand made by the Zuni Indians. They're turquoise set in sterling silver, and if you flip them over"—she took the earring from Helen's grasp and pointed to a tiny signature—"they're signed by the person who made them."

"Oh, I love them," Helen said, hugging Kathryne. "Thank you so much."

"I'm glad. Everybody wears them in Taos." She put her hand on the doorknob leading into her private office. "Is there anything pressing I need to tend to?"

"Nothing pressing. Like I said, I figured you might need a little time to recover from a month of shopping, but after seeing you and listening to your adventure, it sounds like you did a little more than wander around gathering souvenirs. I've never seen you look so good. Now I'm jealous. I'm going back to the gym."

"Oh, that reminds me. Make sure, from now on until I move, I get out of here at three. I'm joining the gym. I'm not about to fall back into my old habits, and," Kathryne gave Helen a firm look, "no more donuts." She paused, and then added. "And if you see Ron, I've got a little something for him, too. Want to see?"

"What is it?"

"It's called a bolo tie."

After arranging the wooden snake near her computer, Kathryne sat down and started surfing the Internet. It couldn't hurt to make a few inquiries about pets—like what kind of dog would be good around horses, and could a dog get along with a cat if she wanted one to keep mice out of the barn?

Once more she felt a little twinge of doubt, wondering if she were rushing things, but browsing through the American Kennel Club's web page turned out to be more fun than she'd expected. The only bad thing that came from it—looking at all the dogs made her realize how much she missed Duke.

Before long, an hour had gone by and when Helen brought in a cup of coffee, she suggested the Animal Humane Society, stating that they always had nice dogs up for adoption. Armed with this information, Kathryne's thinking changed.

Why not get two dogs, Kathryne mused, the Weimaraner she'd always wanted since she saw one in a store as a child, and the shepherd-cross looking back at her from the Animal Humane's web site. After all, as soon as the closing papers were signed, she'd be the proud owner of five acres—more than enough room for two dogs.

A sad little face stared back at her as she read the caption. *Pugsy was left at our facility by his broken-hearted military family who were transferred to Germany. He's a four-year-old male pug who needs special care . . .* She scrolled down, leaning that the pug needed daily medication. "I could do that," she murmured. "Small dogs are great to snuggle with when watching TV or a movie." Although she'd never been a TV watcher, she thought she might start as there wasn't much to do at night all alone in the cabin.

Page after page contained adorable pictures of unwanted dogs of all ages. She was reading about a Dalmatian that had been neglected after the child who owned it decided it wasn't as cute when it grew up when the buzzer sounded on the intercom. "Yes," Kathryne answered, glancing at the various homeless animals on her computer screen thinking that three or even four dogs wouldn't be so bad.

"There's a delivery here for you. Shall I bring it in?"

Kathryne shrugged. "Sure." She flipped through a few more pictures on the Internet, turning when she heard the door open. "My gosh . . . flowers?"

"Flowers," Helen repeated with a big smile. She carried them to Kathryne's desk, placed them down, then added, "and a card."

Kathryne gave her a quick glance before she gazed at the colorful bouquet. The vase was in the shape of an old fashioned, brass spittoon. It was filled to the point of spilling with bluebells, tiny white daisies, bright red button-mums, and several other beautiful specimens, all resembling the wildflowers she had picked from John's meadow. "Do we know who they're from?"

Helen spun on her heels and strolled to the door. "Yes we do." Helen stopped just before pulling it closed. "Somebody must have had a really nice time in New Mexico?"

Smiling, Kathryne reached for the small envelope in the plastic fork, feeling a little giddy. In all her married life, Doug had never sent flowers. To him, they were a waste of money. *Why spend money on something that doesn't last? They'll be dead in a few days. Don't be so sentimental. Just go and buy yourself something nice. You pick it out—I'm terrible at choosing gifts.*

Her fingers shook ever so slightly as she removed the card. Much to her astonishment, after she read the short note, her throat tightened with an unexpected bout of emotion. Swallowing, she whispered, "Just a little reminder of what's waiting for you when you return. Love, John."

She held the tiny card to her heart and repeated, *"Love John."*

John reached over to the other seat and ruffled the fur on Duke's neck. It had been a long day teaching eight city kids how to ride. He was glad Hank had returned. The steady paycheck would buy the supplies he needed to renovate the hunting shack until he received the rest of the money from the sale of the cabin at closing.

While he'd been busy, he hadn't thought about the note he'd sent with the flowers. But now, as he headed toward Taos to get some supplies, with nothing to do but think, he began to doubt he'd used the right words.

"Love, John," he muttered, shaking his head. He glanced over at Duke for a second before turning his attention back to the road. "I just had the best week of my life, and now she probably thinks I'm crazy . . . or a stalker . . . or just plain love-starved. I should have asked Norman. He would have known the right thing to say."

John gave his dog another quick look, completely disgusted with himself. Duke gave a loud yawn, then sank down on the roomy front seat of the old pickup, resting his head over the arm rest. A moment later he was sound asleep. John heaved an annoyed sigh and flicked on the radio.

The mellow twang of a steel guitar filled the cab, reminding him of the way Kathryne had felt in his arms when they'd put on the stereo and danced, cheek-to-cheek, in the middle of the afternoon the day before she left. One thought led to another and soon he was thinking about sexy, lacy underwear and sleeping naked.

"Damn it," he grumbled, stepping on the brakes. "I missed my turn." He waited until a two-door sedan drove by, and then turned. Barring any more sensual distractions or traffic problems, he'd finish his shopping and head for home . . . alone for the weekend.

Kathryne stood in her office gazing out the window for a long time. Somehow a simple little card had changed everything. Gone was her carefree, buoyant feeling—the feeling she contributed to her decision to have a noncommittal sexual relationship with John—replaced with a sense of guilt that she'd given him the wrong impression.

"Noncommittal," she scoffed. "Who was I kidding?"

She glanced over her shoulders at the flowers on her desk, then back at the card in her hand. "Love, John," she murmured, fastening her gaze on the words. "It's too soon," she added softly, trying to ignore the excited little flutter that tickled her heart every time she said the words. Instead, she turned back to stare out the windows, not seeing the park, but instead a distant mountain peak dusted with snow.

"It's just too soon," she whispered.

★ ★ ★ ★ ★

John heard the phone ringing at the same time he slipped his key in the back door. In three long strides he grabbed the receiver, placing it to his ear. "Hello?"

His serious expression quickly changed to one more cheerful and relieved. "You liked them, then. That's good."

He walked over to the refrigerator and opened it, holding the phone in the crook of his neck. "I'm glad. I've never bought flowers in one town and had them sent to another, so I was kind of worried if they'd do it like I wanted."

He took a beer out, then put it back and reached for the bottle of grape juice. Norman had warned him that some women don't care for a man who has to have a beer every night, so it was a habit he'd gladly break if it meant Kathryne might like him more for it.

"So, how was your flight? Good. No, Duke is outside taking a break. I took him with me to Taos after work. We just got home. Yeah, I have eight kids this week and six more coming on Saturday. You know, gotta stay busy."

He listened as she told him about her day, smiling when she repeated what Helen had said about her hair. When she paused, he took a deep breath, determined not to sound like a love-sick fool.

"I miss you," he said casually. "It's not the same around here." Then feeling like he'd said too much, he quickly added with a teasing laugh. "Yeah, my stalls are getting messy again."

The American Airline's jet landed in Albuquerque exactly on schedule Friday afternoon. Doug quickly exited the first class section of the plane, slinging his carryon over his shoulder. He held his briefcase up like a shield as he pushed past an older couple.

"Excuse me," he muttered as he continued on his way. He

184

glanced at his watch before he pulled his cell phone out of his jacket pocket, keying in a preprogrammed number. "Hey, this is Doug . . . yeah. Just landed." He glanced around the lobby, and then spotted the man he called. "Yeah, I see you."

Doug clicked his phone closed, and after he hoisted his bag to a more comfortable position, hurried toward the man. Doug extended his hand. "Ben, it's good to finally meet you face-to-face."

"Did you bring the contract?"

Doug patted his briefcase. "I've got everything we need right here."

Vicky glanced at the clock on the opposite wall of the small reception area of USIB. It was nearly four on Friday afternoon, and although Doug had said she didn't need to come in when he was gone, she felt responsible for making sure things got done—even if it was just making sure the office was neat and tidy for Monday. Besides, there wasn't the budget to hire a cleaning service, and since his divorce, the one that cleaned the complex had orders to leave Doug's office alone.

She put away several pens and tidied up the top of her desk. Her desk—her very own desk with her name neatly printed on a small brass sign. Next to it stood a little brass cardholder filled with business cards that had taken three weeks to arrive. She picked several up, pausing to place them in her purse she kept in the bottom drawer.

Tomorrow she'd mail one to her mother. Her new position was a far cry from the meaningless job she'd had in records. And in spite of her affair with the boss, she felt proud of her advancement. Her heart did a little painful lurch. Doug was handsome and rich, but he wasn't the man she'd first thought him to be.

She pulled a feather duster out of the supply closet and

quickly ran it around the two reception chairs, the small table and the silk plant, and then the arms of the chair partially hidden by the huge plant. Satisfied her area was clean and neat, she opened the door to Doug's office, wondering if he'd ever consider hiring a cleaning service. She bent over and picked up a crumpled piece of paper, swearing under her breath as a run inched up her pantyhose.

Early Saturday morning, Norman stepped out of his friend's shop for a breath of fresh summer air. He loved this time of the year. Warmer days brought more shoppers, and more shoppers brought more revenue. He loved straw hats, sandals, and best of all, Hawaiian shirts and Bermuda shorts.

As he sprayed some window cleaner on the large glass pane, his thoughts turned to other fond memories—summer days spent up at the cabin with his sister and best friend. For a moment, his heart twisted with remorse and he wished John had accepted his help. He had just finished wiping the glass clean with a paper towel when a rapid thrumming sound caught Norman's attention.

Shading his eyes, he glanced up to see a white and gold helicopter. The words *Enchantment Development* were boldly printed on the side. He watched it head north until it disappeared over the distant treetops, taking with it his good mood.

John had sold the cabin, and now some developer was scanning the area like a giant bird of prey looking for a piece of forestland to clear for more houses. In his opinion, there were too many subdivisions already—all trying to turn his sleepy little town into a big city.

Thinking about cities reminded him of Kathryne. As much as he enjoyed meeting her, and as delighted as he was that the cabin went to someone so nice—practically family—it still wouldn't be the same. The hunting shack was too far to just pop over, and he certainly couldn't visit the old cabin whenever he felt like it. He wouldn't be able to sit in Elle's chair and remember happier times ever again. He wouldn't get to see Duke much either. *No,* Norman decided with a sad sigh. *Nothing would ever be the same.*

Putting aside the cleaner and towels, Norman picked up a broom. He began to whistle a little tune while he swept away a few leftover leaves, waving at Sheriff Roberts when he drove by.

John looked up from chopping wood to see Sheriff Roberts's SUV rolling to a stop before the house. Duke got up from where he slept by the front door, and wagging his tail, barked once in greeting and then lumbered down the steps. While the sheriff petted Duke, John leaned the ax against the block. "Howdy, Jeff. What brings you up here?"

"Just a little business, John." The sheriff shook John's outstretched hand. "Can we talk for a minute?"

John's smile faded, replaced by a puzzled frown. "Sure. Come on in."

The sheriff shook his head. "This isn't something I want to do John, but I've got an eviction notice here." He took a folded paper out of his back pocket and held it out.

"What the hell . . . ?" John unfolded the paper and, after reading it, glanced over at his friend. "There's got to be a mistake."

"That's what I was hoping, but it's all there in print."

"I paid this weeks ago," John added. "The entire past due amount."

The sheriff pushed his tan cowboy hat back off his forehead, heaving a sigh. "How'd you pay it, John?"

"Money order. I got it from Lucy over at the Circle K." John's frown deepened. "What does this mean, Jeff?"

"It means USIB is saying they didn't get it. Did you get one of those receipt requested forms? You know, they're green, and there's a place where they sign for it?"

"No. I didn't think to. Like I said, I sent it out as soon as I got the money. It had plenty of time to get there." John stepped up on the front porch. "Come on in, I'll show you my copy."

John watched the sheriff drive away, and then glanced again at the paper still clenched in his hand. If USIB didn't get the money, who did? And, what could he do to prove he'd sent it? Angry and frustrated, he tossed some feed to the animals, and then went inside to take a quick shower.

On the way to his room, he noticed a business card peeking out from under the sofa. Stopping, he picked it up and glanced at the name. It was Kathryne's, but something on the card hardened his features. Tossing it on the kitchen table, he grabbed the phone off the wall and keyed in Norman's number. "Hey, can you come out here?" His dark brows snapped together. "I know Larry asked you to watch the shop this weekend, but it's serious. I'd really appreciate it if you could get here as soon as you can. Yeah, thanks."

Monday morning, Kathryne thumbed through a fifteen-page contract—the last of three she needed to scan for discrepancies. The intercom beeped. "Yes, Helen."

"I've got a man called Norman holding on line—"

"Got it," she said, hoping she didn't sound rude.

"Norman? What a wonderful surprise. Oh, I'm fine . . . and yourself? Well, certainly you can ask me for some legal advice. No. It's absolutely no bother. I still owe you for the dance lessons. What's happening?"

Kathryne listened intently, trying to be all business, trying not to think about what she could lose if the USIB's claim was valid. "How much time did the sheriff say John had?" she asked.

"Thirty days isn't much, but we'll take what we can get. Yes, it's very serious, but don't let John do anything rash. If they enforce the eviction, I want you to see to it that he complies . . . yes, until I find out what's happening, he has no choice."

She took a patient breath. "Norman, calm down and try not to worry. If we have to go to court, we'll go. No, you won't have to come to Baltimore. USIB has to file in your county, so if there's a hearing, it'll be held in Taos." Kathryne leaned back in her chair, listening to Norman, wishing she could stop him from being so upset.

"Norman," she interrupted. "As of this moment, I don't want you or John to speak to anyone at USIB. Yes, that's right. I'll handle it, but I need a favor. No, I don't need their address. I'll explain later, but I know exactly where they are and who's behind this."

She paused again when Norman said he had something else to tell her. Listening carefully, she closed her eyes and gave a long sigh. "What did he say when he found out?"

Listening while Norman told her word for word what John said, she inwardly groaned. "I wish he'd called me," she said softly, "to let me explain. Yes, I'm sure, but let me at least tell you what's going on."

And she did as best she could. She couldn't deny that she knew Doug held the papers on John's land, but she reassured Norman that she and her ex were totally separated in all business dealings and that she'd do everything she could to stop him. "Just remember we're in this together. I'll get back with you soon. Yes, I miss you too."

The moment she hung up, she buzzed Helen. "Find Ron and have him come by A-S-A-P, then call Frank Edwards's office and see when he and I can get together. Yes, explain that I need his legal opinion on a case I've been given and that I'd like to take him to Murphy's for dinner tonight to discuss it, if at all possible. Helen, stress that it's very important. Yes. Thanks."

Ron straightened his tie, then stepped into the reception area of Kathryne's office. "Hi, Helen, is she in?" he asked, taking a tissue to blow his nose.

Helen nodded. "She's waiting for you. Go on in."

Kathryne turned away from the window the moment she heard the door open. Her junior partner stood in the doorway, looking pale and tired. His eyes were a little red, as was his nose. "Ron, I'm glad you came so quickly. Please sit down. You look terrible. Aren't you feeling well?"

"No, I've got a cold, but you look great. You've lost weight," he muttered, sitting on the edge of the chair, and then, as if he just realized what he said, he immediately cleared his throat and blushed.

"Thank you." She went to the bar and took a small crystal glass from the shelf, filling it with ice, then motioned to the variety of liquor in small decanters. "Would you like a drink?"

"N-no thanks, Ms. Sheldon. I'm taking antibiotics."

"Water?"

Again, he declined.

She filled the glass with bottled water than carried it to her desk. She sat, folding her hands before her. "Explain to me why you didn't tell me who's behind USIB the moment you found out?"

Ron cleared his throat again, then sniffed. "I didn't find out until after you left." He visibly swallowed, then loosened his tie. "I told Helen, and I asked her if she thought I should disclose the information, but then you hadn't had a vacation for so long, and we knew you'd be back in a little over a week, and . . . well, maybe it wasn't the best decision, but we talked it over and decided to wait."

Kathryne took a sip of water. "I can appreciate that, but now we've got a bigger problem. USIB denies receiving payment. Doug has initiated foreclosure procedures." She pulled out a box of tissue and offered it to the young man. "I'm sorry you've been ill, but are you feeling well enough to assist me with this?"

"Absolutely." He grabbed a tissue and blew his nose.

Doug stepped into the elevator of the office complex with a very satisfied smile. A few weeks ago he'd toyed with the idea of using the Hawkins Ranch to persuade Kathryne to come back to him, but after his weekend meeting with Ben Griego, he'd decided no woman was worth that much money. One hundred acres could provide enough land to build four hundred homes, netting approximately one hundred and twenty million dollars. With his share of thirty-six million he could retire comfortably any place his heart desired.

Griego and Sons, of Enchantment Development Incorporated, would be ready to act upon their offer as soon as the eviction was enforced and the final papers signed. An additional survey would have to be preformed, as well as a title search, before the subdivision paperwork could be submitted to the county, but that was the responsibility of the developer. If it all went smoothly, the first installments would exchange hands in about two and a half to three weeks.

"Good morning, Mr. Wilcox," Vicky said with a cheerful smile.

Doug stopped at her desk, totally unaware that a man sat in the corner chair, glancing through a magazine. "Vicky. We're sleeping together. You can call me Doug."

He frowned at the blush that crept up her neck, and the way she kept looking over his shoulder. He turned, his gaze falling on the well-dressed middle-aged man holding a black briefcase. "Oh, hey Frank, this is an unexpected surprise." Doug hurried and opened the door to his office. "Come on in."

"Care for a drink?" Doug asked as he went to the side bar and poured a small amount of Scotch into a glass.

"Not this time, Doug. I'm here on business."

"Well then, let's sit down." Doug took a sip, frowning as he took his place behind his desk, waiting until Frank sat. "Sound's serious. How can I help you?"

"I'm here representing John W. Hawkins at Kathryne's request, Doug. She'd represent Mr. Hawkins herself, but feels there's a conflict of interest."

"How so?"

"It seems she's in possession of a signed and notarized purchase agreement between herself and Mr. Hawkins for a parcel of land that, for reasons unknown, your company claims to have in foreclosure."

Doug nearly choked, placing his glass down on the desk with a thud. "Claims? It *is* in foreclosure. Mr. Hawkins is a deadbeat. He was given notice weeks ago and failed to pay. When his grace period expired, he was served with an eviction notice. In a few weeks he'll be evicted—forcibly, if he resists." Doug shoved away from his desk and stood. "I don't know what Kathryne's trying to pull, but I've done everything by the book."

Frank opened his briefcase and lifted out several pieces of paper. "These are copies of the agreement between Mr. Hawkins and Kathryne. As you can see, they predate your eviction notice, a copy of which I've reviewed and have included for your convenience. I also have a copy of a money order, made out to USIB for the sum of six-thousand dollars, and a sworn statement from the store clerk verifying the purchase."

"You've been busy, Frank, but I don't care what you have there," Doug replied firmly. "I've never deposited any funds from Mr. Hawkins. If I had, we wouldn't be having this conversation."

Frank met Doug's angry gaze, holding out the papers. "You'll swear to that in court?"

Doug placed his palms on the top of his desk and leaned toward Frank. "I'll not only swear to it, I'll let you look at the corporate checking account if you don't believe me. And I don't need your copies. A purchase made by a second party isn't valid without the first party's consent. I bought Mr. Hawkins's mortgage. That makes me the first party. I assure you, I gave no such consent."

Frank put the papers on Doug's desk, and then withdrew a long, blue voucher check, placing it on Doug's desk. "Kathryne's prepared to pay the total amount due, including the amount of interest that would be accrued in the twelve years before its expiration to expedite an amicable settlement regarding this matter."

Doug picked up the check and stared at it for several moments. "Sixty-two thousand, four-hundred and fifty-three dollars." He tore it in half and then in quarters, tossing the pieces at Frank. "Not interested."

Frank patiently closed his briefcase and stood. "I wish you'd reconsider, Doug. You know I don't want to see this come between you and Kathryne."

"You tell her that she hasn't got a case."

Frank moved several of the papers he'd placed on Doug's desk, pulling out a copy of a recorded land division. "Kathryne asked me not to use this unless you refused to cooperate."

"What is it," Doug snarled, snatching it from Frank's hand. "Another prenuptial agreement?"

"I'm sorry," Frank said, frowning. "I'm not following you. This has nothing to do with—"

Doug held up his hand, stopping Frank. "Yeah, yeah, I know. I was just mouthing off. Just show me the paper."

"Kathryne anticipated your refusal to comply, and even though I have advised her against it, she is willing to extend her generous offer for an additional forty-eight hours." Frank handed Doug a copy of the recorded deed with a legal description that separated five acres from the original one hundred. "As you can see from the legal description of the five acres, it's located in the northeast corner of the—"

"Yeah, yeah, I got it."

Frank stood to leave. "If you'd like to discuss this matter further, I'll be in my office." He turned and opened the door. "Good day, Doug."

Vicky had stepped back the moment the doorknob turned. Pretending to straighten some magazines on the table, she accepted Frank Edward's business card with a weak smile.

"If Mr. Wilcox changes his mind, my numbers are on that card. Don't lose it."

"N-no, sir, I won't." She frowned, waiting until he left before she went to her desk, sank down in her chair and heaved a sigh of relief. Maybe now Doug would be forced to do the right thing.

CHAPTER THIRTEEN

John drummed his fingers on the small round table where he and Norman sat drinking a cup of coffee. He'd agreed to come to town, to have coffee with Norman, and to await Kate's arrival. He hoped there'd be a little time to talk with Kate alone, but with Norman being in such a state of nerves, he doubted he'd get the chance.

"When Kate gets here," Norman began, leaning closer, "everything will be just fine, you'll see."

John put down the latte Norman insisted he try. "Are you trying to convince me or yourself?"

Norman's shoulders sagged. "Don't tease me, Johnny, not now, not when I'm so totally stressed."

John smiled. "Norm." He waited until Norman lifted his head, meeting his gaze. "I don't know what I'd do without you. You know that, don't you?"

Norman's eyes grew watery, and his chin quivered ever so slightly as he reached across the table and put his hand on top of John's. "It's I who's dependent on you, John. I don't have many friends, no family, no one except you."

John carefully moved his hand out from under Norman's. "Don't go getting mushy, on me, Norm, all right? And as far as that family thing goes, you're like a brother to me, and don't forget it." John glanced around, a little uncomfortable with Norman's show of affection. "I'm not planning on going anywhere without you."

195

"You say that, but it's not true," Norman muttered. "The road to the hunting shack is barely passable using a four-wheel drive. My little car will never make it."

"Well, we'll just have to find you a second car," John said, taking a sip of his coffee.

"Another car? Are you crazy? Have you seen the price of gas these days?" Norman shook his head as he crossed his arms over his chest. "I'll just have to get used to the fact that the only time I'll get to see you is when we're working." Norman heaved another sad sigh. "Maybe you could bring Duke to work once in awhile."

John wished he could say something to make Norman feel better, but the truth of the matter was he couldn't think of anything. Ever since he'd found Kathryne's card, he'd felt as if the wind had been knocked out of his sails. He knew he wasn't a lady's man—had only ever been with Ellie. But with Kate, he'd felt renewed—almost like he used to feel back in his younger days.

He glanced at his watch, and then heaved an impatient sigh. "She should be getting here any minute."

"There they are. I recognize her car. Boy, she sure likes those SUVs," Norman said, standing to wave out the window, his mood surprisingly improved. "It's so good to see her again."

John watched her park. Then she stepped out of the car, followed by a tall, dark-haired man with a moustache. "Yeah, she looks good," he said, frowning, unable to shrug aside his feeling of betrayal. He stood and headed toward the door, opening it and standing aside to let them enter.

"Kate," he said calmly, nodding his greeting.

"Hello, John," she said cheerfully before turning to her companion. "John, Norman, this is Frank Edwards, a good lawyer and a good friend. He'll be representing us—you, actually—as we haven't signed the final papers. Even though it will be a week, maybe two, before we can have a hearing, we thought it best to get an early start so that we're all on the same page."

"Pleased to meet you," John said, shaking Frank's hand. "Norman, why don't you buy Frank a cup of coffee while I have a word with Kate."

"Ah, sure," Norman replied, leading Frank toward their table.

"I'm really tired, John. I didn't sleep well last night, and then our flight was late. Can it wait until later when we have dinner together?"

He held the door open for her to step outside. "It's important, Kate."

"Norman warned me that you felt like this, but I assumed after he explained it to you, you'd be over it."

"Over it?" John heaved a sigh and looked over the top of her head for a moment before returning his gaze to hers. "Why didn't you tell me your ex was USIB?"

Kathryne shook her head. "I didn't know it at the time. I didn't find out until after you'd agreed to sell. Besides, I thought you knew Doug and I were through," she said, feeling a little hurt and a little angry at the same time, even though she was expecting this kind of reaction. "I can't believe you'd think I could be that devious."

"What would you think? USIB is owned by your ex. You're both at the same address."

"Not exactly. Doug's office is on the other side of the complex. It's a big building, John. I rarely see him, and certainly never by choice." She folded her arms and turned her back to him, hoping he would see how deeply he'd hurt her. "Regardless, do you think I'm the kind of person who would offer to buy your ranch, give you a deposit, and then have my ex foreclose?"

"I'm trying to tell you, I don't—didn't know what to think. Selling the cabin is all I was planning on. Losing the land . . .

well, that's different. It kind of hit me below the belt. I'm sorry. After seeing your card, I just figured—"

She spun, her gaze locking with his, ready to put him straight. "You figured wrong. If I was in cahoots with Douglas, and I assure you I'm not, I wouldn't have given you the money in the first place. I wouldn't have come out here, and I certainly wouldn't have befriended you and Norman. I would have stayed in Baltimore and just waited to foreclose."

She stepped around him to go back inside, but he caught her arm in a firm but gentle grasp.

"Kate, I'm sorry. Maybe I'm not as smart as you. I don't know how the law works, except I know what's right and what's wrong, plain and simple, and what your ex is trying to do is wrong. I guess with everything happening, I jumped to conclusions." He stared at her for several long moments. "I should have known you couldn't do anything like that." He let her go, but she didn't leave. "Aren't you going to slap me or something?" When she still didn't move, he gave a hopeful smile. "Does this mean you forgive me?"

"John Wayne Hawkins, I don't know how I feel. One moment I think you're the most wonderful man in the world, and then the next, I'm thinking you're a jack—" She folded her arms over her chest, stopping herself before she said something she'd regret. "I suppose you had good reason to be worried, but you should have called me. Didn't you tell me it was always better to talk things out?"

A gentle smile spread across his face. "Yes, ma'am, I did, and it is."

She gave him a skeptical glance, and then finally smiled. "Then start practicing what you preach."

"Ben, yeah, it's me, Douglas Wilcox. Great. No, there's no problem . . . well maybe just a little one. No, no, let me explain."

Douglas spent the next twenty minutes going over all the details of his meeting with Frank Edwards, holding nothing back.

"Yes, it's serious. Taos is a hick town—no offense meant, of course, but I'm worried that as soon as the judge is made aware that Kathryne is willing to pay the entire amount of the contract, including interest . . ." Doug shrugged his shoulders as he paced before the large glass windows in his office. "Well, since this is only a hearing in Magistrate Court . . . I'm thinking the judge will simply rule in her favor. Yeah, I'm pretty sure that's what will happen."

Doug listened intently for several moments. "I realize there's a lot riding on this . . . for both of us, but what you're suggesting isn't exactly something I want to get involved with."

Holding the phone slightly away from his ear, he winced, then nodded. "Calm down. No, I realize the seriousness of the situation." His frown deepened. "No, I don't want out. I was just hoping we could come up with something that could change things. You know . . . maybe a bribe. Money talks, you know." He would have laughed, but couldn't quite manage it.

"Yes, I won't worry. Look, it's best that I don't know exactly how you'll handle things, all right? I trust you'll do whatever's necessary to make sure we both profit from our efforts. If anything changes, I'll call you immediately. Goodbye."

Doug put the receiver back in the cradle, grabbing the silk handkerchief from his back pocket to dab at the beads of sweat dotting his brow. After several moments and two long, deep breaths, he filled a glass with ice and added a liberal amount of Scotch, downing the drink in two swallows, thinking that ignorance wasn't bliss.

John glanced at the receiver. "Damn," he muttered, then placed it in the cradle. He'd spoken with Kathryne almost every evening since her return, and each time he was hoping she'd end their conversation with a spoken *I love you,* but she never did. Their conversation had taken a professional turn, and he hated it. Had his accusation ruined their chance for a meaningful relationship? Had he hurt her more deeply than he realized?

If he didn't know better, he was beginning to think she'd never say it, and he sure as hell didn't want to say it again in case she felt pressured to say it back. Hell, she was probably tired of men, especially men who questioned her character and put her on the defensive.

And why was he in such a hurry? Once she moved into the cabin, he'd make sure they spent lots of time together. Besides, maybe she thought love and marriage were old fashioned. Maybe she just wanted a relationship without commitment. He could do that. A license didn't necessarily mean a relationship that lasts. Right?

"What do I know?" he muttered, yanking off his shirt. A few moments later he stood in the shower, trying to think of a way to make her love him.

Kathryne sighed. She'd just had a conversation with John, and it left her feeling empty—made her wish he was here, or better yet, made her wish he'd invite her to spend the night at his cabin. Lately it seemed like each time they talked, it felt strained, as if he were trying hard not to say the wrong thing. Had she been too hard on him? Did she scare him off by voicing her opinion too strongly?

If it hadn't been for Douglas and his stupid attempt to cheat John out of his land, John would have never accused her of betrayal. She gave a disgusted laugh. She knew all about betrayal—learned it from Doug. Almost as fast as she thought it, she realized how John must have felt. Even though his feelings weren't justified, he had still experienced them, and she could relate to that. So much so she immediately felt dreadful that she hadn't been more understanding.

She glanced at the phone, remembering her brief conversations with John—wishing she hadn't been so formal—so business like. She would have vindicated herself, saying she was just being professional because of the circumstance, but deep down she knew it wasn't true. She was acting childish, and vowed to stop it immediately.

She picked up the receiver and dialed John's number in the hopes of inviting him out for dinner and maybe even a dance or two. After a few disappointing minutes, she put the phone down then began to get ready for bed, wondering if he hadn't pick up because she'd hurt his feelings.

A few moments later her mood lightened. John didn't have caller ID.

Glancing at the gathering clouds, John checked each child's saddle, adjusting stirrups and reins with encouraging words to ensure the children enjoyed their trail ride. But his mind wasn't entirely on his work. It wasn't because of his early telephone conversation with Frank, although Frank had delivered interesting news about a company called Enchantment Development. No, John decided. Even a construction company—a big construction company—couldn't cloud his light-hearted feeling.

Kathryne had also called. Called and apologized. Never in his life would he have expected her to apologize to him. And when he tried to tell her he should be the one apologizing, she reminded him he already had, the day she'd arrived. After that, they fell into their usual conversation, easy, comfortable, with a little teasing thrown in. Just the kind of talk he could do all day. Especially with Kathryne.

"Are you guys ready?" he asked the kids as he swung up on Sunny. When they all shouted yes, he pushed his hat down a little tighter on his forehead and led them out of the stable towards the well-worn trail, glancing cautiously at the thick clouds gathering over the distant mountain peaks. "Looks like we might need our slickers on the ride home," he added as they disappeared down the trail.

Kathryne sat across from Frank, idly tapping her pen on the pad of paper. "It just doesn't make sense," she started. "Why would Doug pursue this? Surely he's aware the judge is going to rule in our favor."

"Maybe he's in denial," Frank stated matter-of-factly. "When I met with him, he said something really strange."

"What did he say?" she asked curiously.

"When I gave him John's deed to the five acres, Doug said something like, 'what's this? Another prenuptial agreement?' "

Frank frowned when Kathryne gave a short burst of laughter. "Personally," he began again, still frowning, "I think he's gone off the deep end, and it very well might have something to do with the divorce. Maybe he's jealous. Maybe he thinks there's something between you and John, and he's just being stubborn and trying to give you a hard time."

Kathryne tried to look contrite, feeling bad, but not too bad, that Doug still stung from her prenuptial incident in the restaurant. She took a breath, forcing down an uncommon bout of mirth. "I don't know how he could think that. I didn't even know John when Doug and I divorced." She gave a little sigh. "I didn't even know the cabin was for sale, and I especially never dreamed I'd be moving to New Mexico." She leaned forward. "Trust me, Frank, all of this was the farthest thing from my mind. I thought I'd continue with the firm until the day I died."

"Well, something's got him all worked up. I think there's more to it than just a simple foreclosure." Frank checked his watch then stood. "It's getting late, and I want to do some snooping around before five. I spoke with John this morning and told him I had a lead on Enchantment Development, a construction firm out of Santa Fe that's been looking to buy land in the area."

"Do you think they've got something to do with Doug's weird behavior?"

Frank shrugged his shoulders. "Who knows, but it won't hurt to do a little investigating." He pushed in his chair and smiled. "Did you know that before I became a lawyer, I was a cop?"

This time Kathryne didn't stop her amazed laughter. "You? The man who complained so ferociously about a parking ticket that we all thought you'd take your appeal to the Supreme Court?" She shook her head doubtfully. "I would never have believed it."

Frank grinned. "Believe it. I used to have to spend my days off in court waiting for the judge, and when he'd finally get there, the defendant's lawyer would ask for a postponement. Many cases are moved so many times, it's impossible for the arresting office to make an appearance. When he doesn't show, the case is automatically dismissed. That's where I learned you can fight almost any ticket and get away with it." His grin turned even more smug. "And, that's one of the reasons I became a lawyer. You know the old expression. If you can't fight 'em, join 'em."

Kathryne gathered up her notes and purse, following her friend to the door leading out of the small conference room they'd been using at the hotel. "Snooping? That doesn't sound very professional for an ex-cop or a lawyer," she teased. "What are you planning?"

"I'm planning on speaking to a few realtors. My guess is that they'd know the approximate value of John's land. Money prompts lots of men to do strange things."

Kathryne followed him to the elevator, stepping inside and selecting their floors. "Do you think Doug wants it so he can sell it? If so, why'd he turn down my offer?"

"Maybe it wasn't enough." The door opened on Frank's floor, but before he stepped out, he gave Kathryne a reassuring smile. "The case is in our pocket, Kate. I'm just naturally suspicious."

"You're making me crazy with all this, but I trust you, Frank. Do whatever you need to on end this." She returned his smile as the elevator door slowly closed. A moment later her cell phone rang. "Hello? Hi, Norman—please, calm down. I can barely understand you. You're in the lobby? Yes, I'll be right there."

Kathryne frantically pushed the stop button on the elevator, then pressed lobby several times as she dropped her cell phone into her purse. The moment the door opened, Norman greeted her, looking wretched.

"Oh, Katie, I'm so glad I found you. I'm just going crazy."

"Where is he?" she asked as Norman grabbed her arm and together they quickly headed toward the glass doors.

"John took him to the hospital."

John stood by the window in the small surgical waiting room. It was dark, and rain turned the different colored lights from the traffic and street signs into a blur, but he wasn't really interested in anything outside. His mind was on the elderly man he'd brought in over an hour ago—a man he'd grown to admire and respect—a man who had no idea his accident really wasn't an accident.

John heard the elevator doors open and instantly recognized Norman's voice coming from the hall, reassuring Kate that her father would survive. However, John wasn't so certain. If he didn't follow the anonymous caller's instructions he'd received via Hank's cell phone, he couldn't be sure Hank, Kate, or Norman would ever be safe again. He'd tried to recognize the voice, but it was useless. Even when he checked the number, he'd hit a brick wall. The call had come from a pay phone.

"Kate," he said, turning the moment she entered the small lounge. He glanced at Norman's worried face and then back at Kate's, strengthening his determination to do and say anything to keep them both safe.

"He's in surgery." John took her hands and held them. "The doctor said he's got a broken leg, and maybe some broken ribs, and that's why it was hard for him to breath. That's why they took him to surgery."

"How? What happened?" she asked, following him to a comfortable looking sofa. She sat down next to him, and he knew she felt thankful he was there.

"I'm not sure," he said truthfully. He hadn't been there—hadn't witnessed what happened. "It was raining, and when I realized he was late getting back from town, I went looking. I think he must have lost control—maybe he swerved to avoid a deer—all I know is that his pickup ran off the road and rolled. He was conscious when I got there, but in a lot of pain."

"Those roads can be so dangerous," Norman added, sitting in the chair across from them.

John squeezed Kathryne's hands between his own, remembering how Hank's cell phone started ringing the moment John arrived. It didn't take a rocket scientist to figure that the people responsible for the accident were watching, as they told him to say nothing and listen. Afterwards, they told him to tell Hank it was a wrong number. "I'm sure he'll be all right. The only thing I noticed right away other than his leg was that he was having a little trouble breathing. Said his side hurt."

Kathryne nodded. "Thank God you found him. How long has he been in surgery?"

"About an hour."

"Will you stay until it's over?" she asked John, and then

looked at Norman. "Will you both stay?"

John gave her a reassuring smile, but before he could say *of course*, Norman emphatically replied.

"We wouldn't leave you alone for the world."

Hank came out of the surgery just fine. His breathing problems vanished as soon as the doctors removed a sliver of rib bone. Except for a few bumps and bruises, his prognosis was good. Kathryne listened carefully to the doctor as he relayed the information. "He'll be out of the hospital in a week, provided he has someone to help him at home."

"I'll see to it," Kathryne assured him.

"I'll be there twenty-four-seven," Norman interjected. "Right John? We'll all be there to help him."

"May I see him?" Kathryne asked.

"Sure, but he's still a little groggy. Don't stay too long. He needs to rest." The doctor stopped Norman from following. "Just family for now, all right?"

"Ah, sure," Norman said, taking a step back at the same time he added. "But really, we're all kind of his family."

John put his hand on Norman's shoulder. "We'll visit tomorrow when he's feeling a little better. For now, we'll let them have some father-daughter time."

Norman looked up and forced a small smile. "Sure, John. Tomorrow. Tomorrow I'll make some homemade cookies and bring some flowers to brighten up his room." Norman rolled his eyes and added, "Poor Hank. Can you imagine spending a week in this place?" He went to the off-white curtains at the side of the large window. "My God, look at these, couldn't they have found a more exciting color?"

John gave a soft laugh and inwardly breathed a sigh of relief that his friend was over his bout of hurt feelings. "Personally, I think this whole place could use a makeover—something with some color—something cheerful."

Norman scoffed. "My gosh, John. If they did that their patients might actually feel better sooner."

Kathryne entered the recovery room and went directly to her father's bed as he opened his eyes. "Hi," she said softly, picking up his hand.

"Hi back," he murmured. "Guess I won't be taking you to the dance. Got to have this damned cast on for twelve weeks. Doc says I've got old bones and they take longer to heal."

Kathryne smiled, blinking back tears. "That's all right. I think I've found someone who can take your place."

Her father frowned and shifted his weight. "I bet I know who it is, too."

Kathryne gave her father an admonishing look. "Aren't you a little old to be so psychic?"

"John's a good man, Kate. He saved my life." He took a ragged breath and closed his eyes. "But, I'm not sure if he knows how to dance."

It was late. John had dropped Kathryne off at the hotel, promising to be back to take her to the hospital as soon as he could get Norman moving in the morning. After he walked Kathryne to her room, he went back to the lobby and asked to borrow a phone.

"Frank? It's John. I'm sorry to be calling so late, but I've got something to tell you that can't wait until morning. No, I'd rather not come up. Can you meet me in the parking lot in a few minutes? Thanks."

John leaned against his pickup waiting for Frank to arrive. He'd awakened the poor man and knew that Frank needed a few minutes to collect himself and get dressed. It wasn't a problem. The easy part was waiting. The hard part would be convincing Frank that he lied.

"I don't believe it for a minute," Kathryne stated, seated across from Frank in the coffee shop of the hotel. By his dark expression, Kathryne felt sure Frank agreed with her. "John's probably never told a lie in his life. Why now?" She shook her head, and then took a sip of hot coffee, glancing at her watch. "When he gets here, I'm going to give him a piece of my mind."

"I wouldn't do that, Kate. Not just yet. I told him I wouldn't tell you until after he dropped you off at the hospital."

She gave an impatient sigh. "All right. I won't say a word, but I'm doing it for your sake, Frank, not John's."

"John made me take this statement last night—said to give it to the judge." Frank opened his briefcase and took out a single document. Kathryne instantly recognized John's bold handwriting. "After I read it, I asked him to reconsider, but he wouldn't. He insisted I take it out there in the parking lot. I was wearing my bedroom slippers."

"This is ludicrous," Kathryne answered, feeling a little anxious as she read the document. There was a lot riding on this hearing—more than she wanted to admit. Frank had made it perfectly clear that if John lost his case, she'd still have the five acres, and she knew her father would always have a place for John at the lodge. But why didn't that make her feel any better? Frank had just said there was no need for any worry. The case was cut and dried. She had nothing to fear, and Frank felt reasonably certain John didn't either.

Not according to the document in her hand. If the judge was disagreeable, John could be held in contempt and fined. "How do we know he wasn't forced to do this?"

"Well." Frank heaved a sigh. "We don't. But for now, he signed it, and as his representative, I'm duty bound to present it as soon as I can call the magistrate and schedule a hearing. I'm hoping I can get it as soon as Thursday."

Kathryne shook her head at the same time she picked up her purse and stood, leading Frank to the cashier. "John isn't a liar," Kathryne stated with more conviction that she felt. "Something's up. I just know it."

CHAPTER FOURTEEN

John took off his Stetson and stepped into Hank's room, nodding at a pretty little nurse just before she left. "Howdy, Hank. How are you feeling?"

"I'd feel better if I didn't think you were such an idiot," Hank grumbled.

John blanched. "I suppose you're so disagreeable because you're in pain. Maybe I should come back some other time."

"Oh, no, you don't," Hank began. "You get yourself over here and tell me why you've tucked your tail and turned coward on us."

John frowned. He didn't like what he'd done, but he sure as hell wasn't a coward. He didn't have a choice. "I don't know what you're talking about, Hank."

"Don't give me that bull crap." Hank shifted his weight, swearing under his breath about being too old to be troubled with a broken leg. "I've been driving these roads practically all my life. A little rain never bothered me before."

"It was raining pretty heavy and—"

"Hog wash," Hank interrupted. "Where's my truck?"

"Junior towed it over to his place." John heaved a loud sigh. "If you're thinking it can be repaired, you're wrong. It's totaled."

Hank gave John a stern look. "I don't give a tinker's damn about that truck. It's insured. It's you I'm worried about. You and Kathryne."

John nodded, feeling wretched. "You don't have to worry,

Hank. As long as I'm around, nothing will happen to Kate."

"What the hell are you saying?" snapped Hank. "John, you're like a son to me. And I like to think I know you as well as any man, but this . . ." Hank shook his head. "I want to know who called."

"Called?" John repeated, but he knew Hank was no fool.

"On my cell the night of the accident. I was a little dazed and in pain, but my ears were still working. I heard a man threaten you."

"That's impossible, Hank—"

"You think? Well, I'll share a little secret with you. I keep my cell earpiece on high since the only time I use it is when I'm driving and you know I like driving with the window open. It's noisy, but the fresh air's worth it."

"Hank—" John clamped his jaw shut the moment Hank raised his hand.

"It was real quiet in the cab after the accident. The rain had stopped, the engine was off." Hank narrowed his eyes. "I heard, John. I heard a man say my accident wasn't an accident at all."

John matched Hank's stern gaze. "Then you know I had no choice."

"That's why you told Frank you lied, isn't it?" Hank raked his fingers through his tousled grey hair. "They said there'd be more trouble if you didn't."

"That's right."

"You're no liar, John. And we both know you're no coward. I just said that to piss you off so you'd tell me the truth. Now, what are you going to do about it?"

"For now, I'm going to do as they say. But I'm not going to take it sitting down. I've got some friends checking out a few things."

"You're going to lose the ranch," Hank confirmed with a sympathetic smile. "Kathryne called and told me Frank got a special hearing for Thursday."

John put on his hat. "Maybe I will, but at least I know my friends will be safe."

Hank leaned up on his elbows, calling out before John could leave the hall. "We stopped being friends a long time ago, John. Now we're family."

A few moments later, the nurse returned with a little plastic cup and a glass of water.

"It's time for your pain medication, Mr. Sheldon."

"I don't need that right now," Hank grumbled. "Hand me that phone, please. I need to make a call."

Vicky hurried after Douglas, trying to balance the heavy briefcase and her purse. A month ago, she would have been delighted to accompany Douglas to court—or any public function, for that matter, but not anymore. Now she suspected she was being used, or, more to the point, flaunted before his ex-wife.

Her suspicions were aroused when Douglas had insisted she wear stiletto heels and a tight-fitting, peach-colored dress that, in her opinion, was cut a little too low for court, and carry a silly briefcase filled with blank paper. Did he think it made her look smarter?

She'd only begun to ascend the dozen steps when she caught her high heel on the step and stumbled. She would have fallen, but a pair of strong arms came around her. When she looked up, a tall, olive-skinned man smiled. His eyes were the strangest shade of blue, and by his higher cheekbones and braided black hair, she suspected she'd just gotten her first glimpse of a real Native American.

"Are you all right, ma'am?" the man asked in a deep, soft voice.

"Y-yes, thank you," she stammered, admiring the navy-blue

western shirt he wore, as well as his black cowboy hat. He had a type of tie she found very interesting and had recently seen on a new friend back in Baltimore. This man's tie appeared to be a bear's claw, held in place with silver leaves. It was v-shaped, and there was a small chunk of turquoise nestled in the curve of the claw.

"That's very pretty," she murmured, aware that she'd been staring. She hurriedly gathered up several sheets of paper, embarrassed that they were blank. She felt sure the man noticed but had been polite enough not to point it out.

"Vicky, get up here."

She tore her gaze away from the man's tie and cast a quick glance at Doug, who scowled at her from the top step, holding the door. He gave a disgusted look, then stormed in to the courthouse where all parties involved were to meet informally for a hearing with the judge.

"May I carry that for you?" the man asked, smiling.

"No," she said quickly . . . too quickly. "I've got it, but thanks for asking." He let go of her arm and smiled, and for a moment she found herself smiling back. "Ah—I'd better go or he'll really get mad."

The dark-haired man's smile faded. "Are you with him?"

"Yes. For now," she replied with a little shrug of her shoulders as she bent down to retrieve the heel of her shoe. "He's my boss, Doug Wilcox."

The nice man seemed to ponder that information for a few minutes before he spoke. "Well, if he gives you any trouble, just tell him it was my fault." He released her, and then touched the brim of his black Stetson. "Name's John if you need anything. John Hawkins."

Vicky swallowed hard, and then hurried up the last few steps. The moment she went inside, Doug caught her by the arm. His fingers tightened painfully. "What did you say to him?"

Vicky stared at Doug, puzzled by his bout of temper. "N-nothing. I tripped, and he helped me. That's all." Doug released her, then strode down the hall.

"Hello Douglas," Kathryne replied politely when Doug entered the courtroom. Vicky from records also came in, carrying a pile of loose papers. She looked a little disheveled, and on closer inspection, she held the spiky heel of her right shoe in her hand. Doug stopped so quickly Vicky bumped into him, getting a dirty look for her blunder. He whispered something and pointed to the next table. She hurried to it, dropping an armful of briefcase and papers on the top.

Kathryne stiffened a little as Douglas's eyes drifted from her eyes down to her breasts, the narrow, concho-studded belt at her waist and then back up to her eyes, briefly scanning the concho earrings in her ears, then dropping down to her pointed-toed boots.

"Good God, Kate, have you looked in a mirror lately? You're looking more and more like Annie Oakley than a corporate attorney. Haven't you gone a little overboard with the southwestern crap?"

She ignored his sarcasm. "You're late, Doug."

Her ex-husband glanced around with an arrogant smirk. "Apparently so is the judge, and you're buddy, Hawkins, but then this is a little backwards town, located in a backwards state, isn't it." He loosened his tie. "If I recall it's nicknamed the land of *mañana*."

"Guess it depends on how you view things." Kathryne glanced past Doug. "Excuse me," she said as she brushed by. She met John halfway. "May I have a word with you in private?" she whispered.

John seemed to hesitate, and then nodded.

"What is going on?" she demanded, keeping her voice low. "You can't—"

"There's no use beating a dead horse, Kate. I've made up my mind."

"You've made up your mind?" she repeated. "Don't you mean you've changed your mind?" She took a calming breath, trying hard to keep her temper in control. What was it with men? One moment they seem rational, and the next . . . "I'm confused. Why wait until just a few days ago to admit you lied? You could have told me at any given time and saved us all the embarrassment."

John stared at her, a tiny muscle ticking above the smooth line of his jaw. "I'm sorry, Kate. I don't want to hurt anybody."

He would have left her to return to the others, but she caught his arm. "I thought I knew you—I thought you were different from most men." She hesitated for a breath of a moment, her eyes searching his. "But apparently I was wrong."

She let go of his arm, and when he stepped aside, she led him back to the table. "You're about to meet my ex," she stated over her shoulder. "Another man I trusted and who deceived me." She gave a little toss of her head. "Who knows? You two could become friends."

If she'd had the nerve to look at John, she would have noticed how her words had cut. Instead, she led him purposely toward Doug. John stood at least a head taller than her ex. "Douglas, meet John Hawkins. John, this is Douglas Wilcox."

"You're late," Doug said with an air of superiority, even though he had to raise his head to met John's steady gaze.

John didn't seem to notice the insult, nor did he offer his handshake. "Your assistant nearly killed herself on the steps. I helped her pick up some papers."

Kathryne watched as John nodded a greeting at Vicky, wondering why it bothered her so much when she knew John was the type of man to help anybody who needed it, friend or foe. He had no way of knowing that Vicky was part of the reason she'd left Doug.

She thought about it for a moment, smiling a little when she thought she should take the time to thank the woman.

"She's not my assistant. She's my secretary," Doug replied, turning to smile at Kathryne. "She's cute, but a little clumsy."

John put his hand in the small of Kathryne's back, giving her a little push toward their table. "Then perhaps you should have had the good manners to help her up the stairs," John said, leaving Doug to stare at his back.

Two hours later, Kathryne slipped off her boots, sinking down on the edge of the bed to rub her aching feet. She'd forgone comfort, taking Norman's advice that the narrow-toed black lizard boots would be more fashionable for court. And the judge had arrived even later than John and Doug, stating that she'd had a flat tire and no one was around to change it.

Kathryne thought about the flat tire she'd had the day she met John, feeling a stab of pain almost equal to the one she felt when she learned Doug had been unfaithful. She heaved an unhappy sigh, reaffirming that she was through with the opposite sex.

Although Frank had offered to take then all to a great steakhouse for dinner, John had refused. By the way she and John exchanged casual glances; she knew it had been a rough few hours for him too, but she couldn't let herself feel sorry for him.

He'd betrayed her trust. Not as badly as Douglas, but nevertheless enough to make her very angry. Her feelings had only intensified after Frank had wanted to go over the case in detail, but once more, John had stated that he'd made his decision and intended to stick to it.

Now, as she slipped out of her clothes and into a comfortable cotton, lightweight robe, she took the silver broach from her hair and shook it loose, catching a glimpse of the little blinking light on the hotel's phone. She picked it up, then pressed the number that would retrieve her message, wishing it was from John and hoping that he'd have some kind of a reasonable explanation about what had happened in court earlier that day.

Ms. Sheldon, my name is Vicky Lewis, and I have some information that you might be interested in. Please call . . . Kathryne held the receiver away from her ear, frowning at it for a moment before she replayed the message. Several minutes went by, and then she punched in the number.

"Hello. Is this Ms. Lewis? Yes. I'm interested." Kathryne listened to the woman's plight. "If you don't mind, I think it would be better if we met away from the hotel. It's ten-thirty. The only place I know that's open is the Last Chance Saloon down the street. I'll meet you there in about twenty minutes. And Ms. Lewis, if this is some kind of a joke—"

Kathryne got to the restaurant before Vicky and chose a private table in the back, as far away from the band and dance floor as she could get, yet a place that offered her a perfect view of the front entrance.

Once seated, she decided to have a cold beer while she nibbled on a bowl of peanuts. Several minutes went by. Kathryne glanced at her Rolex, now nestled in an engraved silver and turquoise band. She'd give the woman another fifteen minutes, and then she'd call John.

She shelled another peanut, tossing the scraps on the table before popping the nut into her mouth. At the same time, the door opened and in stepped Vicky. Kathryne stopped chewing, startled by Vicky's appearance. With her long blond hair up in pigtails, she looked like teenager. She wore a dark windbreaker and jeans, and white sneakers, and didn't appear to be very tall.

Kathryne waved, and Vicky hurried over, slipping off her

jacket to reveal a tan tee with the words, *I went to New Mexico and all I got was this lousy t-shirt,* printed on the front. Kathryne took a sip of beer trying to remember that this child slept with her ex-husband. "Want something to drink?"

"Sure," Vicky replied. Kathryne motioned for the waitress, and Vicky ordered a beer.

"May I see your I.D.?" the waitress asked. She glanced at the girl's driver's license then handed it back. "My gosh, you don't look any older than twelve."

Kathryne braced herself. If the mouthy waitress made even the slightest indication that Kathryne was Vicky's mother, she'd have her job. Only after the woman grinned, and then asked, "You two sisters?" did Kathryne breathe a sigh of relief.

After the waitress left, Kathryne took another sip of beer, raising one skeptical brow. "Well, what's this all about?"

Vicky cautiously glanced around. "I don't know why I'm so nervous. I guess I just really liked my job."

"I'm sorry, I'm not following . . ."

"No, I guess you wouldn't." Vicky leaned back when the waitress placed the bottle of beer on the table, asking if she wanted a frosted glass. "No thanks."

Kathryne took another sip of beer at the same time Vicky took one. Then Vicky leaned on the table and began to speak while she fiddled with the corner of the little cocktail napkin. "You see, Ms. Sheldon. A lady like you has always been respected. I mean, you're a lawyer, you're rich—no one questions your decisions, everyone respects you regardless that you're blond and good-looking."

Kathryne felt a little puzzled. Had Vicky just given her a compliment or had she just been insulted because of her blond hair? "Blond isn't necessarily a bad thing, Ms. Lewis, nor do I think it has any bearing on respect or the lack of it."

Vicky's big blue eyes widened. "Oh, but it does. Do you

remember when you hired me to work in records?"

Kathryne nodded. "That's where most of the apprentices start."

"What?"

Kathryne nodded. "Your resume said you wanted to become an apprentice. You're a legal aid. All my legal aids start in records, and they're encouraged to attend classes on law as they work their way up. The corporation pays for their education, and work hours are adjusted accordingly. Working in records couldn't have been that bad. I've been told it's a great place to review cases while you're sorting and filing them."

Vicky frowned, then took another sip of beer. "That's not what Douglas told me. He told me I'd be stuck there forever, that you didn't like blondes, that . . ." Vicki shrugged. "Oh well, I guess it's all water under the bridge now, right?"

"Right." Kathryne looked at Vicki. This girl didn't steal Doug; he corrupted her.

"You didn't read the handbook I gave you, did you?" Kathryne popped another peanut into her mouth, waiting for an answer.

"No," Vicky muttered, reaching for a nut. "Doug told me I didn't need to—that he'd take care of me."

Kathryne gave an impatient sigh. She was through with Doug, but listening to the lies he'd fed this young woman was almost more than she could stomach. "This isn't why you called me, is it?"

Vicky shook her head. "No. But I want you to know why I did what I did. Remember when I said you had everything any girl could want?"

Kathryne nodded. "Yes, but not everything is as it appears, remember that."

"Oh, I will. I've already learned my lesson. You see, I thought I was going to be in records forever, and then Doug came along and told me how lonely and unhappy he was that you were threatening to divorce him, and that Diana, his secretary, was threatening to quit."

The young woman took another long drink, staring at the bottle. "Then one day he came down to records, and he told me he'd left you and started his own business. He said Diana didn't want to work for him anymore, and he asked me to be his secretary. At the time, he implied that we'd be building a future together."

"Doug is good with words."

"Yes," she murmured. "And making promises." She pulled out a crumpled piece of paper from her pocket. "I'm not only Douglas's personal secretary, I clean the office too." She blushed. "Not every day, but then it doesn't get too dirty."

"Your point?" Kathryne asked impatiently.

Vicky placed the paper on the table. "I found this on the floor one night after he left on a business trip to New Mexico."

Kathryne picked up the paper and read it, recognizing John's bold signature at the bottom of the page. "There was a money order sent with this. Do you know what might have happened to it?"

"In court today I was shocked when that nice man, Mr. Hawkins, admitted to the judge that he'd lied about sending a money order to Doug."

"Why?" Kathryne asked. "What were you expecting?"

"Certainly not that," the young woman confessed. "I was expecting the truth."

"You don't think Mr. Hawkins was telling the truth?" Kathryne watched Vicky closely as she reached into her pocket and pulled out a small white envelope, opened it and then shook out the contents.

"Is this what you're looking for?"

Kathryne fingered the tiny pieces and a few long pink strips of a shredded money order before she lifted her gaze to Vicky's. "Where did you get this?"

"Out of Douglas's shredder when I cleaned his office the night he left to take a land developer from New Mexico out to dinner."

Kathryne's frown deepened. "Why are you doing this for us?"

Vicky sighed. "I may be many things, Ms. Sheldon, but mostly I'm honest. Mr. Hawkins is a nice man, and he doesn't deserve to lose his land to someone who'd lie to make a profit."

Vicky finished her beer, then shrugged on her jacket before she stood. "I don't know why Mr. Hawkins said he didn't pay his delinquent amount because he did. The proof's right there. Good luck," she murmured and turned to leave.

Kathryne caught her sleeve. "What are you going to do? Doug isn't going to be happy you betrayed him."

Vicky's shoulders slumped. "No. He's going to be furious, but at this point I don't care. I've got a little money set aside— enough for a bus ticket back to Baltimore. Then I'll start look- ing for a new job."

Kathryne pulled her rental keys out of her purse along with two of her own business cards. "Vicky, take these keys. They're to the silver Ford Explorer." She jotted a number on the back of one of the cards, and then handed it to the young woman. "This is the license number. It's parked outside, and it's full of gas."

"I can't take your car," Vicky protested. "Especially after all I've done." The young woman looked up and smiled weakly. "But you could give me a ride to the bus stop in the morning if you wanted to."

Kathryne nodded. "I'll be happy to do that, but you're still going to need a way to get home. Buy a bus ticket to Santa Fe. They have a small airport with shuttle flights available. I'll ar- range to have a ticket waiting when you get there. I'll also have a plane ticket to Baltimore waiting for you when you get to the airport in Albuquerque. Now, do you have a number where I can reach you if I need to?"

"Sure." Vicky took out one of her new business cards and looked at it for a moment before writing the number on the back. "Here. I guess I won't be needing these anymore."

Kathryne watched the young woman leave, then picked up the pieces of money order and carefully put them back in the envelope; folded John's crumpled letter and placed them securely into her purse along with Vicky's number. She drank the last swallow of her beer, thinking about what had just happened. Although she didn't doubt the outcome once the judge was given the evidence, it had cost Vicky Lewis a lot to step forward and do what was right.

But what about John? What had made him do what he did?

Checking her watch, Kathryne opened her cell phone and hit the speed dial for the office. "Hi, Helen, it's me. I'm leaving this message so when you get in, you can call this number . . . Her name is Vicky Lewis, the Vicky from records, and before you start complaining, I want you to arrange for her airfare back to Baltimore and have it waiting for her at the airport in Albuquerque. Also, I want you to meet her at the airport in Baltimore and inform her that if she wants it, she can have her old job back. I'll give you details later." Kathryne clicked her phone shut then immediately opened it, pressing another speed key she'd meant to delete a long time ago but was now please she hadn't. "Doug? Yes. I know it's late, but I've got something I want to tell you. No, it can't wait until morning." A satisfied smile played on her lips. "Don't worry. I'm sure after we speak, you'll be able to fall right back to sleep."

Frank sat across from Kathryne in the hotel's coffee shop, adding sugar to his cup. "This better be good, Kate. I'm still on Baltimore time, and it's way past my bedtime."

It didn't take Kathryne long to relay her meeting with Vicky to Frank. "So, we've determined that John lied, and"—she nodded at the envelope—"with that evidence, the judge is sure to overturn her decision. But that's not what concerns me." She leaned a little closer. "I think we should try and find out why John lied."

"I agree, and there's something I need to tell you. You're father left me a message saying that he overheard a man threaten John."

"How's that possible? Was John on the phone at the lodge?"

"No. Someone called Mr. Sheldon's cell phone the night of the accident. They must have been watching because he said it didn't ring until John had been there for several minutes. John answered and that's when your father overheard. It seems he keeps the volume on high when he's driving." Frank took another sip. "But, that's not all. I've been doing a little investigating, and I found something very interesting." He paused for effect. "Enchantment Development has a reputation."

"A reputation? For what?" Kathryne asked with a worried frown.

"Pressuring folks into selling their property." Frank stood and pushed in his chair. "I've got a meeting with the owner in the morning, so we'll see."

Kathryne took the last sip of her coffee. "Meanwhile, I'll try to get hold of John and do a little investigating of my own."

She watched Frank head toward the elevator, confident that her colleague had a good chance at learning who or what was behind John's deception. She checked her watch. It was nearly midnight, and by now John would surely be asleep at his cabin. For a moment she envied him, but felt comforted that soon, all the turmoil of the last few days would be behind her and she'd feel as if she were on vacation every day.

Kathryne slipped the key-card into the slide mounted on her door and stepped inside, still troubled that there had to be something serious going on, or John would never have lied. She hesitated for a moment, checking her watch again. Her shoulders sagged. It was just too late to call John and tell him about Vicky Lewis and the shredded money order. Reluctantly, she decided it should wait until morning.

Glancing over at the bedside table, a little red light blinked impatiently on her phone. Hoping for a message from John she hurried over and asked the operator to retrieve her call.

"Kate? It's Dad. I'm being released tomorrow, and I'd sure like it if you come get me. Call me when you get back."

CHAPTER FIFTEEN

Early the next morning, Kathryne tried to call John while she got dressed, but there wasn't any answer, so she quickly called the lodge. "Norman? Hi, it's Kate. Is John around?"

She tugged on a pair of jeans, holding the phone in the crook of her neck while Norman went to look for John. A moment later, Norman's voice caused her to sink down on the bed. "Well, thanks for trying. How long do you think he'll be gone? All right. Would you ask him to call me the moment he's back? Great, and by the way, did Dad call? Good. Yes, it will be nice to have him home. See you soon."

The short drive to the hospital didn't give Kathryne any time to mentally go over the conversation she planned to have with John, and the one she planned to have with her father. Why did the men in her life feel they couldn't share their troubles with her? Did they think she was too weak? "Good grief," she muttered. "I hope there's a better explanation than that."

She turned into the hospital's parking lot, then drove the SUV closer to the appropriate door and went inside. She smiled the next moment when she heard her father's voice asking the nurse to leave him alone, saying he could put on his own pants.

"Are you being stubborn?" Kathryne asked as she stepped into his room.

"Yes," the nurse answered before Hank could say a word. "I've been trying to tell him they won't fit over his cast, but he won't let me cut them."

Kathryn took the scissors, and then held out her hand. "Give me your pants, Dad."

"Darn it, Kate. I just bought these. Maybe we could have Norman bring an old pair from the lodge."

"We can do that, if you'd like, but it'll take a couple of hours."

Her father frowned. "I've had about as much of this place as I can stand. Especially the food." He gave her his new jeans. "Go ahead, but try and cut along the seam so I can mend them."

She laughed. "Since when have you become so frugal?"

"Never you mind. It's not the money. It's the fact that they're real comfortable, and since I wear a popular size, the store's always out of them."

A little while later, with his daughter's help, Hank was dressed and sat in a wheelchair. "What do you mean, you're going to hire a nurse? What kind of nonsense is that? I've got Norman, for God's sake, and he's better than two women put together."

Kathryne laughed. "I'm sure, but even Norman needs a day off now and then."

"That's true, but then I was hoping you'd cancel your hotel and move in until you're ready to move over to John's cabin."

"That would be nice, but Frank and I have to leave for Albuquerque the day after tomorrow or we'll miss our flight." Kathryne wheeled her father down the hall, and with the help of a big, burly male nurse, got him easily into the back seat of the car, his broken leg propped up on a pile of pillows. "I borrowed those from the hotel," she said with a sly grin.

"Borrowed or pilfered?" Hank countered with an even slyer grin.

"Borrowed. I'll return them later tonight when I get back . . . after dark, so no one will notice."

It wasn't long before they were on the road to the lodge. "I had a very strange meeting with Doug's secretary last night." Aware that she'd piqued her father's interest, she relayed everything she'd learned, ending by telling him that Frank planned to meet with a man named Ben Griego of Enchantment Development, who might know something about Doug's attempt to swindle John out of his land.

"Doug isn't smart enough to do something like that. You've got proof of that with your shredded money order. Any fool would have burned it."

"Dad," Kathryne scolded. "That's no way for a retired trial lawyer to talk."

He gave a good-humored laugh. "I was just trying to get your goat," he mused, looking out the backseat window and growing more serious. "I knew John was lying the whole time."

"So did I, but he's a stubborn man and even though I tried, I couldn't get him to talk to me about it." She gave a heavy sigh. "It seems I have that problem with all the men I care about."

"What are you talking about?" her father asked with a concern frown. "We're getting along just fine."

"Are we? I'm not so sure. Frank told me you called him and that you heard someone threaten John." She gave him a brief, stern look in the rearview. "Didn't you think I'd be interested in that little bit of information?"

"Well, yes, but I guess I just wasn't thinking." He leaned forward and patted her shoulder. "I'm sorry, Kate. I'll try to be more considerate in the future."

Stunned that her father had given in so easily, Kathryne was momentarily at a loss for words. "There's something else that really bothers me," she said, waiting for her father to coax her on.

As if on cue, he asked, "What?"

"John and I were becoming very good friends. We could talk about almost anything, and then just like that," she snapped her fingers, glancing at her father in the rearview mirror, "he stopped talking to me. In fact, he avoided me."

Had she not been driving, she would have seen the worry in her father's brown eyes. "Don't be too hard on him, hon. Sometimes a man does silly things when he's backed up against a wall."

"Is he backed up against a wall, Dad? Is that why he lied? Is there something else you're not telling me?"

"Listen to me, Kate, but don't go getting upset."

"I won't," she said, thankful her voice didn't expose the spark of fear his tone ignited.

"I think my accident wasn't an accident, and that's why that man called John."

"My God," she gasped, stepping on the brake.

"What the hell are you doing?" her father asked, hanging on to the back of the seat when she came to a screeching halt.

"I'm going back to town. I'm taking you to the sheriff's office so you can tell them what you just told me."

"Kathryne, stop. Take a breath and think about it." He raked his fingers through his hair. "Geez, had I known you were going to blow things out of proportion, I'd have never told you."

Her mouth dropped open for a moment. "Are you kidding me? You just said your accident wasn't an accident, and in my books that means someone was trying to kill you. You don't think that warrants police involvement?"

"Yes, but not just yet. And I don't think they wanted to kill me, Kate. I think whoever did this wanted to scare John, and by all I've seen and heard, it worked." He put his hand on her shoulder and gave it a little squeeze. "For now, you've got to keep this to yourself. If it leaks out, we could all be in danger."

Her father grew quiet, but now his silence troubled her. "Are you all right, Dad?"

"Your story got me to thinking, that's all."

"About what?"

"That's what's bothering me," he said with a bewildered

smile. "I'm not really sure—just a hunch." He squinted against the bright sun as it poured in through the window. "Mind if I roll this down?" he asked. "I need some fresh air."

"No, not at all. I'll shut off the air conditioner and roll mine down too."

Hank made small talk on the trip home, but it didn't alleviate her tension. She tried to think where it had all gone wrong between herself and John, aware that she was as responsible for their strained relationship as he was. She shouldn't have over-reacted. And he shouldn't have lied.

No matter what troubled him, both of them were equally at fault, but that didn't help matters. She needed to talk with him. Not just about Vicky and the evidence, but about other things too. Like why he lied, and if he did so, as her father said, because his back was against a wall, why he didn't share it with her. Maybe, just maybe, she could have helped.

She was still deeply in thought when they turned on the drive leading to the lodge.

"Well, here we are," Hank announced. "Park up there by the front door." Norman came out the next instant and together they got her father safely into the lodge and into his private quarters, where a wheelchair waited.

"I rented this the moment I found out you broke your leg," Norman said with a satisfied smile. "You're not the kind of man to stay in bed for long, Hank."

Hank smiled, trying out the chair. "This is great. See, Kate. I told you there's no need to worry about a nurse." Hank glanced at Norman. "I think Kate could use a cup of your special chocolate. Right, Kate?"

Kathryne blinked, aware that her father used the chocolate to get rid of her. "I suppose so." She shrugged, then motioned to Norman. "Take me to your kitchen."

The moment she left his room, Hank wheeled himself over

the bedside table where his cell phone nestled in the charger. He grabbed it and scrolled to *received calls,* disappointed to see an *unavailable call* on the day of his accident. "Damn," he muttered, setting it back in the charger.

He reached for his other phone, picking up the receiver and dialing a number. "Yes, I'm a customer of yours, and I was wondering something. Is there a way to find a number even if it's marked unavailable?"

John tied his horse to a nearby tree, removing his Stetson. He took a handkerchief from his back pocket and wiped the sweat from his forehead. It was nearly noon, and already the day felt unusually hot. He checked his watch, but at the same time he heard a rustling close by. A moment later, a man rode up on a buckskin gelding.

"Hey, John. Sorry, I'm late." The man glanced around. "You're right. No one can find us here, that's for sure."

"That's the plan," John said, taking hold of the horse's reins while his friend Jarrell dismounted. "Were you able to find out who's trying to kill my friends?"

Jarrell shook his head. "Nope, but I found something that's almost as good." Jarrell held up a small plastic bag containing a small piece of white paper. "After I towed Hank's truck to the yard, I quickly found that the brake fluid had been drained." Jarrell gave John a big smile, showing his white teeth, made even whiter by the deep rich color of his Native American skin. "I found this."

John held out his hand.

"Hey, bro, not so fast. I've got more to tell you."

"What is it?" John asked, growing a little impatient.

"It's a near-perfect print of a man's index finger."

John nodded in approval. "How'd you manage it?" he asked with a skeptical grin.

"Hey, Johnny. You're not the only brother who has friends. Remember Chino's boy, Joey?"

"Yeah. How's he doing? I haven't seen him in ages."

"Well, there's a reason for it. He's all grown up. He's been in Santa Fe at the New Mexico State Police Academy, but that's not the best part."

John gave his friend a sideways glance. "Must I ask?"

Jarrell laughed. "Joey just graduated, and he's been assigned to the crime lab. He told me how to lift a print." Jarrell wiggled the sack then dropped it into John's hand. "Now all we have to do is take that to Joey . . . correction . . . Officer Crow, and he'll tell us who it belongs to. If the guy's been tagged before, you'll soon have your man."

"I can't believe it," Norman cried, hugging Kathryne and then John and then Frank Edwards in the main room of the Silver Creek Lodge. When he went to hug Hank, he held up his hand, thwarting the emotional assault. "I can't believe someone would try and hurt us. We'd never hurt a fly, would we, John?"

"Nope," John said with a kind smile. "Well, maybe I would, but you wouldn't."

Norman laughed, but it was clear he was still upset that someone had tried to harm Hank. "It's a miracle, Hank, a miracle. I tell you that it's all going to be over soon." Norman clasped his hands together in happiness. "Let's celebrate. I'll make us a special dinner with all the trimmings. And I've got a special bottle of wine I've been saving for just such an occasion."

Frank gave a half smile. "I'd like to stay, Norm, but I think I'd better get that print to Santa Fe for identification. After my meeting with Ben Griego, I wouldn't be surprised if it didn't belong to one of his sons."

Kathryne handed Frank the keys to her rental. "You've got

the map John gave you?" she asked as she and John walked him toward the door.

"Yes, and I've got my cell if I get confused."

"Yeah, right. A man asking for driving instruction," she said sarcastically.

John grinned. "The police academy is right off the highway. You can't miss it. It's got lots of police cars parked around it. And if you do manage to get lost, just speed a little and they'll find you."

Laughing, Frank shook his head. "Thanks for the advice, but I'm certain I'll be able to find it." He took Kathryne's hand. "You two stay safe."

Kathryne reached up and placed a chaste kiss on Frank's cheek. "We will, and you drive safely too. We'll be waiting for your call."

John slipped his arm around Kathryne, and together they walked out onto the huge porch to wave goodbye to Frank. "Pray we get some answers," Kathryne murmured as the tail-lights of the SUV disappeared down the winding drive.

John turned Kathryne, holding her just close enough to rest his hands on her hips. "Well, I guess I owe you . . . big time." He lifted her hand and placed a kiss on the back. "You know, in my culture, if someone saves your life, your life is theirs to do with as they wish."

"I didn't exactly save your life," she confessed. "Your friend Chino helped, and you saved my dad's life, so—"

John's smile widened as he placed his fingers over her mouth to stop her. "Maybe, but your dad's not Navajo, so he doesn't have my beliefs, and Chino's not as cute as you, so you're getting the prize."

"Prize?" she repeated. "I like the sound of that. Tell me. What kind of prize?"

His gaze was intense, filling her with anticipation, making her feel all warm and tingly inside.

"A wish. Anything your heart desires."

"Anything?" she asked with a cunning smile.

He nodded, never looking away, and, she could tell he tried very hard not to spoil the moment by laughing. "Anything, but there's a catch."

Kathryne feigned disappointment. "I knew it. There's always something in the fine print." She heaved an exaggerated sigh. "All right, what's the catch?"

"You only get *one* wish." He moved a little closer and kissed the tip of her nose. "Well, do you have something in mind?"

Kathryne gave a little shrug, hoping he couldn't see behind her bogus look of innocence. "Oh, give me a little time. Maybe I'll think of something."

Frank called before ten the next morning. Kathryne took the call and listened intently, aware that she'd have to tell John, Norman, and her father every little detail. "This is great news," she said. "I'm sure they'll be surprised, but that's because they underestimated our determination to learn the truth." She smiled at Norman, who looked as if he were about to have a stroke, said her goodbyes, and hung up the phone.

"Well?" Norman asked anxiously.

Kathryne smiled at Norman, then turned to John. "They got a match, and it's just as Frank suspected. Jerry Griego. Ben Griego's oldest son."

Norman sank down into the nearest chair in utter relief. "Thank God," he murmured. The next instant he bounded up. "I've got to go tell Hank. He'll be so happy."

Kathryne watched as Norman hurried out of the room. "Well, it looks like you've got your ranch back, Mr. Hawkins."

"Yes it does, but that's not the best part," he said pulling her into his arms. "The best part is that we're going to be neighbors." He gave her a tight hug before holding her at arm's length. "What happens now?"

"Well, since the conspiracy is exposed, the judge's decision will be overturned."

"What about your ex?"

Kathryne shrugged. "I don't know. Doug could end up doing some time if he's implicated."

John's features suddenly went from concerned to exuberant. "I've got a great idea."

Kathryne gave him a skeptical glance. "I can't stay and let someone else close my cases and pack, John. No matter how badly I want to stay."

"I wouldn't dream of getting in your way," he said cheerfully. "Take all the time you need. When you're ready, I'll come to Baltimore with Red and my flatbed. We'll load up your things, and you can see a little of the countryside on the way back."

Kathryne thought about it for several moments, and then nodded. "As crazy as it sounds, it also sounds great. I don't think I've ever driven across America in my entire life. Even when I was a child I flew from Maryland to New Mexico with my parents. A moving company brought our things."

"Well, then, neighbor, it's high time you did."

Frank finished packing, glad that Norman had talked him into spending his last night enjoying the benefits of the Silver Creek Lodge, including a refreshing swim, a relaxing massage and a fabulous dinner of roasted duck with orange sauce. He'd slept soundly, taken a long, hot shower and was now looking forward to breakfast. Norman had promised a surprise.

"Let me get this straight," Frank began, snapping his suitcase shut after he let Kathryne into his suite. "We . . . you and I, are going to ride in a big rig with John into town because the rental has a flat tire? Why don't we just change it?"

"John would have done that, but the spare is missing. I guess I forgot to check before we left Albuquerque."

Frank tugged on his ear absently. "It's a crazy plan, and I'm not sure why we're taking a big rig when we could just take his pickup, but if you're cool with it, I guess I am too. When do we leave?"

"John has to finish getting the SUV on the flatbed, but it shouldn't take too long. I'd say we'll be leaving within the hour."

"Great. I'll wait downstairs. Norman said something about baking something for breakfast. I'm dying to know what he's made. The man's quite a chef. Shall I save some for you?"

Smiling at Frank's eager expression, Kathryne declined. "Thanks, but no thanks. I've got to finish packing." She went into her own room and placed her new boots in the box and then piled it on top of her largest suitcase. A little while later, she went outside just as John finished securing the SUV on the flatbed.

"Are you ready?" he asked, motioning toward Red. "It's getting late, and we still have to fix the flat."

"I'm ready, but I'd better go get Frank. Norman's been feeding him his special cinnamon rolls."

A few minutes later, Kathryne emerged with her arm looped through Frank's. "You're really going to enjoy the trip. Isn't he, John?"

"I think so," John added opening the door to the tractor. "Climb on in."

Frank smiled like a little boy getting his first pony ride, then grabbed the handrail and pulled himself up.

"My gosh," he murmured. "It's huge. Look at that! There's cupboards and a clothes closet."

"Yes, there is," Kathryne said. "And, there's a little refrigerator, satellite radio . . . a television . . . and a bed . . ."

"A bed?" Frank repeated, looking down at her from his perch

on the passenger seat.

Kathryne nodded and held up two fingers. "Two of them."

Frank's snoring nearly drowned out the country-western music on the radio. After John had stowed their luggage in the second, smaller bunk that hung over the bed, Frank had asked John question after question about truck driving, and John had patiently explained everything in detail.

Frank decided to recline on the bed only after they'd reached the main road, commenting on how comfortable it was. Five minutes later, he fell asleep.

"Are you angry with me for not checking to see if there was a spare?" Kathryne asked, reaching across to put her hand on John's shoulder. The moment he turned and grinned, she had her answer.

"I could never get angry at you," he said nonchalantly. "I've got to get fuel and have the oil changed in town. Besides, if I didn't honor my duty to you, I would dishonor my ancestors. My grandfather was a proud man and a respected chief. He'd find a way to get revenge."

Kathryne laughed at John's expression. "If you're thinking that this is my one and only wish, think again. This is just a little favor."

John grinned. "My grandfather wouldn't have let me narrow it down to just one, so you'll still get your wish."

"I saw his picture on your dresser." Kathryne tucked a strand of hair behind her ear. "He looked like a sweet old man."

John feigned a shudder. "Hey, looks can be deceiving. You never met my grandfather. He used to scare me when I was a child. He had things like rattlesnake rattles and crows' feathers and bears' teeth that he kept in a little sack. He told me they were good-magic and gave him great power. Later I learned from my mother how he came by his *power*, and it wasn't as nearly as exciting as my grandfather led me to believe."

"Grandparents are allowed to stretch the truth, John."

"He did that and more." John shook his head and grinned. "Mother said he found the crow's feathers after one landed on a power pole and got zapped. On a trip out to Window Rock they stopped at a curio shop on old route 66 and he bought the rattlesnake tail, and the bear's teeth were really from a goat he'd slaughtered."

"Are you serious?" she asked, finding it all amusing.

"Very serious. But let me tell you, to a seven-year-old boy, they looked enough like the real thing to make me believe my grandfather was magical."

"How old were you when you learned the truth?"

John grew quiet and the humor left his features. "It was after his funeral. Mom and I were sitting in his old mobile home, talking about old times and collecting his things, when the subject came up. I was nineteen and about to begin my second tour in Vietnam. I wanted to see him—to say goodbye, but I didn't make it back in time."

"I'm sure he would have understood."

John's smile didn't quite hide the pain flickering in the depths of his blue eyes. "I've always hoped so."

"Well," Frank began, shaking John's hand. "It was a pleasure meeting you, John, and as far as the ride . . . it was great. I slept like a baby. If ever I give up practicing law, I'm going to go buy a big truck and tour America."

"Let me know when you're ready and I'll teach you how to drive." John put his arm around Kathryne. "Or maybe if you ask real nice, Kate will teach you."

Frank turned to Kathryne. "You know how to drive that thing?"

She felt her cheeks warm with a blush. "John taught me. I

have to tell you Frank, it's a rush."

Frank laughed at her expression. "Lawyer, truck driver, what's next?"

"Try country homeowner," Kathryne said proudly. "I'm selling the firm to move out here permanently. Dad and I are going to be business partners again." She cast him a sideways glance. "You wouldn't be interested in buying in, would you?"

Frank laughed. "I'm not, but I might know someone who would. I'll call them as soon as we get back." He checked his watch. "Well, I'll go check on the tire repair while you two say your goodbyes."

John took hold of Kathryne's hand. "I'm going to miss you."

She gazed into his eyes, smiling. "You like to dance, right?"

"Absolutely," he said, his eyes twinkling, "especially in the afternoons."

Her lips quivered, but she didn't dare laugh at his devilish expression. She wasn't at all sure that when she disclosed the rest of her plan, he'd comply. "You said that you still owed me a favor, a special wish, right?"

"That's right."

"Then if I wished you'd take me to a dance, you'd do it with no questions asked?"

"No questions asked."

"Even if it meant you might have to take a little trip to get to this dance?"

His dark brows came together, but the devil still danced in his eyes as he placed his hand over his heart, looking every bit the Navajo Chieftain by the way he lifted his chin. "I meant what I said. I will do my duty and take you to this dance."

"Oh, I'm so glad," she cried, wrapping her arms around his neck and kissing his cheek. "It's in three weeks, and when you bring Red out to Baltimore to pick up all my stuff, we'll get you fitted for a tux."

He placed his fingers over her mouth, his gaze much more intense. "Baltimore? The dance is in Baltimore?"

She nodded. "The Summer Ball. It's an annual affair put on by my corporation and everybody I know—my best friend Liz— she'll be there with her husband, and my mother, and all my aunts and uncles will be there. Everyone I know will be there with their dates, even determinedly single Helen, my devoted secretary. You'll get to meet the whole family, and before you refuse, there's no way I *can't* attend. I have to attend—this one last time."

John's brows snapped together, causing her to chatter on.

"I just thought we might kill two birds with one stone." She shrugged and gave a weak smile. "Doesn't that sound like fun?"

"Which part?" John asked dryly. "You were saying a lot all at once."

"Why, all of it, especially the part where we make the trip back to New Mexico together." She smiled nervously when John looked like he might protest, "We'll be even." She paused, frowning before her features brightened. "No, wait . . . I'll owe you one . . . a big one."

CHAPTER SIXTEEN

The Summer Ball extravaganza was definitely one of the most prestigious events of the year. As soon as Kathryne arrived back at work, she'd called her mother again, hoping that there was some slim chance she'd be able to get out of hosting the ball. But it was useless. She'd tried twice, and each time her mother and stepfather gave her the many reasons she needed to be there, and if their guilt trip wasn't enough, the moment she returned to work, Helen had reminded her about the annual bonuses.

Her fate was sealed. As owner and senior partner in the firm, it was her privilege to give out the bonuses and the various awards earned by the staff and junior partners. Only Christmas was looked forward to more, and then only because of the parties and the additional paid week off that didn't count against the days they saved for their usual vacations. Before he left, her father had made it a policy—insisting that happy employees stayed, and it was a policy she'd strictly enforced, even when Doug had wanted to abolish it.

Her thoughts of Douglas reluctantly dragged her back to the dreaded ball. She hadn't heard a word from him since he'd lost the lawsuit. However, she had no doubt he'd be bitter about it and bitter that she wouldn't renew his lease.

The only good thing about hosting the ball this year was the fact that Doug wasn't invited. Since the divorce, he was no longer a partner or an employee. She wouldn't have to worry about him causing a scene by bringing a mere child as his date. Vicky had quit USIB and taken back her old job in records.

And even though Kathryne hated to admit it, she'd feel less stressed about having John as her date if Douglas wasn't around.

Kathryne took a sip of coffee and let her gaze and thoughts wander back to John and their week alone at the ranch. She smiled at her memory of the night the fluke storm blew in. When she'd panicked about the damage the next morning, John came to her rescue, hammer in hand, stating that there was no need to worry, he'd have things patched up by nightfall.

And he did. And later that night, they'd shared a quiet evening together, designing a new gazebo and hot tub area she wanted to build in the back yard. Although John wasn't a college graduate, nor a law school graduate, he had qualities Doug could never hope to have. Qualities like honesty and loyalty and compassion—and he was darned good with repairs.

Usually, thoughts of John made her feel better, but not tonight. Nothing could chase away her feelings of gloom over the impending ball. Reluctantly, she went inside, not really looking forward to eating another meal alone. She glanced at the clock. It was only six p.m. back in New Mexico. She picked up her phone and dialed John's number.

"Hey," she began. "What have you been doing? Yes, I miss you too. No, no cases this week, in fact I've got all my loose ends tied up. It feels good, and on the other hand, it's a little scary too. Law is all I know." She smiled, listening as he told her she knew how to drive a big truck and could always get a job cleaning stalls.

"Why, thank you," she said, "for the compliments." She sank down on the sofa. "I spoke with Frank today, and I wanted to let you know that there wasn't enough evidence to implicate Doug. Well, he's exonerated for several reasons. First, under oath, he stated that he refused to listen to Ben Griego's suggestions on how they might deal with you, and second, because he had no prior knowledge that the Griego family had applied unwarranted pressure to several other families in an attempt to acquire land."

She smiled. "You'd forgive the Grim Reaper. Hey, do you own a tux?" she asked, realizing that he probably didn't. "Don't worry about it. I'll arrange to have one here waiting for you. What do you mean you can't stay here? Why not? Can't you leave the truck at the truck stop? I'll send a car for you."

She heaved an impatient sigh. "John, why do you want to stay in a hotel? No one will care if you stay with me." She gave a little, almost desperate laugh. "My mother? This is about my mother? I'm a big girl. She won't care."

But all the reasoning in the world didn't change his mind. He was set against staying in her home, preferring to stay at a hotel until they were on their way to New Mexico. "All right," she finally agreed. "I'll make the arrangements and call you tomorrow. Yes, I'm looking forward to seeing you too. Good night."

Kathryne looked at the phone still resting in her lap. "Yes, I'm looking forward to seeing you too," she repeated in a witchlike voice, thoroughly disgusted with herself. The longer she was away from John, the more she missed him, but she was scared to death to think it was love.

They'd only known each other for a little over a month. It couldn't be love. Hadn't some of her friends warned her to be careful? Especially when on the rebound.

"Damn," she muttered angrily. "I should have just blurted it out. John Wayne Hawkins, I love you. That's what I should have had the guts to say . . . not murmur a weak *goodnight.*" She thought about hitting the redial button, but then decided against it.

She dropped the receiver into the cradle and then stared at it for several more frustrating minutes. "If you'd just tell me how you feel, John, I'd tell you how I feel."

It dawned on her a second later. Maybe that's what he wanted. Maybe he was afraid of getting hurt, too? She snatched up the receiver and punched the button. A moment later she got a busy signal.

Determined, she waited ten minutes then tried again, delighted when he answered. "John?" she said a little breathlessly. "I just wanted you to know something." She took a calming breath unaware that she'd paused so long, he asked if she was still there. "Yes, I'm here."

Kathryne closed her eyes and silently prayed for the courage to speak her mind. "John Hawkins, I've only ever said this to one other man in my entire life, and we both know that I've come to regret it. So don't make me regret what I'm about to say. I-I think I love you, John . . . and if you ever make me regret it, I'll . . . I'll . . . well, just don't, all right? Just don't."

Before she realized what she'd done, she slammed down the receiver.

John's dark brows snapped together as he stared at the phone for several moments before he placed it in the cradle. But his frown didn't stay for long. Slowly a smile spread across his face as he tried to recall each and every word.

"Who was that?" Norman asked, taking another sip of his hot tea.

Overjoyed, John did the first thing that came to mind. He grabbed Norman and physically lifted him out of the chair and gave him a big bear hug. The look on his friend's face only added to his happiness. "It was Kathryne."

"B-but she just called," Norman interjected, looking a little uncomfortable. "John, you can put me down now."

"Oh, sorry, Norm." John tried to help Norman straighten his shirt, but Norman slapped at his hands.

"What in the world has come over you, John? I don't think I've ever seen you like this. What could Kathryne have possibly said that—"

"She loves me."

Norman took a step back when John took one forward.

"Did you hear me, Norm? She loves me. She just said so."

Norman looked bewildered. "That's great, John. Absolutely great, but I already knew that. Didn't you?"

John stared at his friend. "You knew?"

Norman smiled and nodded. "Of course. My God, John, the woman couldn't keep her eyes off you. Every time I saw the two of you together, it was as plain as day."

Norman sat back down and took another sip of tea. "I'm surprised you never noticed."

John's good mood faded just a little. "Why didn't you say something about it?"

Norman looked horror-struck. "I'd never do that—I'd never interfere in your private life. You know that."

John felt totally confused. "I had no idea."

"Really?" Norman asked, turning his attention back to his tea. "Well, I think we're missing one important point here, don't you?"

"For God's sake, Norman, will you just use plain English and say what you mean?" John began to pace, something he didn't usually do, but for some reason, tonight it made him feel a little better. "Sometimes you're so damned frustrating."

"That doesn't change the fact that a beautiful woman called you, long distance, all the way from Maryland to open her heart to you, and you never opened your mouth." Norman gave a superior sniff. "Of course, you're going to see her in a week, so I guess you could tell her how you feel then."

It dawned on John that what Norman had said was true, and now instead of dialing her right back, he'd spent the last five minutes arguing with Norman, who had known about her feelings all along.

"Crap," John grumbled, reaching for the phone. He dialed Kathryne's number at the same time he headed for his room.

"Where are you going?" Norman protested.

"This is private," John said a moment before he closed the door.

"But John, aren't we in this together?"

"Nope." The phone began to ring and the instant Kathryne answered, all thoughts of Norman vanished from John's mind.

Kathryne anxiously awaited John's arrival, checking her reflection one more time. The strapless rose-chiffon fit her well. The Grecian bodice flattered her figure, and the tanning salon had done a great job of hiding her farmer's tan. Tight-fitting to just above her hips, the long skirt flared out in soft, gentle folds.

A sweep of delicate chiffon flowers, a deeper color than the gown, started at the top of her left breast and cascaded downward, across her ribs, ending with a swash of chiffon that flowed down her right hip.

Her hair was a mass of soft curls, piled loosely on the top of her head. She smiled, pleased with the style. Doug had always been too short for her to dream of wearing her hair in such a manner.

But then there was nothing about Doug that compared to John. John was tall, considerate and in his own gentle way, stronger than any man she'd ever known. She had just put on a delicate starburst necklace of pearls and diamonds that matched her earrings when the doorbell rang. Peeking through the little security scope in the door, she pressed the intercom. "Yes, Bill?"

"I've a delivery for you, Ms. Sheldon. I believe it's a corsage for your ball."

Kathryne hurried over to her purse, pulled out a ten-dollar

bill, and then opened the door. "My gosh," she said, gazing at the beautiful white flowers through the frosty plastic container. She took the package and pressed the bill into the young man's hand.

"I can't accept this, Ms. Sheldon. The man, who gave me those, has already given me a very generous tip."

"He has?" She smiled. John was also a very generous man. She held out the ten-dollar bill. "I'm sure he won't mind if you get two."

The young man's smile was worth it. "Gee, thanks." He turned to leave, and then stopped. "Oh, the man . . . Mr. John, he's downstairs waiting for you and," the boy gave her a knowing nod. "He a nice looking man, but he's not from around here is he?"

"No, Bill, he's from New Mexico."

"I thought he was from the west." Bill gave a knowing nod.

"Really?" she asked, aware that Bill was waiting to tell her his opinion. "How could you tell?"

"He's wearing the best-looking tux I've ever seen, a huge silver belt buckle, a silver broach-thing at his neck, and black cowboy boots."

The ballroom at the hotel was ablaze with rich summer colors. Round tables, covered with crisp white cloths and bright red napkins dotted the majority of the hall. Centerpieces of yellow, white, red and purple flowers added a vivid splash of color, reflecting on the pure white china and sparkling crystal. The orchestra had been placed to the rear of a huge, raised dance floor above which hung a large sparkling, crystal ball.

Banners of bright green leaves and clusters of colorful flowers were strewn around the walls and on the long table where the board of directors and senior partners would make their speeches and pass out the awards and bonuses.

John and Kathryne had arrived early to make sure there weren't any last minute disasters, but everything looked beautiful and appeared to be under control. In thirty minutes the first of the guests would arrive, her mother and stepfather, her friends; everyone whom she cared about—except Hank. It would be difficult to say goodbye, but she couldn't dwell on what she was leaving, preferring to look ahead to her new home and her new relationship with her father.

She had just finished speaking to the person in charge of the dinner placements when she felt John's gentle grasp on her arm. When she turned he frowned. "Are you doing all right?" he asked, his dark brows drawn together.

"Yes, why?"

"You look kind of pale. Can I get you something to drink?"

She gave him her best smile, ignoring her nervous stomach. "No, I'm fine. Really."

"Did you eat anything today?" he asked, apparently still not convinced that she was well.

"Breakfast." She would have turned to rearrange her files containing the awards, but he stopped her.

"What time?"

"Seven, I think."

"That was twelve hours ago." He shook his head. "Kate, let me go get you a candy bar. What would it hurt?"

She laughed at his exasperated expression. "My waist line, that's what. Now stop worrying. Dinner will be served promptly at eight."

"Well, if you're certain." He strolled to the closest table, looking down at the beautiful place setting. "I was hoping you could help me out a little."

She couldn't prevent the smile that teased her lips when she noticed his slight blush.

"Anything. Just tell me what it is." She slipped her arm

through his, watching as he pointed at the arrangement of silverware.

"Which ones do I use, and for what?"

Kathryne had just finished with John's quick course in etiquette when she saw Ron standing in the far corner looking rather lost. "John, come with me, I'd like you to meet Ron. He's such a nice young man." She took a step then hesitated. "Oh my gosh, look who just arrived . . . without a date."

John looked over at the entrance instantly recognizing the young woman he'd helped on the steps of the courthouse, just as Kathryne waved. "Vicky, over here."

"Are you match-making?"

Kathryne smiled. "Of course. Now hurry."

A little while later, Kathryne led John toward an older couple. "Mom, this is John Hawkins, my friend from New Mexico." Kathryne felt as if she were sixteen, introducing her prom date. "John, this is Louise, my mother and her husband George, my stepfather."

"I'm pleased to meet you both," John replied, shaking Louise's hand gently and then Richard's a little more vigorously. "Kate has told me a lot about you."

"So you're the man who's stolen our daughter away from us," Louise replied with a slight smile. Kathryne froze, holding her breath for a second. John didn't know it, but he was being tested.

"Knowing your daughter the short time I have, I doubt that anyone could make her do anything she didn't want to do." John matched her mother's stare. "She's a very special lady."

"Indeed," Louise replied, a smile softening her features. He'd passed the first round. Kathryne put her hand over her stomach and then nearly sighed in relief, thinking she should have brought some antacids.

"John taught me to drive an eighteen wheeler," Kathryne said to George.

Louise's grey brows shot up. "Did you?"

"Yes. She picked it up quickly."

"She didn't run over anything, did she?" Louise asked. "She could never back out of our driveway without running over a shrub or two."

"No, ma'am. She managed to keep the dirty side down."

George leaned a little closer to his wife. "He means she kept the undercarriage down—that she didn't roll it, my love."

Louise glanced at George for a split second then gave a stiff laugh. "Good, I'd hate to think of the money you'd have to invest in new shrubs if more than one wheel ran over them."

"So, Kate," came Douglas's voice. "Did John give you a CB handle too?"

Kathryne spun. Doug stood there, looking as handsome as ever in his black tux with a petite redhead on his arm. It took Kathryne only a moment to remember the woman as the younger sister of one of the senior partners. Her hopes of getting through the evening unscathed vanished. "Ah, yes, he did, but that's not important now." She held out her hand. "Aren't you Elizabeth Roberts? I thought so. Welcome."

Kathryne felt proud of the way John handled himself. Not a soul would have guessed he wasn't born into a family that had five course dinners and used more than two forks. He was polite, gracious when spoken to, and funny on several occasions.

He sat quietly when she gave her speech and handed her the appropriate award at the appropriate time. She didn't know what she'd have done without him. His strength gave her strength, and even though at first she'd felt a little nervous, she began to relax and started to enjoy herself.

By the time she finished with the last of the bonuses, it was time for the orchestra to take up their instruments and begin the first waltz of the evening—the one she and Douglas usually shared to encourage all the other guests to begin dancing. Her stepfather rose and led her mother out onto the floor.

"Kate," John said, drawing her attention. He stood next to her chair, waiting for her to accept his unspoken invitation to dance. Then she saw Douglas stand, and much to her dismay, he walked directly toward her, leaving his date alone at their table.

She rose on trembling legs, slipping her cold hand into John's warm one.

"Ah, excuse me, cowboy," Doug replied with a sarcastic smile. "Or is that an incorrect idiom? You're only half *cowboy*. The other half is Indian, isn't it?" He didn't give John time to respond, and those closest were beginning to grow uncomfortable, especially Kathryne. A little muscle tightened above the firm set of John's jaw at the same time her heart jumped into her throat.

Doug shook his head. "Wow, it must be tough . . . you know . . . the identity thing."

"It's not," John said smoothly, unaware that the music had stopped and a small crowd had gathered. "It's easy. Just like it's easy to tell a jackass from a gentleman."

Doug's face went beet red as he pursed his lips and straightened his black bow tie. In the next instant, he took a swing at John. The crowd gasped, and Kathryne stopped breathing. Doug's sucker-punch missed, but he quickly recovered his balance and swung again. John easily blocked Doug's swing, planting one of his fists square in the middle of Doug's face. Doug's head snapped back, and he would have tumbled to the floor if Frank Edwards hadn't caught him and eased him over to a chair.

"Son of a bitch," Doug muttered as he held a thick napkin to his bleeding nose. "You're gonna be thorry you laid a hand on me."

"You all right, John?" Frank asked, but Kathryne could hardly make out what he said. The room began to spin. She met John's gaze a second before it started to get dark. The last thing she knew she was being lifted, floating and smelling John's spicy cologne.

John reluctantly released his hold on Kathryne the moment the paramedics arrived. They placed her on the gurney, and John was forced to step back when Louise and Richard crowded around their unconscious daughter. Liz was there, and Helen, and only when John felt strong fingers close around his upper arm, did he turn away.

"She's in good hands," Frank said softly as the paramedics lifted her into the ambulance. "Come on, there's nothing you can do, and I doubt anyone would let you anyway. Let's go get a drink."

"Thath's the man," Douglas said, still holding a bloody napkin to his nose. "He'th the one who athaulted me. Thumeone needth to call the copths." He sat on the curb, and let one of the paramedics examine his nose. "I think he broke a tooth."

"What happens now," John asked. "Should I wait for the police?"

"I think there are enough witnesses to justify what you did, John. It's a simple case of self-defense. There's no use waiting. Doug's harmless."

Numbly, John followed Frank out into the parking lot and over to a red Cadillac sedan. "That son of a bitch," John ground out as he slid into the car, watching when Douglas staggered up and pointed his direction.

Frank purposely turned up the radio as he backed out and

headed toward the road. "Yup, he's that for sure."

Kathryne sat up in her hospital room, disorientated at first. She placed her hand on her aching head and sagged back down, feeling sick to her stomach. The sun peeking in through the blinds told her she'd been there all night. She blinked several times, and then Dr. David Anderson strolled in with a smile. "What happened? Why am I here?"

"Well, hello there, sleeping beauty. I was wondering if you were going to wake up soon." The kindly grey-haired doctor glanced at his watch and at the same time gently picked up her wrist. "I've got other patients you know, Kate. An old man like me needs his sleep. You gave us all a scare last night."

His smile told her he was teasing, but she didn't feel like laughing. The last thing she remembered was being angry, and then frightened that someone was going to get hurt. Without warning, the room had grown overly warm and then everything started to tilt. She didn't remember anything after that, except that John caught her a second before everything went black.

"What time is it?" she asked.

"A little after six. I just got here, but the nurse said you slept soundly all night after I left." Dr. Anderson put her arm down, retrieved her chart, and then sat on the edge of the bed. "Well, young lady, your color is coming back, your blood pressure is a little high, but all in all you're as healthy as a horse."

She smiled then. "Thanks."

He seemed to look at her longer than normal, causing her to raise her eyebrows in question. "There's more?"

He nodded. "You're dehydrated, and if I didn't know better, you've lost weight since I last saw you."

"I needed to lose some weight . . . so I did."

"Did you take any pills, or worse"—he gave her a stern look—"did you starve yourself?"

"No, I worked it off." She held up her hands where small calluses had replaced the once healing blisters. "When you're busy, time goes by quickly and food isn't so important. Besides, your partner told me to. I had an appointment a couple of months ago, but you were out sick."

"Really, were you having a problem?"

She leaned back against the pillows. "Irregular periods, hot flashes, some anxiety attacks. I was told to take it easy, no spicy foods, and to lose some weight." She waved her hand over her flat tummy. "I did what I was told."

"Yes, I can see, and you look great. A little fatigued around the edges, but I guess that's to be expected. You're mother said you collapsed at the corporate dance."

"Yes, I suppose I did. It must have been the crab dip."

"Well, if it was, it only affected you. However, my dear, there's something I need to ask you."

"Ask away," she murmured, stifling a yawn.

"What did my associate prescribe? Your chart's at my office."

Kathryne filled him in, then agreed to let the nurse take a blood sample, with Dr. Anderson's promise that she could go home as soon as they got the results.

"What's it for?" she asked skeptically.

"Just want to check to see if you're anemic," he replied patting her hand. "There's a nice-looking man out in the waiting room. They tell me he's been there most of the night, and I believe them. He's wearing a very stylish tux. I'm assuming he's a friend of yours?"

Kathryne sat more upright. "Yes, he is," she said with a frown. "Is he all right?"

"He's not the one they brought in on a gurney," he replied with a knowledgeable grin. He stood and smiled down at her. "Now you rest, and I'll check in on you this evening."

"David," she protested over the clanking of breakfast trays in the hall. "I want to go home. I was hoping you'd release me."

Her old friend shrugged his shoulders. "What's your hurry? You've got nurses to see to your every need." A nurse came in with her covered tray and he stopped her and lifted the lid. He feigned a shiver then quickly replaced the cover. "And I hear the food's outstanding." His soft laughter could be heard as he stepped out into the sterile corridor. Then a moment later he peeked around the corner. "May I say hello to your Navajo friend?"

"How did you know?" she asked, looking around the nurse as she set down the breakfast tray.

"Not too many folks from Baltimore wear their hair in a long braid, or boots; but I think it was the cowboy hat that did it for me."

She laughed at Dr. Anderson's expression. "Yeah, me too. That and his sexy blue eyes."

"Blue eyes? Really? Well he's out there holding a small fortune in flowers. Is he a keeper?"

Kathryne shrugged her shoulders as she lifted the lid, grimacing at the stiff scrambled eggs and limp bacon. "If I manage to catch him, I might keep him."

"All right, what's his name?"

"John. His name is John, but don't send him in until I get a brush and a mirror."

A few moments later there was a soft knock on Kathryne's hospital room door, and then John came in, smiling when their gazes met.

"Hi." He walked over to her bed carrying a huge vase of flowers and then placed them on the little table by her bed. He took off his hat and set it on the guest chair in the corner. "I thought you might need something in here to cheer the place up. I don't know about you, but hospitals give me the willies."

"The willies?" she asked, taking his hand when he sat on the side of the bed. She leaned forward, accepting his kiss. Her gaze landed on John's hand. "Does your hand hurt?"

His grin was almost evil. "Nope, but I bet Doug's nose does."

Her smile faded. "Doug won't take this lying down—"

"He did last night," John teased.

"John," she scolded, trying hard not to laugh. "This is serious. Doug could drum up some false charges and cause trouble—"

John put two fingers over her mouth. "Frank's taking care of it. He got statements from several guests last night before we left. It's a clear case of self-defense, Kate. Doug took a swing at me first. It's not my fault he missed and then stumbled into my fist."

Kathryne laughed at his innocent expression, gently caressing his bruised knuckles. "Well, if you really want to know. I'm proud of the way you handled it."

He raised a dark brow. "You are? So let me get this straight. When you're proud, you faint?"

"Yes." She nodded at first, then quickly shook her head. "No, I don't usually faint. I think it was the crab dip. It tasted funny to me, but that's not what I meant. I meant I was really proud of you last night. You looked fabulous, and no one there would ever dream that this was your first ball. And I'm especially proud of the way you handled Douglas." She paused then added, "You're looking at me like you don't you believe me."

"Kate, you're an attorney. You know more fancy words than I could possibly look up in a thesaurus. I would have thought you'd want me to settle it with words, not actions."

She lifted his hand and placed a kiss on the bruised knuckle. "I think we all appreciated a little action . . . for a change."

CHAPTER SEVENTEEN

It was almost dark when John came to visit. Much to Kathryne's surprise, she'd slept most of the afternoon and felt well rested and anxious to be released. John sat on the side of the bed, tucking a tendril of hair behind her ear, taking a moment to caress her cheek. "When can we break you out of this joint?" he asked.

"Ah-hem," came a gruff voice. Dr. Anderson stood in the open doorway, smiling. "Am I interrupting?"

Kathryne looked past John and smiled. "Of course. But since it's you, I'll let it slide this time. The two of you have met, I assume?"

"Sure have," the doctor stated. He looked at John and grew a little more serious. "May I have a moment with my patient, John?"

Kathryne felt John's fingers tighten on hers a moment before he stood, and when she looked up his features had hardened, almost as if he expected bad news. "Sure. I'll wait in the hall. Just let me know when you're done."

Dr. Anderson closed the door after John left, then came back and sat beside her.

"All right, your expression is scaring me. Out with it." Kathryne felt her heart pick up its pace and her palms suddenly grow moist.

"Kate," David began, taking her cold hand in his. "Gosh, I think I've known you almost all your life?" His gray brows came together, but his smile was strangely reassuring. "Some folks around here think I'm too old to practice medicine, that I should retire, but I'm just not ready yet. It's a big decision—one that needs to be made carefully and in the right frame of mind. My wife can't make it for me," his smile widened. "Although she'd like to. No, something that serious is my decision and my decision alone. You see, although it will have some affect on my family, it will affect me the most. Therefore, only I can determine if it's time."

He covered her hand with his other one. "Remember that little blood test I had you take this morning?"

"Yes," she murmured softly, comforted by the way he kept smiling and the way he kept tight hold of her hand. "Am I anemic?"

"No, my dear, you're pregnant."

"What?"

"You're pregnant." He nodded for emphasis.

Kathryne stared at her good friend for a long time. A baby? She was going to have a baby? "My God," she breathed. "I'm forty-four . . . how can I have a baby? I'm in menopause."

David's laugh brought her gaze to his. "Apparently not," he said, taking off his glasses to clean them. "Apparently you didn't have a complete understanding of the medication you were on." He reached over and got her chart. "My associate gave you birth control pills to regulate your periods." Again, David grinned. "Birth control pills prevent pregnancy, but there's a little catch."

"Yes?" she asked, still a little dazed by the news. "What catch?"

"If you're going to have sex, and you want to avoid getting pregnant, you've got to keep taking them." He chuckled again, and then put on his glasses before he grew more serious. "Kate, I'm going to be honest with you. Pregnancy, especially a first pregnancy . . ."

She tried to interrupt.

"Let me finish. I know you were pregnant before, but that was nearly twenty-five years ago. That much time elapsing makes this pretty darned near a first for you. Now, where was I?"

He scratched his ear and then began again. "Oh, yes. I want you to know that you could pull this off without a hitch. But I also want you to know that there could be complications. I'd hate to have a repeat of what happened. If you're going to keep this baby, you're going to have to follow my orders to the letter. I'll work with your obstetrician very closely."

"I don't have one," she said softly, her mind filled with a thousand questions.

"That's the least of our problems right now," David added.

She nodded, still unable to completely fathom what was happening, but trying to listen to everything he said.

"If you choose not to continue the pregnancy, I'll—"

"Abortion?" she whispered, feeling ill. Immediately it wasn't an option.

He caught her hand and gave it another squeeze. "Were you listening when I told you the little story about my retirement?"

"Yes."

"Well, there was a reason I rattled on like that, especially when you were thinking you were dying of something." He took a deep breath and let it out slowly. "You're not a girl anymore, Kate . . . but, you're not over the hill either. You've got every chance in the world to have a healthy, happy baby, but I want the choice to be yours." He nodded toward the door. "Not that fellow out there, not your folks." He lightly tweaked her nose. "No one but you. Trust me, dear. You're going to be the one who'll have to deal with morning sickness, stretch marks, dirty diapers, leaking breasts, *and* staying up all night."

Kathryne watched as her doctor stood, letting go of her hand to retrieve her chart. "I'm going to go now, so you can have some time to digest this news. There's no hurry to make your decision. I want you to take all the time you need. The only stipulation I'm going to put on you is that you make the decision that's *best* for you." He glanced at this watch. "Now I've really got to go."

"More patients?" she asked, thankful for his support.

"Nope. I'm late for my golf game." He went to the door, pausing with his hand on the knob. "Shall I have that fellow come back in or send him packing?"

Kathryne took a calming breath. "He's come an awful long way to be sent packing. He's a good man, David. You'd better send him in."

The doctor paused then added. "How about I let you go home?"

"That would be great."

"You've got to promise not to over-do until I get you on some good vitamins."

"I promise."

David's dark brows came together again. "Kate, I feel it's best if you come to your decision without any pressure." He gave her a fatherly smile. "Get my point?"

She nodded. "I agree. For now this will be our little secret."

John came back in a few minutes later. "That doctor's a real nice guy." He sat down on the side of the bed and picked up Kathryne's hand. "You look like your old self. There's a little color back in your cheeks."

"I'm feeling better too. The good news is that I can go home this afternoon. The bad news is that the movers are going to be at the penthouse in about thirty minutes, and I have to wait for the release papers to be processed."

"I don't see the problem. I'll just go over to your penthouse and get them started." John stood, then picked up his hat. "Call me as soon as you're ready to leave, and I'll pick you up."

"That would be great. I've already packed most of my precious things, and I'm pretty certain the movers know exactly what to do."

He gave her a wide smile. "Maybe so, but if I don't get moving, it's not going to get done the way I want it done. I don't want anything blowing out of those crates half way between here and New Mexico."

When John left, Kathryne called Norman for the number of the drugstore in Taos, reassuring him that everything was quite all right and that she was anxious to share some news with him. Afterwards, she called Dr. Anderson at his office and gave him the number, sharing with him her decision to go through with the pregnancy. "Life has given me a second chance, and I'm not about to throw it away," she said, fighting back happy tears.

David told her he was delighted with her decision and that he'd call the drugstore and she'd have everything she needed by the time she got there. He also stated that he'd call around and locate a good obstetrician for her. If none could be found in Taos, then certainly there would be one in the larger city of Farmington.

"Kate," the good doctor said, just before they hung up. "I'm happy for you."

She had just finished signing some insurance papers when her bedside phone rang. "Yes?"

"Hi, love. It's Mom. We brought a few things. You know, comfortable shoes and clothing. We didn't think you'd want to wear your evening gown home. We're in the lobby. Are you feeling well enough to have visitors?"

"Of course." Kate hurried into the bathroom and ran a brush though her hair, pausing to glance at her profile in the mirror.

With a bright smile, she hurried back to bed to await their arrival.

John finished speaking with the men Kate had hired. According to the man in charge, they knew exactly what to do and would begin immediately. A quick glance at his watch told him it was nearing the time Kate expected to be released. Although he kept busy, he worried that the doctor may have given her some bad news, and that's why she hadn't called.

He glanced out the window of her apartment for the tenth time, then decided he'd give her a call instead, but the phone rang in his hand.

"John?"

"Yes," he replied. "Who's this?"

"It's Louise, Kathryne's mother."

From her tone, it wasn't a social call. John's heart missed a beat. His mind filled with memories—the time the doctor called and told Ellie they'd found a lump, and then the time a different doctor called and told him that Ellie's cancer had returned.

John swallowed hard, forcing himself back to the present, to be calm and listen. "How are you?"

"I'm fine. It's Kathryne we need to worry about. Richard and I are sending a car for you. We'd like to speak to you if you don't mind."

"No, not at all."

It seemed as if only a few minutes had passed when the bellhop told him a limo waited. He grabbed his black Stetson and jammed it on his head. "Lead the way."

John slipped into the back seat of the long black limo, his face like stone. He hadn't been in a vehicle like this since the day he'd buried Ellie. The driver asked him if he wanted anything to drink, then closed the door and took his place behind the wheel.

Time seemed to crawl as they worked their way through the busy city. Fifteen minutes later, the limo pulled into a circular driveway before a stately, red brick mansion. John opened the door and reached into his wallet, pulling out a ten-dollar bill.

"What's your name, pal?"

"Omar," the young black man said with a bemused smile. "Nice hat."

"Yeah, yours is nice too," John stated, looking at the young man's immaculate uniform. "Well, my name is John, and thanks for the ride." He pressed the money into Omar's hand, turning so quickly he missed the man's startled expression.

John climbed the stairs, but before he could lift the brass knocker, the door opened and a young female servant in a crisp black and white uniform asked him in. "Please, come this way."

Louise and George waited for him by the pool at the back of the huge house. "Louise, George," John acknowledged with a nod, taking off his hat. "Nice place you've got here."

"Sit down, John." George motioned to the chair across from his own. Then waved a different servant over who carried a glass of ice and a pitcher of fresh lemonade. "Lemonade?"

"Yes, thank you." His stomach tightened with dread when Louise and George exchanged worried glances while a glass was filled and placed before him. The servant refilled George's glass, but Louise shook her head.

After the woman left, Louise leaned forward, her features unreadable. "Just what are your intentions concerning my daughter?"

John thought he hadn't heard correctly. He felt like a teenager being drilled by an untrusting parent. "I beg your pardon?"

Louise scooted a little closer to her husband, her face a mask of concern. "We want to know exactly how you feel about Kath-ryne. Are you in love with her?"

John took a moment to look at them, trying to tell himself

that they were only concerned parents, not busy-bodies. "Yes. I'm in love with your daughter. Now you're going to answer a question for me."

"Fair enough," Louise stated with a nod.

"Did she ask you to ask me that?"

"Of course not," Louise said frowning. "She doesn't even know you're here."

"Then what business is it of yours?"

Louise gasped at the same time her hand flew up to toy with the silk scarf around her neck. "It's my business because she's my only child, and she's pregnant. I assume, since she's divorced and has been in New Mexico *alone* with you, that it's your child. But now, after seeing your expression I'm beginning to think Kate didn't want you to know."

Louise cast a quick glance at her husband then turned back to John. "Regardless who the father is, this is a vulnerable time for her, and I don't want her upset or confused. It's her decision concerning this child, hers and hers alone."

John's jaw had gone slack. Kate was pregnant—with his child. A million emotions raced around his skull, all of them tripping over one question. Why hadn't she told him? "W-what do you mean, the decision is hers? The decision about what?"

"Whether she should have this baby or if she should have an abortion." Louise's gaze was hard and firm. "She's not a young woman. Babies conceived later in life can have problems . . . all types of problems. Kate has no experience with children. She's devoted her life to her career." She clutched her hands together. "Now this," she murmured, obviously upset. "There could be complications. I won't have her risk her health, nor will I allow you to encourage her in any way to make a decision that has the potential of ruining her life."

George's tone matched his wife's. "Do you realize that when the child graduates from high school, if you're still in the picture, you'll be eligible for social security benefits—provided there are any left?"

Although John met George's stern gaze, he couldn't believe that the man thought he cared about social security when he'd just found out he was going to be a father. He was still too stunned to see their reasoning. He lifted the glass and took a sip, hoping it would calm him down and soothe his suddenly dry throat. "I-Is she in any immediate danger?" he asked when he could trust his voice.

George put his arm around his wife, who looked like she was ready to burst into tears. "Not presently, but Dr. Anderson is concerned that there might be as the pregnancy progresses."

Louise moved closer to the edge of her seat. "You see, Kate lost a child a long time ago. It was still born late in the seventh month . . ."

Kate's voice that rang in John's ears. *I remember being angry— angry that everyone kept calling my baby it.* "She," John murmured.

"What?" Louise asked.

"The baby . . . it was a baby girl, not an *it.*"

Louise cleared her throat uncomfortably, then continued to retell the story. "Are you listening to me?" Louise asked, setting her glass down with an audible thud. "It was devastating—for all of us, but especially for Kate. Babies are for young people— it's insane for her to even consider keeping this child, and if for some reason she decides to try, then moving to New Mexico is out of the question. If something happened, I doubt she'd survive it this time."

John picked up his hat and stood, aware that George and Louise weren't through talking. "I'm sorry to cut this short, but I've got to go." He put on his hat and started to leave, but George, looking a little flustered, grabbed his arm.

"John, I know Louise sounds a little like an overbearing parent, but I'm not sure it's wise to confront Kate at this time."

"George," John began, "I understand your concern, but there's something you both need to learn about me. When I want your opinion, I'll ask for it."

John looked down at George's fingers until the older man loosened his grip. "Now, if it's not too much trouble, could I borrow a phone?"

"What for?" Louise asked, rising from her chair.

"To call a cab."

Louise and George exchanged worried glances, and then Louise whispered something in her husband's ear. He seemed to hesitate for a moment then nodded. "Our driver will take you to the hospital. Kathryne's been released, and she can ride home with Omar."

Once on the main road, John leaned forward and slid the privacy panel open to speak to the driver. "Hey, Omar," he said meeting the young man's gaze in the rearview mirror. "I know they gave you your orders, but can you do a favor for me and take me to the truck stop over on Interstate Ninety-Five, exit fifty-seven to pick up my rig? There's an extra ten bucks in it for you."

"Sure." The man grinned and shook his head. "I'll be happy to, John." He waited until the panel was back in place, then murmured, "Pick up your rig? What's a rig?"

John wasn't sure why Omar refused to take his money, but he thanked him, and then shook his hand, aware that the young man's eyes were glued to Red. "Would you like to look inside?" he asked.

"Oh, yeah," Omar replied, climbing in the moment the big truck was unlocked. "Wow, you could live in here." Omar's grin split his dark face. "It's cool, way cool," he said, then stepped down. "Thanks, John."

"It's nothing, but I'd appreciate it if you wouldn't tell the Sheldons where you dropped me off, all right?"

"Hey, no problem, brother." Omar pretended to zipper his mouth, lock it, and throw away an imaginary key. "My lips are sealed."

"John," Kathryne said, surprised to see him so soon, but even more surprised by the way he looked at her. She finished tying her hair back, and then patted the side of the bed, waiting for him to put his hat on the other chair. "Is there something wrong?"

"I don't know—is there?" he asked, sitting beside her.

Her smile was brilliant. "No. I'm feeling great, and David said I'm good to go. I was just about to get dressed when you came."

"That's a relief, but there's something we need to talk about first."

"My, you look so serious." Kathryne narrowed her gaze. "Did my mother corner you? She's been asking about you, and I think she wants to make sure you're good enough for her only daughter."

"Am I?" he asked. He smiled, but there was still a shadow of concern deep in his eyes.

"Of course. Why would you think differently?"

"I guess when a man finds out something that would change his life in a way he never dreamt possible, it's rather unsettling."

"Oh, no," she murmured, pressing her fingertips against her mouth. "My mother told you about the baby, didn't she?"

John nodded. A tiny muscle jumped above the tight set of his jaw. "She doesn't want you to have our baby. She wants you to get an abortion." He paused, and then right before her eyes he seemed to change. His eyes seemed to be a little watery and his jaw a little tight. Suddenly she realized he was afraid.

"John?" she asked, but he stopped her with a quick shake of his head.

"Let me finish, Kate." He took a deep breath. "I've always wanted children, but if it means I could lose you . . . I mean if I had to make a choice, I'd want you over a child."

Kathryne swallowed to ease the sudden dryness in her throat. "My mother's a headstrong woman. She's concerned about my health, that's all. But that doesn't matter, John. Ultimately it's my . . . our decision."

"Yes, that's true. It's your body, but it's our child." John said, taking her hand between his. "I don't know what you're thinking right now, and maybe part of me is afraid to ask. But know this, Kate. I love you. I loved you before the baby, and I'll always love you, no matter what." He swallowed hard, and she could see he was extremely upset. "If there's a chance . . . if there's a chance that you'd be healthy and we could still have a healthy baby . . . I'd be a good husband and a good father."

Kathryne couldn't speak. Had John just proposed? "Y-you would," she agreed, fighting back the sudden urge to cry. "You'd be a wonderful husband and a wonderful father. That's for sure."

"And you'd be a wonderful wife and a wonderful mother," he said softly, lifting her chin with his knuckle. "Marry me Kate, and if the doctor says you're going to be all right, let's have this baby."

Happy tears streamed down her cheeks. "All right. We'll get married, and . . . and have our baby."

John tipped his head, forcing her to meet his gaze. "If we both agree that we love each other and that we'll be good parents, why are you crying?"

Kathryne sniffed. "I'm not so worried about being a mother." More tears trickled down her cheeks. "David said he'd find a good doctor for me, and I'll be taking some vitamins, so I'm sure I'll have a healthy baby."

"Well then, what is it, Kate? Don't you love me?"

Her head snapped up. "Oh, I do. Absolutely. But loving someone and living with that person are two different things."

John scooted around so he could hold her in his arms. "Kate. I'm trying to understand what it is you're saying, but you're sounding a lot like Norman right now."

She giggled, then reached for a tissue and blew her nose before she looked up at him. "Don't you see? My mother was worried you wouldn't be good enough for me. But, I'm afraid I won't be good enough for you. I can't cook. I know nothing about children and apparently less about what it takes to be a good wife. I'm afraid that I won't measure up to Ellie, that I'm never going to be the kind of wife a man like you needs."

"Where did you get that notion?"

"I thought I was a good wife to Douglas, but then he cheated on me and I realized that maybe it wasn't just his fault, but that maybe I drove him to it."

John laughed out loud. "Yeah, and thank you for that." He shook his head, then pulled out several more tissues and handed them to her. "Here, dry your eyes, Momma. Doug *ain't* worth it."

"Where are you going?" Kathryne asked when John stood and put on his new black Stetson.

"I have few errands to do, but don't you worry. You get dressed. I'll be right back, and then I'll take you out of this place." He headed toward the door. "Did I ever tell you that hospitals give me the willies?"

Dressed in the clothes her mother had brought, Kathryne flipped through a magazine while she sat, cross-legged on the bed. She glanced impatiently at her watch, wondering what was taking John so long.

She tried to get interested in an article about one of her

favorite movie stars, but there seemed to be some kind of a commotion taking place in the hall. People seemed to be chatting and laughing and acting very unprofessional, piquing Kathryne's curiosity. She rose, slipped on her shoes and walked to the door to peek around the corner. Only when she walked down the short hall, did she discover a dozen nurses crowded around the window.

"John," she murmured then hurried back to her room. She went straight to the window and opened the blinds. "Oh my," she breathed, her heart swelling with pride. Red was parked in front of the *Patient Pick Up* sign. The flatbed appeared to be loaded with all her things. Parts of wooden crates showed under the bright blue tarp.

Delighted, she sank down on the bed and anxiously awaited his arrival. Several minutes later the voices in the corridor seemed to grow even more excited and more cheerful. When the lady across the hall came out of her room and smiled, Kathryne couldn't resist. She carefully peeked around the doorway.

Her mouth dropped open. John was surrounded by nurses, each carrying several helium balloons in various colors of pink, yellow and baby-blue. All sizes, and shapes, with several touting congratulatory comments. Two of the pink ones had *It's A Girl* on them, and two of the blue had *It's A Boy*.

The balloon John held was huge and metallic and had colorful ribbon streamers hanging down from it. But what warmed her heart the most were the words on the sides. *We're Having a Baby* had been printed in bright, glittery hot pink and blue letters.

But that wasn't all. One elderly nurse-volunteer pushed a cart overloaded with flowers, and a square package wrapped in pink and blue paper, and covered in bows. Before she could comprehend all that was going on, they were in her room and gathered around.

Amid the giggles and smiles of all the nurses, Kathryne's gaze locked on John's. His bemused expression was tinged with arrogance. He muttered several polite *excuse mes,* and pressed forward until he stood by her bed. After tying his balloon to the bedrail, he took the package off the cart and placed it in her lap. "Open it," he said with a grin.

Doing as John asked, Kathryne felt a little uncomfortable with everyone looking on, but she quickly unwrapped the box and took off the lid. A moment later a bright smile spread across her features as she first held up a magazine on motherhood, then one titled *Diesel Mechanics,* another titled *Farm and Ranch,* and lastly a thick book of baby names.

EPILOGUE

"Oh, goodness gracious," Norman said in a soft voice. "It just can't be that terrible." He shifted the squalling infant to his left shoulder, and then picked up a clean diaper. "Shush," he whispered, kissing the tiny cheek before he laid the baby on the changing table in the newly decorated nursery in the newly renovated cabin. Norman made funny faces and cooing sounds as he took off the old diaper, gently washed the baby's bottom, and then expertly replaced the diaper with a fresh one. "There. Uncle Normie made everything better for his little sweet pea."

Kathryne's heart warmed at the loving expression Norman had on his face as he carefully wrapped the infant in a soft receiving blanket and cradled him in his arms. The baby instantly stopped crying. Kathryne cast a quick glance up at John, who also stood at the door, his arm around her, his expression as loving as Norman's.

Duke rested nearby in the hall, completely tolerant of the Weimaraner pup that chewed on his tail. Pugsy the pug and Dottie the Dalmatian sat patiently, watching Kathryne, peeking into the room now and then to see what everyone was so interested in.

Norman glanced up and upon seeing John and Kathryne, grinned. "Isn't this fun?" he asked, his eyes dancing with pure pleasure.

Kathryne laughed. "I never quite thought of changing dirty diapers as fun, but having this baby has been the best experience of my life."

"Our life," John amended. "You know, Norm. Johnny's only been home a few days, and I don't think I've gotten to hold him more than twice."

Norman straightened, his expression changing to defensive. "That's not true, Big John. You're exaggerating. I'm here to help, and that's what I'm doing."

"Norm," John said patiently. "Do you think we could forego using *big* before my name?" John ignored his wife's giggle. "It makes me think of lumber jacks and wrestlers."

"Well how are we to tell the two of you apart—the baby and you, I mean?" Norman replied with a worried frown, rocking back and forth.

"Well, he's twenty-one inches long and I'm—"

"Big," Norman interjected. "I can just see it. In a few years I'll call out your name and little Johnny will answer when I was really speaking to you, and vice versa. We'll all be walking around in a state of confusion. And then there are other problems that could arise, John. Problems we didn't think about when we chose little Johnny's name."

John smiled patiently, leaning against the door jam, his arm still snuggly around his wife. "I'm almost afraid to ask, but what kind of problems?"

"Problems like checking accounts and credit cards. Do you realize how difficult it's going to be keeping them separated? You know how banks are, John. They never get anything right, especially if the names are the same. And what about dental and doctor records? Those get mixed up all the time."

John left Kathryne and went to Norman who reluctantly placed the baby in John's arms, coaching John on the proper way to hold an infant. "Hold his head, John, and support his little back. Ah, look at him. Isn't he the cutest thing since Dukey was a pup?"

This time John laughed, reminded how Norman had changed all their dogs' names. Dottie was usually called Dolly and Walter the Weimaraner was called Wally. It seemed the only one that had escaped a name change was Pugsy. But there was another problem with Pugsy. Norman was always trying to sneak him into his car.

"I reckon that's true, but you've forgotten something, Norm," John said.

Norman's gaze flew from the baby to John. "I did?"

"Yes. We didn't use my middle name."

"Oh, I thought we decided to do that. When did we change our minds?"

John glanced at Kathryne, who came over and put her arm around Norman's shoulders. "Like you, we were concerned that making the baby a junior could possibly complicate his adult life more than we wanted."

Norman's shoulders sagged with relief. "Whew, that was a smart decision. I was a junior, you know, and for years, until Dad passed, our accounts were always messed up."

"John told me all about that." Kathryne met John's gaze, and at that moment, John knew he had to be the luckiest man in the world.

"Norm," John began at his wife's urging. "We decided to use Alexander as Johnny's middle name. John Alexander Hawkins."

Norman gasped. He covered his heart with his clasped hands as happy tears filled his eyes. He first looked at Kathryne and then back at John, and then tipped his head slightly to the side, his expression so happy, it nearly brought tears to John and Kathryne's eyes.

"Oh, my gosh," Norman breathed. "This is more than I could have ever hoped for. I don't know what to say."

"There's no need to say anything. Babies' names should always include the names of special people in the family," Kathryne added. "It's what families who love each other do."

Norman stepped closer and being careful not to squeeze the baby, wrapped John and Kathryne in his arms. "This is so wonderful, I could just cry. But wait . . ."

John and Kathryn exchanged cautious glances.

"What?" they said in unison.

Norman's smile returned, and at the same he time gave a little sigh of relief. "I was just worried that Johnny's initial might spell something weird. You know, kid's with initials like CAT or BM get teased all the time in school, but we're good." He nodded for emphasis. "There's nothing much they can do with John Alexander Hawkins."

John shook his head in bemused disbelief, and then headed toward the door with his wife and son, while Norman chatted on and on about what kinds of toys little babies liked, and maybe he'd buy a pony next spring, and a swing set . . . sand box . . . and much, much more.

ABOUT THE AUTHOR

Donna MacQuigg is a second generation native of New Mexico and has lived there all her life. Donna has previously published six historical romances, three Scottish Medieval romances, and three western romances. As a youngster, she spent nearly every weekend camping with her family in the beautiful mountains of the Santa Fe National Forest—which lends a good measure of authenticity to the setting of this story. She's also an avid equestrian and raised Arabian horses for over 25 years with her husband and two children. Her newest hobby is taking her six-month-old standard poodle to obedience and agility classes.

Visit her Web site at www.donnamacquigg.com. She enjoys receiving your comments at donnamacquigg@yahoo.com.